Anglo-Saxon Grammar

Exercise Book

With Inflections, Syntax, Selections for Reading, and Glossary

C. Alphonso Smith

Alpha Editions

This edition published in 2024

ISBN : 9789367248942

Design and Setting By
Alpha Editions
www.alphaedis.com
Email - info@alphaedis.com

As per information held with us this book is in Public Domain. This book is a reproduction of an important historical work. Alpha Editions uses the best technology to reproduce historical work in the same manner it was first published to preserve its original nature. Any marks or number seen are left intentionally to preserve its true form.

PREFACE.

THE scope of this book is indicated in § 5. It is intended for beginners, and in writing it, these words of Sir Thomas Elyot have not been forgotten: "Grammer, beinge but an introduction to the understandinge of autors, if it be made to longe or exquisite to the lerner, it in a maner mortifieth his corage: And by that time he cometh to the most swete and pleasant redinge of olde autors, the sparkes of fervent desire of lernynge are extincte with the burdone of grammer, lyke as a lyttell fyre is sone quenched with a great heape of small stickes."—*The Governour*, Cap. X.

Only the essentials, therefore, are treated in this work, which is planned more as a foundation for the study of Modern English grammar, of historical English grammar, and of the principles of English etymology, than as a general introduction to Germanic philology.

The Exercises in translation will, it is believed, furnish all the drill necessary to enable the student to retain the forms and constructions given in the various chapters.

The Selections for Reading relate to the history and literature of King Alfred's day, and are sufficient to give the student a first-hand, though brief, acquaintance with the native style and idiom of Early West Saxon prose in its golden age. Most of the words and constructions contained in them will be already familiar to the student through their intentional employment in the Exercises.

For the inflectional portion of this grammar, recourse has been had chiefly to Sievers' *Abriss der angelsächsischen Grammatik* (1895). Constant reference has been made also to the same author's earlier and larger *Angelsächsishe Grammatik*, translated by Cook. A more sparing use has been made of Cosijn's *Altwestsächsische Grammatik*.

For syntax and illustrative sentences, Dr. J. E. Wülfing's *Syntax in den Werken Alfreds des Grossen, Part I.* (Bonn, 1894) has proved indispensable. Advance sheets of the second part of this great work lead one to believe that when completed the three parts will constitute the most important contribution to the study of English syntax that has yet been made. Old English sentences have also been cited from Sweet's *Anglo-Saxon Reader*, Bright's *Anglo-Saxon Reader*, and Cook's *First Book in Old English*.

The short chapter on the Order of Words has been condensed from my *Order of Words in Anglo-Saxon Prose* (Publications of the Modern Language Association of America, New Series, Vol. I, No. 2).

Though assuming sole responsibility for everything contained in this book, I take pleasure in acknowledging the kind and efficient assistance that has been so generously given me in its preparation. To none do I owe more than to Dr. J. E. Wülfing, of the University of Bonn; Prof. James A. Harrison, of the University of Virginia; Prof. W. S. Currell, of Washington and Lee University; Prof. J. Douglas Bruce, of Bryn Mawr College; and Prof. L. M. Harris, of the University of Indiana. They have each rendered material aid, not only in the tedious task of detecting typographical errors in the proof-sheets, but by the valuable criticisms and suggestions which they have made as this work was passing through the press.

C. ALPHONSO SMITH.

LOUISIANA STATE UNIVERSITY,
BATON ROUGE, September, 1896.

PREFACE TO THE SECOND EDITION.

IN preparing this enlarged edition, a few minor errors in the first edition have been corrected and a few sentences added. The chief difference between the two editions, however, consists in the introduction of more reading matter and the consequent exposition of Old English meter. Both changes have been made at the persistent request of teachers and students of Old English.

Uniformity of treatment has been studiously preserved in the new material and the old, the emphasis in both being placed on syntax and upon the affinities that Old English shares with Modern English.

Many obligations have been incurred in preparing this augmented edition. I have again to thank Dr. J. E. Wülfing, Prof. James A. Harrison, Prof. W. S. Currell, and Prof. J. Douglas Bruce. To the scholarly criticisms also of Prof. J. M. Hart, of Cornell; Prof. Frank Jewett Mather, Jr., of Williams College; and Prof. Frederick Tupper, Jr., of the University of Vermont, I am indebted for aid as generously given as it is genuinely appreciated.

C. ALPHONSO SMITH.

    August, 1898.

PREFACE TO THE FOURTH EDITION.

AMONG those who have kindly aided in making this edition free from error, I wish to thank especially my friend Dr. John M. McBryde, Jr., of Hollins Institute, Virginia.

C. ALPHONSO SMITH.

UNIVERSITY OF NORTH CAROLINA,
   Chapel Hill, February, 1903.

PART I.

INTRODUCTION.

CHAPTER I.
HISTORY.

1.

The history of the English language falls naturally into three periods; but these periods blend into one another so gradually that too much significance must not be attached to the exact dates which scholars, chiefly for convenience of treatment, have assigned as their limits. Our language, it is true, has undergone many and great changes; but its continuity has never been broken, and its individuality has never been lost.

2.

The first of these periods is that of OLD ENGLISH, or ANGLO-SAXON,1 commonly known as the period of *full inflections. E.g.* **stān-as**, *stones;* **car-u**, *care;* **will-a**, *will;* **bind-an**, *to bind;* **help-að** (= **ath**), *they help.*

It extends from the arrival of the English in Great Britain to about one hundred years after the Norman Conquest,—from A.D. 449 to 1150; but there are no literary remains of the earlier centuries of this period. There were four2 distinct dialects spoken at this time. These were the Northumbrian, spoken north of the river Humber; the Mercian, spoken in the midland region between the Humber and the Thames; the West Saxon, spoken south and west of the Thames; and the Kentish, spoken in the neighborhood of Canterbury. Of these dialects, Modern English is most nearly akin to the Mercian; but the best known of them is the West Saxon. It was in the West Saxon dialect that King Alfred (849-901) wrote and spoke. His writings belong to the period of Early West Saxon as distinguished from the period of Late West Saxon, the latter being best represented in the writings of Abbot Ælfric (955?-1025?).

3.

The second period is that of MIDDLE ENGLISH, or the period of *leveled inflections*, the dominant vowel of the inflections being **e**. *E.g.* **ston-es, car-e, will-e, bind-en** (or **bind-e**), **help-eth**, each being, as in the earlier period, a dissyllable.

The Middle English period extends from A.D. 1150 to 1500. Its greatest representatives are Chaucer (1340-1400) in poetry and Wiclif (1324-1384) in

- 5 -

prose. There were three prominent dialects during this period: the Northern, corresponding to the older Northumbrian; the Midland (divided into East Midland and West Midland), corresponding to the Mercian; and the Southern, corresponding to the West Saxon and Kentish. London, situated in East Midland territory, had become the dominant speech center; and it was this East Midland dialect that both Chaucer and Wiclif employed.

NOTE.—It is a great mistake to think that Chaucer shaped our language from crude materials. His influence was conservative, not plastic. The popularity of his works tended to crystalize and thus to perpetuate the forms of the East Midland dialect, but that dialect was ready to his hand before he began to write. The speech of London was, in Chaucer's time, a mixture of Southern and Midland forms, but the Southern forms (survivals of the West Saxon dialect) had already begun to fall away; and this they continued to do, so that "Chaucer's language," as Dr. Murray says, "is more Southern than standard English eventually became." See also Morsbach, *Ueber den Ursprung der neuenglischen Schriftsprache* (1888).

4.

The last period is that of MODERN ENGLISH, or the period of *lost inflections*. E.g. *stones, care, will, bind, help*, each being a monosyllable. Modern English extends from A.D. 1500 to the present time. It has witnessed comparatively few grammatical changes, but the vocabulary of our language has been vastly increased by additions from the classical languages. Vowels, too, have shifted their values.

5.

It is the object of this book to give an elementary knowledge of Early West Saxon, that is, the language of King Alfred. With this knowledge, it will not be difficult for the student to read Late West Saxon, or any other dialect of the Old English period. Such knowledge will also serve as the best introduction to the structure both of Middle English and of Modern English, besides laying a secure foundation for the scientific study of any other Germanic tongue.

NOTE.—The Germanic, or Teutonic, languages constitute a branch of the great Aryan, or Indo-Germanic (known also as the Indo-European) group. They are subdivided as follows:

North Germanic: Scandinavian, or Norse.

Germanic

East Germanic: Gothic.

Old High German, (to A.D. 1100,)

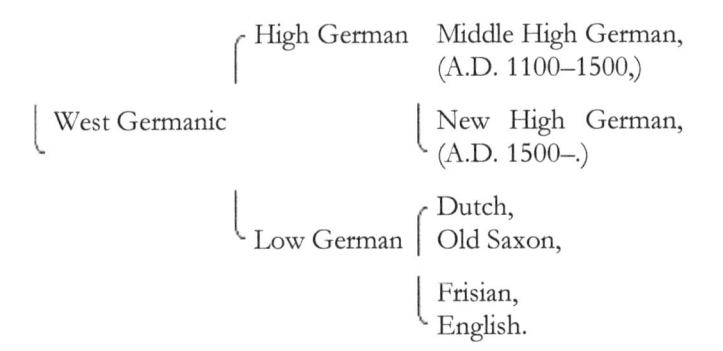

```
                    ┌ High German  ┌ Middle High German,
                    │              │ (A.D. 1100–1500,)
┌ West Germanic     │              │
│                   │              └ New High German,
│                                    (A.D. 1500–.)
│
                    └              ┌ Dutch,
                      Low German   │ Old Saxon,
                                   │ Frisian,
                                   └ English.
```

1. This unfortunate nomenclature is due to the term *Angli Saxones*, which Latin writers used as a designation for the English Saxons as distinguished from the continental or Old Saxons. But Alfred and Ælfric both use the term *Englisc*, not Anglo-Saxon. The Angles spread over Northumbria and Mercia, far outnumbering the other tribes. Thus *Englisc* (= *Angel* + *isc*) became the general name for the language spoken.

2. As small as England is, there are six distinct dialects spoken in her borders to-day. Of these the Yorkshire dialect is, perhaps, the most peculiar. It preserves many Northumbrian survivals. See Tennyson's *Northern Farmer*.

CHAPTER II.
Sounds.

Vowels and Diphthongs.

6.

The long vowels and diphthongs will in this book be designated by the macron (–). Vowel length should in every case be associated by the student with each word learned: quantity alone sometimes distinguishes words meaning wholly different things: **fōr**, *he went*, **for**, *for*; **gōd**, *good*, **God**, *God*; **mān**, *crime*, **man**, *man*.

Long vowels and diphthongs:

    ā as in f*a*ther: **stān**, *a stone*.

    ǣ as in m*a*n (prolonged): **slǣpan**, *to sleep*.

    ē as in th*ey*: **hēr**, *here*.

- ī as in mach*i*ne: **mīn**, *mine*.
- ō as in n*o*te (pure, not diphthongal): **bōc**, *book*.
- ū as in r*u*le: **tūn**, *town*.
- ȳ as in German gr*ü*n, or English gr*ee*n (with lips rounded):1 **brȳd**, *bride*.

The diphthongs, long and short, have the stress upon the first vowel. The second vowel is obscured, and represents approximately the sound of *er* in *sooner, faster* (= *soon-uh, fast-uh*). The long diphthongs (ǣ is not a diphthong proper) are **ēo, īe**, and **ēa**. The sound of **ēo** is approximately reproduced in *mayor* (= *mā-uh*); that of **īe** in the dissyllabic pronunciation of *fear* (= *fĕ-uh*). But **ēa** = *ǣ-uh*. This diphthong is hardly to be distinguished from *ea* in *pear, bear*, etc., as pronounced in the southern section of the United States (= *bæ-uh, pæ-uh*).

7.

The short sounds are nothing more than the long vowels and diphthongs shortened; but the student must at once rid himself of the idea that Modern English *red*, for example, is the shortened form of *reed*, or that *mat* is the shortened form of *mate*. Pronounce these long sounds with increasing rapidity, and *reed* will approach *rid*, while *mate* will approach *met*. The Old English short vowel sounds are:

- a as in *a*rtistic: **habban**, *to have*.
- æ as in m*a*nkind: **dæg**, *day*.
- e, ę as in l*e*t: **stelan**, *to steal*, **sęttan**, *to set*.
- i as in s*i*t: **hit**, *it*.
- o as in br*oa*d (but shorter): **God**, *God*.
- ǫ as in n*o*t: **lǫmb**, *lamb*.
- u as in f*u*ll: **sunu**, *son*.
- y as in m*ü*ller (with lips rounded)1: **gylden**, *golden*.

NOTE.—The symbol **ę** is known as *umlaut*-**e** (§ 58). It stands for Germanic *a*, while **e** (without the cedilla) represents Germanic *e*. The symbol **ǫ** is employed only before **m** and **n**. It, too, represents Germanic *a*. But Alfred writes **manig** or **monig**, *many*; **lamb** or **lomb**, *lamb*; **hand** or **hond**, *hand*, etc. The cedilla is an etymological sign added by modern grammarians.

The letters ę and ǫ were printed as shown in this e-text. The diacritic is not a cedilla (open to the left) but an ogonek (open to the right).

Consonants.

8.

There is little difference between the values of Old English consonants and those of Modern English. The following distinctions, however, require notice:

The digraph **th** is represented in Old English texts by **ð** and **þ**, no consistent distinction being made between them. In the works of Alfred, **ð** (capital, **Ð**) is the more common: **ðās**, *those*; **ðæt**, *that*; **bindeð**, *he binds*.

The consonant **c** had the hard sound of *k*, the latter symbol being rare in West Saxon: **cyning**, *king*; **cwēn**, *queen*; **cūð**, *known*. When followed by a palatal vowel sound,—*e, i, æ, ea, eo*, long or short,—a vanishing *y* sound was doubtless interposed (*cf.* dialectic *kʸind* for *kind*). In Modern English the combination has passed into *ch*: **cealc**, *chalk*; **cīdan**, *to chide*; **l ce**, *leech*; **cild**, *child*; **cēowan**, *to chew*. This change (*c* > *ch*) is known as Palatalization. The letter **g**, pronounced as in Modern English *gun*, has also a palatal value before the palatal vowels (*cf.* dialectic *gʸirl* for *girl*).

The combination **cg**, which frequently stands for **gg**, had probably the sound of *dge* in Modern English *edge*: **ęcg**, *edge*; **sęcgan**, *to say*; **brycg**, *bridge*. Initial **h** is sounded as in Modern English: **habban**, *to have*; **hālga**, *saint*. When closing a syllable it has the sound of German *ch*: **slōh**, *he slew*; **hēah**, *high*; **ðurh**, *through*.

9.

An important distinction is that between voiced (or sonant) and voiceless (or surd) consonants.[2] In Old English they are as follows:

Voiced.	Voiceless.
g	h, c
d	t
ð, þ (as in *th*ough)	ð, þ (as in *th*in)
b	p
f (= v)	f
s (= z)	s

It is evident, therefore, that **ð** (**þ**), **f**, and **s** have double values in Old English. If voiced, they are equivalent to *th* (in *th*ough), *v*, and *z*. Otherwise, they are pronounced as *th* (in *th*in), *f* (in *f*in), and *s* (in *s*in). The syllabic environment will usually compel the student to give these letters their proper values. When occurring between vowels, they are always voiced: **ōðer**, *other*; **ofer**, *over*; **rīsan**, *to rise*.

NOTE.—The general rule in Old English, as in Modern English, is, that voiced consonants have a special affinity for other voiced consonants, and voiceless for voiceless. This is the law of Assimilation. Thus when *de* is added to form the preterit of a verb whose stem ends in a voiceless consonant, the **d** is unvoiced, or assimilated, to **t‿sęttan**, *to set*, **sętte** (but **tręddan**, *to tread*, has **tredde**); **slǣpan**, *to sleep*, **slǣpte**; **dręncan**, *to drench*, **dręncte**; **cyssan**, *to kiss*, **cyste**. See § 126, Note 1.

Syllables.

10.

A syllable is usually a vowel, either alone or in combination with consonants, uttered with a single impulse of stress; but certain consonants may form syllables: *oven* (= *ov-n*), *battle* (= *bæt-l*); (*cf.* also the vulgar pronunciation of *elm*).

A syllable may be (1) weak or strong, (2) open or closed, (3) long or short.

(1) A weak syllable receives a light stress. Its vowel sound is often different from that of the corresponding strong, or stressed, syllable. *Cf.* weak and strong *my* in "I want my lárge hat" and "I want mý hat."

(2) An open syllable ends in a vowel or diphthong: **dē-man**, *to deem*; **ðū**, *thou*; **sca-can**, *to shake*; **dæ-ges**, *by day*. A closed syllable ends in one or more consonants: **ðing**, *thing*; **gōd**, *good*; **glæd**, *glad*.

(3) A syllable is long (*a*) if it contains a long vowel or a long diphthong: **drī-fan**, *to drive*; **lū-can**, *to lock*; **slǣ-pan**, *to sleep*; **cēo-san**, *to choose*; (*b*) if its vowel or diphthong is followed by more than one consonant:3 **cræft**, *strength*; **heard**, *hard*; **lib-ban**, *to live*; **feal-lan**, *to fall*. Otherwise, the syllable is short: **ðe**, *which*; **be-ran**, *to bear*; **ðæt**, *that*; **gie-fan**, *to give*.

NOTE 1.—A single consonant belongs to the following syllable: **hā-lig**, *holy* (not **hāl-ig**); **wrī-tan**, *to write*; **fæ-der**, *father*.

NOTE 2.—The student will notice that the syllable may be long and the vowel short; but the vowel cannot be long and the syllable short.

NOTE 3.—Old English short vowels, occurring in open syllables, have regularly become long in Modern English: **we-fan**, *to weave*; **e-tan**, *to eat*; **ma-cian**, *to make*; **na-cod**, *naked*; **a-can**, *to ache*; **o-fer**, *over*. And Old English long vowels, preceding two or more consonants, have generally been shortened: **brēost**, *breast*; **hǣlð**, *health*; **slǣpte**, *slept*; **lǣdde**, *led*.

Accentuation.

11.

The accent in Old English falls usually on the radical syllable, never on the inflectional ending: **bríngan**, *to bring*; **stā́nas**, *stones*; **bérende**, *bearing*; **ídelnes**, *idleness*; **fre͂ondscipe**, *friendship*.

But in the case of compound nouns, adjectives, and adverbs the first member of the compound (unless it be **ge-** or **be-**) receives the stronger stress: **héofon-rīce**, *heaven-kingdom*; **ǫ́nd-giet**, *intelligence*; **sṓð-fæst**, *truthful*; **gódcund**, *divine*; **éall-unga**, *entirely*; **blī́ðe-līce**, *blithely*. But **be-hā́t**, *promise*; **ge-béd**, *prayer*; **ge-fḗalīc**, *joyous*; **be-sǫ́ne**, *immediately*.

Compound verbs, however, have the stress on the radical syllable: **for-gíefan**, *to forgive*; **of-línnan**, *to cease*; **ā-cnā́wan**, *to know*; **wið-stǫ́ndan**, *to withstand*; **on-sácan**, *to resist*.

NOTE.—The tendency of nouns to take the stress on the prefix, while verbs retain it on the root, is exemplified in many Modern English words: *préference, prefér; cóntract* (noun), *contráct* (verb); *ábstinence, abstaín; pérfume* (noun), *perfúme* (verb).

> 1. Vowels are said to be round, or rounded, when the lip-opening is rounded; that is, when the lips are thrust out and puckered as if preparing to pronounce *w*. Thus *o* and *u* are round vowels: add *-ing* to each, and phonetically you have added *-wing*. E.g. *go^wing, su^wing*.

> 2. A little practice will enable the student to see the appropriateness of calling these consonants voiced and voiceless. Try to pronounce a voiced consonant,—*d* in *den*, for example, but without the assistance of *en*,—and there will be heard a gurgle, or *vocal* murmur. But in *t*, of *ten*, there is no sound at all, but only a feeling of tension in the organs.

> 3. Taken separately, every syllable ending in a single consonant is long. It may be said, therefore, that all closed syllables are long; but in the natural flow of language, the single final consonant of a syllable so often blends with a following initial vowel, the syllable thus becoming open and short, that such syllables are not recognized as prevailingly long. *Cf.* Modern English *at all* (= *a-tall*).

CHAPTER III.
INFLECTIONS.

Cases.

12.

There are five cases in Old English: the nominative, the genitive, the dative, the accusative, and the instrumental.1 Each of them, except the nominative, may be governed by prepositions. When used without prepositions, they have, in general, the following functions:

(*a*) The nominative, as in Modern English, is the case of the subject of a finite verb.

(*b*) The genitive (the possessive case of Modern English) is the case of the possessor or source. It may be called the *of* case.

(*c*) The dative is the case of the indirect object. It may be called the *to* or *for* case.

(*d*) The accusative (the objective case of Modern English) is the case of the direct object.

(*e*) The instrumental, which rarely differs from the dative in form, is the case of the means or the method. It may be called the *with* or *by* case.

The following paradigm of **mūð**, *the mouth*, illustrates the several cases (the article being, for the present, gratuitously added in the Modern English equivalents):

	Singular.	*Plural.*
N.	**mūð** = *the mouth.*	**mūð-as** = *the mouths.*
G.	**mūð-es**2 = *of the mouth* (= *the mouth's*).	**mūð-a** = *of the mouths* (= *the mouths'*).
D.	**mūð-e** = *to* or *for the mouth.*	**mūð-um** = *to* or *for the mouths.*
A.	**mūð** = *the mouth.*	**mūð-as** = *the mouths.*
I.	**mūðe** = *with* or *by means of the mouth.*	**mūð-um** = *with* or *by means of the mouths.*

Gender.

13.

The gender of Old English nouns, unlike that of Modern English, depends partly on meaning and partly on form, or ending. Thus **mūð**, *mouth*, is masculine; **tunge**, *tongue*, feminine; **ēage**, *eye*, neuter.

No very comprehensive rules, therefore, can be given; but the gender of every noun should be learned with its meaning. Gender will be indicated in the vocabularies by the different gender forms of the definite article, **sē** for the masculine, **sēo** for the feminine, and **ðæt** for the neuter: **sē mūð, sēo tunge, ðæt ēage** = *the mouth, the tongue, the eye*.

All nouns ending in **-dōm, -hād, -scipe,** or **-ere** are masculine (*cf.* Modern English wis*dom*, child*hood*, friend*ship*, work*er*). Masculine, also, are nouns ending in **-a**.

Those ending in **-nes** or **-ung** are feminine (*cf.* Modern English good*ness*, and gerundial forms in *-ing*: see*ing* is believ*ing*).

Thus **sē wīsdōm**, *wisdom*; **sē cildhād**, *childhood*; **sē frēondscipe**, *friendship*; **sē fiscere**, *fisher(man)*; **sē hunta**, *hunter*; **sēo gelīcnes**, *likeness*; **sēo leornung**, *learning*.

Declensions.

14.

There are two great systems of declension in Old English, the Vowel Declension and the Consonant Declension. A noun is said to belong to the Vowel Declension when the final letter of its stem is a vowel, this vowel being then known as the *stem-characteristic*; but if the stem-characteristic is a consonant, the noun belongs to the Consonant Declension. There might have been, therefore, as many subdivisions of the Vowel Declension in Old English as there were vowels, and as many subdivisions of the Consonant Declension as there were consonants. All Old English nouns, however, belonging to the Vowel Declension, ended their stems originally in **a, ō, i,** or **u**. Hence there are but four subdivisions of the Vowel Declension: **a**-stems, **ō**-stems, **i**-stems, and **u**-stems.

The Vowel Declension is commonly called the Strong Declension, and its nouns Strong Nouns.

NOTE.—The terms Strong and Weak were first used by Jacob Grimm (1785-1863) in the terminology of verbs, and thence transferred to nouns and adjectives. By a Strong Verb, Grimm meant one that could form its preterit out of its own resources; that is, without calling in the aid of an additional syllable: Modern English *run, ran; find, found;* but verbs of the Weak

Conjugation had to borrow, as it were, an inflectional syllable: *gain, gained*; *help, helped*.

15.

The stems of nouns belonging to the Consonant Declension ended, with but few exceptions, in the letter **n** (*cf.* Latin *homin-em, ration-em*, Greek ποιμέν-α). They are called, therefore, **n**-stems, the Declension itself being known as the **n**-Declension, or the Weak Declension. The nouns, also, are called Weak Nouns.

16.

If every Old English noun had preserved the original Germanic stem-characteristic (or final letter of the stem), there would be no difficulty in deciding at once whether any given noun is an **a**-stem, **ō**-stem, **i**-stem, **u**-stem, or **n**-stem; but these final letters had, for the most part, either been dropped, or fused with the case-endings, long before the period of historic Old English. It is only, therefore, by a rigid comparison of the Germanic languages with one another, and with the other Aryan languages, that scholars are able to reconstruct a single Germanic language, in which the original stem-characteristics may be seen far better than in any one historic branch of the Germanic group (§ 5, Note).

This hypothetical language, which bears the same ancestral relation to the historic Germanic dialects that Latin bears to the Romance tongues, is known simply as *Germanic* (Gmc.), or as *Primitive Germanic*. Ability to reconstruct Germanic forms is not expected of the students of this book, but the following table should be examined as illustrating the basis of distinction among the several Old English declensions (O.E. = Old English, Mn.E. = Modern English):

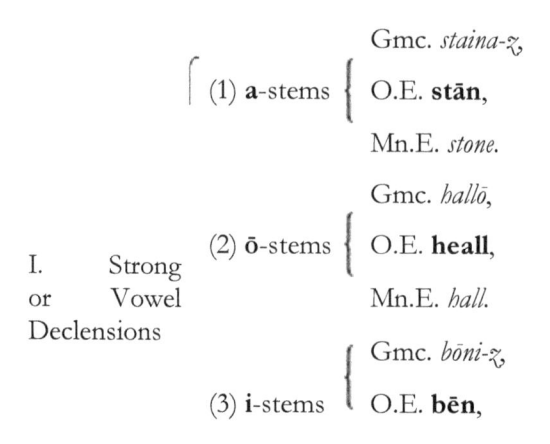

I. Strong or Vowel Declensions

(1) **a**-stems
- Gmc. *staina-ʒ*,
- O.E. **stān**,
- Mn.E. *stone*.

(2) **ō**-stems
- Gmc. *hallō*,
- O.E. **heall**,
- Mn.E. *hall*.

(3) **i**-stems
- Gmc. *bōni-ʒ*,
- O.E. **bēn**,

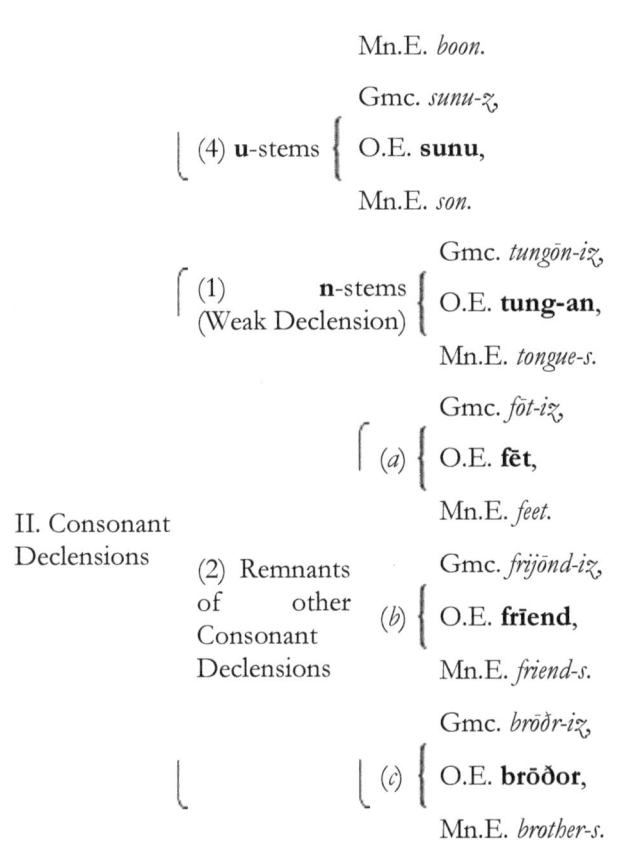

			Mn.E. *boon.*
	(4) **u**-stems		Gmc. *sunu-z,* O.E. **sunu,** Mn.E. *son.*
	(1) **n**-stems (Weak Declension)		Gmc. *tungōn-iz,* O.E. **tung-an,** Mn.E. *tongue-s.*
II. Consonant Declensions	(2) Remnants of other Consonant Declensions	(a)	Gmc. *fōt-iz,* O.E. **fēt,** Mn.E. *feet.*
		(b)	Gmc. *frijōnd-iz,* O.E. **frīend,** Mn.E. *friend-s.*
		(c)	Gmc. *brōðr-iz,* O.E. **brōðor,** Mn.E. *brother-s.*

NOTE.—"It will be seen that if Old English **ēage**, *eye*, is said to be an **n**-stem, what is meant is this, that at some former period the kernel of the word ended in **-n**, while, as far as the Old English language proper is concerned, all that is implied is that the word is inflected in a certain manner." (Jespersen, *Progress in Language*, § 109).

This is true of all Old English stems, whether Vowel or Consonant. The division, therefore, into **a**-stems, **ō**-stems, etc., is made in the interests of grammar as well as of philology.

Conjugations.

17.

There are, likewise, two systems of conjugation in Old English: the Strong or Old Conjugation, and the Weak or New Conjugation.

The verbs of the Strong Conjugation (the so-called Irregular Verbs of Modern English) number about three hundred, of which not one hundred remain in Modern English (§ 101, Note). They form their preterit and frequently their past participle by changing the radical vowel of the present stem. This vowel change or modification is called *ablaut* (pronounced *áhplowt*): Modern English *sing, sang, sung; rise, rose, risen*. As the radical vowel of the preterit plural is often different from that of the preterit singular, there are four *principal parts* or *tense stems* in an Old English strong verb, instead of the three of Modern English. The four principal parts in the conjugation of a strong verb are (1) the present indicative, (2) the preterit indicative singular, (3) the preterit indicative plural, and (4) the past participle.

Strong verbs fall into seven groups, illustrated in the following table:

Present.	Pret. Sing.	Pret. Plur.	Past Participle.

I.

Bītan, *to bite*:

Ic bīt-e, *I bite* or **Ic bāt**, *I bit*. **Wē bit-on**, *we bit*. **Ic hæbbe ge4-biten**, *I have bitten*.
shall bite.3

II.

Bēodan, *to bid*:

Ic bēod-e, *I bid* or **Ic bēad**, *I bade*. **Wē bud-on**, *we bade*. **Ic hæbbe ge-boden**, *I have bidden*.
shall bid.

III.

Bindan, *to bind*:

Ic bind-e, *I bind* or **Ic bǫnd**, *I bound*. **Wē bund-on**, *we bound*. **Ic hæbbe ge-bund-en**, *I have bound*.
shall bind.

IV.

Beran, *to bear*:

Ic ber-e, *I bear* or **Ic bær**, *I bore*. **Wē bǣr-on**, *we bore*. **Ic hæbbe ge-bor-en**, *I have borne*.
shall bear.

V.

Metan, *to measure*:

Ic met-e, *I measure* or *shall measure.*	Ic mæt, *I measured.*	I Wē mǣt-on, *we measured.*	Ic hæbbe ge-met-en, *I have measured.*

VI.

Faran, *to go*:

Ic far-e, *I go* or *shall go.*	Ic fōr, *I went.*	Wē fōr-on, *we went.*	Ic eom5 ge-far-en, *I have (am) gone.*

VII.

Feallan, *to fall*:

Ic feall-e, *I fall* or *shall fall.*	Ic fēoll, *I fell.*	Wē fēoll-on, *we fell.*	Ic eom5 ge-feall-en, *I have (am) fallen.*

18.

The verbs of the Weak Conjugation (the so-called Regular Verbs of Modern English) form their preterit and past participle by adding to the present stem a suffix6 with *d* or *t*: Modern English *love, loved; sleep, slept.*

The stem of the preterit plural is never different from the stem of the preterit singular; hence these verbs have only three distinctive tense-stems, or principal parts: *viz.*, (1) the present indicative, (2) the preterit indicative, and (3) the past participle.

Weak verbs fall into three groups, illustrated in the following table:

PRESENT.	PRETERIT.	PAST PARTICIPLE.

I.

Fremman, *to perform*:

Ic fremm-e, *I perform* or *shall perform.*	Ic frem-ede, *I performed.*	Ic hæbbe ge-frem-ed, *I have performed.*

II.

Bodian, *to proclaim*:

Ic bodi-e, *I proclaim* or *shall proclaim.*	Ic bod-ode, *I proclaimed.*	Ic hæbbe ge-bod-od, *I have proclaimed.*

III.

Habban, *to have.*

Ic hæbbe, *I have* or *shall* **Ic hæf-de,** *I had.* **Ic hæbbe ge-hæf-d,** *I have have. had.*

19.

There remain a few verbs (chiefly the Auxiliary Verbs of Modern English) that do not belong entirely to either of the two conjugations mentioned. The most important of them are, **Ic mæg** *I may*, **Ic mihte** *I might*; **Ic cǫn** *I can*, **Ic cūðe** *I could*; **Ic mōt** *I must*, **Ic mōste** *I must*; **Ic sceal** *I shall*, **Ic sceolde** *I should*; **Ic eom** *I am*, **Ic wæs** *I was*; **Ic wille** *I will*, **Ic wolde** *I would*; **Ic dō** *I do*, **Ic dyde** *I did*; **Ic gā** *I go*, **Ic ēode** *I went*.

All but the last four of these are known as Preterit-Present Verbs. The present tense of each of them is *in origin* a preterit, *in function* a present. *Cf.* Modern English *ought* (= *owed*).

> 1. Most grammars add a sixth case, the vocative. But it seems best to consider the vocative as only a *function* of the nominative *form*.
>
> 2. Of course our "apostrophe and *s*" (= *'s*) comes from the Old English genitive ending **-es**. The *e* is preserved in *Wednesday* (= Old English **Wōdnes dæg**). But at a very early period it was thought that *John's book*, for example, was a shortened form of *John his book*. Thus Addison (*Spectator*, No. 135) declares *'s* a survival of *his*. How, then, would he explain the *s* of *his*? And how would he dispose of *Mary's book*?
>
> 3. Early West Saxon had no distinctive form for the future. The present was used both as present proper and as future. *Cf.* Modern English "I go home tomorrow," or "I am going home tomorrow" for "I shall go home tomorrow."
>
> 4. The prefix **ge-** (Middle English *y-*), cognate with Latin *co* (*con*) and implying completeness of action, was not always used. It never occurs in the past participles of compound verbs: **oþ-feallan**, *to fall off*, past participle **oþ-feallen** (not **oþ-gefeallen**). Milton errs in prefixing it to a present participle:
>
>> "What needs my Shakespeare, for his honour'd bones,
>>
>> The labour of an age in piled stones?
>>
>> Or that his hallow'd reliques should be hid
>>
>> Under a star-*ypointing* pyramid."
>>
>> —*Epitaph on William Shakespeare.*

And Shakespeare misuses it in "Y-ravished," a preterit (*Pericles* III, Prologue l. 35).

It survives in the archaic *y-clept* (Old English **ge-clypod**, called). It appears as *a* in *aware* (Old English **ge-wær**), as *e* in *enough* (Old English **ge-nōh**), and as *i* in *handiwork* (Old English **hand-ge-weorc**).

5. With intransitive verbs denoting *change of condition*, the Old English auxiliary is usually some form of *to be* rather than *to have*. See § 139.

6. The theory that *loved*, for example, is a fused form of *love-did* has been generally given up. The dental ending was doubtless an Indo-Germanic suffix, which became completely specialized only in the Teutonic languages.

CHAPTER IV.
ORDER OF WORDS.

20.

The order of words in Old English is more like that of Modern German than of Modern English. Yet it is only the Transposed order that the student will feel to be at all un-English; and the Transposed order, even before the period of the Norman Conquest, was fast yielding place to the Normal order.

The three divisions of order are (1) Normal, (2) Inverted, and (3) Transposed.

(1) Normal order = subject + predicate. In Old English, the Normal order is found chiefly in independent clauses. The predicate is followed by its modifiers: **Sē hwæl bið micle lǣssa þonne ōðre hwalas**, *That whale is much smaller than other whales*; **Ǫnd hē geseah twā scipu**, *And he saw two ships*.

(2) Inverted order = predicate + subject. This order occurs also in independent clauses, and is employed (*a*) when some modifier of the predicate precedes the predicate, the subject being thrown behind. The words most frequently causing Inversion in Old English prose are **þā** *then*, **þonne** *then*, and **þǣr** *there*: **Ðā fōr hē**, *Then went he*; **Ðonne ærnað hȳ ealle tōweard þǣm fēo**, *Then gallop they all toward the property*; **ac þǣr bið medo genōh**, *but there is mead enough*.

Inversion is employed (*b*) in interrogative sentences: **Lufast ðū mē?** *Lovest thou me?* and (*c*) in imperative sentences: **Cume ðīn rīce**, *Thy kingdom come*.

(3) Transposed order = subject ... predicate. That is, the predicate comes last in the sentence, being preceded by its modifiers. This is the order observed in dependent clauses:1 **Ðonne cymeð sē man sē þæt swiftoste hors hafað**, *Then comes the man that has the swiftest horse* (literally, *that the swiftest horse has*); **Ne mētte hē ǣr nān gebūn land, siþþan hē frǫm his āgnum hām fōr**, *Nor did he before find any cultivated land, after he went from his own home* (literally, *after he from his own home went*).

21.

Two other peculiarities in the order of words require a brief notice.

(1) Pronominal datives and accusatives usually precede the predicate: **Hē hine oferwann**, *He overcame him* (literally, *He him overcame*); **Dryhten him andwyrde**, *The Lord answered him*. But substantival datives and accusatives, as in Modern English, follow the predicate. The following sentence illustrates both orders: **Hȳ genāmon Ioseph, ǫnd hine gesealdon cīpemǫnnum, ǫnd hȳ hine gesealdon in Ēgypta lǫnd**, *They took Joseph, and sold him to merchants, and they sold him into Egypt* (literally, *They took Joseph, and him sold to merchants, and they him sold into Egyptians' land*).

NOTE.—The same order prevails in the case of pronominal nominatives used as predicate nouns: **Ic hit eom**, *It is I* (literally, *I it am*); **Ðū hit eart**, *It is thou* (literally, *Thou it art*).

(2) The attributive genitive, whatever relationship it expresses, usually precedes the noun which it qualifies: **Breoton is gārsecges īgland**, *Britain is an island of the ocean* (literally, *ocean's island*); **Swilce hit is ēac berende on węcga ōrum**, *Likewise it is also rich in ores of metals* (literally, *metals' ores*); **Cyninga cyning**, *King of kings* (literally, *Kings' king*); **Gē witon Godes rīces gerȳne**, *Ye know the mystery of the kingdom of God* (literally, *Ye know God's kingdom's mystery*).

A preposition governing the word modified by the genitive, precedes the genitive:2 **On ealdra manna sægenum**, *In old men's sayings*; **Æt ðǣra strǣta ęndum**, *At the ends of the streets* (literally, *At the streets' ends*); **For ealra ðīnra hālgena lufan**, *For all thy saints' love*. See, also, § 94, (5).

> 1. But in the *Voyages of Ohthere and Wulfstan*, in which the style is apparently more that of oral than of written discourse, the Normal is more frequent than the Transposed order in dependent clauses. In his other writings Alfred manifests a partiality for the Transposed order in dependent clauses, except in the case of substantival clauses introduced by **þæt**. Such clauses show a marked tendency to revert to their Normal *oratio recta* order. The norm thus set by the indirect affirmative clause seems to have

proved an important factor in the ultimate disappearance of Transposition from dependent clauses. The influence of Norman French helped only to consummate forces that were already busily at work.

2. The positions of the genitive are various. It frequently follows its noun: **þā bearn þāra Aðeniensa**, *The children of the Athenians.* It may separate an adjective and a noun: **Ān lȳtel sǣs earm**, *A little arm of (the) sea.* The genitive may here be construed as an adjective, or part of a compound = *A little sea-arm*; **Mid monegum Godes gifum**, *With many God-gifts = many divine gifts.*

CHAPTER V.
PRACTICAL SUGGESTIONS.

22.

In the study of Old English, the student must remember that he is dealing not with a foreign or isolated language but with the earlier forms of his own mother tongue. The study will prove profitable and stimulating in proportion as close and constant comparison is made of the old with the new. The guiding principles in such a comparison are reducible chiefly to two. These are (1) the regular operation of phonetic laws, resulting especially in certain Vowel Shiftings, and (2) the alterations in form and syntax that are produced by Analogy.

(1) "The former of these is of physiological or *natural* origin, and is perfectly and inflexibly regular throughout the same period of the same language; and even though different languages show different phonetic habits and predilections, there is a strong general resemblance between the changes induced in one language and in another; many of the particular laws are true for many languages.

(2) "The other principle is psychical, or mental, or *artificial*, introducing various more or less capricious changes that are supposed to be emendations; and its operation is, to some extent, uncertain and fitful."[1]

(1) Vowel-Shiftings.

23.

It will prove an aid to the student in acquiring the inflections and vocabulary of Old English to note carefully the following shiftings that have taken place in the gradual growth of the Old English vowel system into that of Modern English.

(1) As stated in § 3, the Old English inflectional vowels, which were all short and unaccented, weakened in early Middle English to *e*. This *e* in Modern English is frequently dropped:

Old English. Middle English. Modern English.

Old English	Middle English	Modern English
stān-as	ston-es	stones
sun-u	sun-e	son
sun-a	sun-e	sons
ox-an	ox-en	oxen
swift-ra	swift-er	swifter
swift-ost	swift-est	swiftest
lōc-ode	lok-ede	looked

(2) The Old English long vowels have shifted their phonetic values with such uniform regularity that it is possible in almost every case to infer the Modern English sound; but our spelling is so chaotic that while the student may infer the modern sound, he cannot always infer the modern symbol representing the sound.

Old English. Modern English.

ā	*o* (as in *no*)2	**nā** = *no*; **stān** = *stone*; **bān** = *bone*; **rād** = *road*; **āc** = *oak*; **hāl** = *whole*; **hām** = *home*; **sāwan** = *to sow*; **gāst** = *ghost*.
ē	*e* (as in *he*)	**hē** = *he*; **wē** = *we*; **ðē** = *thee*; **mē** = *me*; **gē** = *ye*; **hēl** = *heel*; **wērig** = *weary*; **gelēfan** = *to believe*; **gēs** = *geese*.
ī (ȳ)	*i* (*y*) (as in *mine*)	**mīn** = *mine*; **ðīn** = *thine*; **wīr** = *wire*; **mȳs** = *mice*; **rīm** = *rime* (wrongly spelt *rhyme*); **lȳs** = *lice*; **bī** = *by*; **scīnan** = *to shine*; **stig-rāp** = *sty-*

		rope (shortened to *stirrup*, **stīgan** meaning *to mount*).
ō	*o* (as in *do*)	**dō** = *I do*; **tō** = *too, to*; **gōs** = *goose*; **tōð** = *tooth*; **mōna** = *moon*; **ðōm** = *doom*; **mōd** = *mood*; **wōgian** = *to woo*; **slōh** = *I slew*.
ū	*ou* (*ow*) (as in *thou*)	**ðū** = *thou*; **fūl** = *foul*; **hūs** = *house*; **nū** = *now*; **hū** = *how*; **tūn** = *town*; **ūre** = *our*; **ūt** = *out*; **hlūd** = *loud*; **ðūsend** = *thousand*.
ǣ, ēa, ēo	*ea* (as in *sea*)	**ǣ**: **sǣ** = *sea*; **mǣl** = *meal*; **dǣlan** = *to deal*; **clǣne** = *clean*; **grǣdig** = *greedy*.
		ēa: **ēare** = *ear*; **ēast** = *east*; **drēam** = *dream*; **gēar** = *year*; **bēatan** = *to beat*.
		ēo: **ðrēo** = *three*; **drēorig** = *dreary*; **sēo** = *she*, **hrēod** = *reed*; **dēop** = *deep*.

(2) Analogy.

24.

But more important than vowel shifting is the great law of Analogy, for Analogy shapes not only words but constructions. It belongs, therefore, to Etymology and to Syntax, since it influences both form and function. By this law, minorities tend to pass over to the side of the majorities. "The greater mass of cases exerts an assimilative influence upon the smaller."[3] The effect of Analogy is to simplify and to regularize. "The main factor in getting rid of irregularities is group-influence, or Analogy—the influence exercised by the members of an association-group on one another.... Irregularity consists in partial isolation from an association-group through some formal difference."[4]

Under the influence of Analogy, entire declensions and conjugations have been swept away, leaving in Modern English not a trace of their former existence. There are in Old English, for example, five plural endings for nouns, **-as**, **-a**, **-e**, **-u**, and **-an**. No one could well have predicted[5] that **-as** (Middle English *-es*) would soon take the lead, and become the norm to which the other endings would eventually conform, for there were more **an**-plurals than **as**-plurals; but the **as**-plurals were doubtless more often employed in everyday speech. *Oxen* (Old English **oxan**) is the sole pure survival of the hundreds of Old English **an**-plurals. No group of feminine nouns in Old English had **-es** as the genitive singular ending; but by the close of the Middle English period all feminines formed their genitive singular in *-es* (or *-s*, Modern English *'s*) after the analogy of the Old English masculine and neuter nouns with **es**-genitives. The weak preterits in **-ode** have all been leveled under the **ed**-forms, and of the three hundred strong verbs in Old English more than two hundred have become weak.

These are not cases of derivation (as are the shifted vowels): Modern English *-s* in *sons*, for example, could not possibly be derived from Old English **-a** in **suna**, or Middle English *-e* in *sune* (§ 23, (1)). They are cases of replacement by Analogy.

A few minor examples will quicken the student's appreciation of the nature of the influence exercised by Analogy:

(*a*) The intrusive *l* in *could* (Chaucer always wrote *coud* or *coude*) is due to association with *would* and *should*, in each of which *l* belongs by etymological right.

(*b*) *He need not* (for *He needs not*) is due to the assimilative influence of the auxiliaries *may*, *can*, etc., which have never added *-s* for their third person singular (§ **137**).

(*c*) *I am friends with him*, in which *friends* is a crystalized form for *on good terms*, may be traced to the influence of such expressions as *He and I are friends*, *They are friends*, etc.

(*d*) Such errors as are seen in *runned*, *seed*, *gooses*, *badder*, *hisself*, *says I* (usually coupled with *says he*) are all analogical formations. Though not sanctioned by good usage, it is hardly right to call these forms the products of "false analogy." The grammar involved is false, because unsupported by literary usages and traditions; but the analogy on which these forms are built is no more false than the law of gravitation is false when it makes a dress sit unconventionally.

> 1. Skeat, *Principles of English Etymology*, Second Series, § 342. But Jespersen, with Collitz and others, stoutly contests "the theory of sound laws and analogy sufficing between them to explain everything in linguistic development."

2. But Old English **ā** preceded by **w** sometimes gives Modern English *o* as in *two*: **twā** = *two*; **hwā** = *who*; **hwām** = *whom*.

3. Whitney, *Life and Growth of Language*, Chap. IV.

4. Sweet, *A New English Grammar*, Part I., § 535.

5. As Skeat says (§ 22, (2)), Analogy is "fitful." It enables us to explain many linguistic phenomena, but not to anticipate them. The multiplication of books tends to check its influence by perpetuating the forms already in use. Thus Chaucer employed nine *en*-plurals, and his influence served for a time to check the further encroachment of the *es*-plurals. As soon as there is an acknowledged standard in any language, the operation of Analogy is fettered.

PART II.

ETYMOLOGY AND SYNTAX.

The Strong or Vowel Declensions of Nouns.
The a-Declension.

CHAPTER VI.

(*a*) **Masculine *a*-Stems.**

[O.E., M.E., and Mn.E. will henceforth be used for Old English, Middle English, and Modern English. Other abbreviations employed are self-explaining.]

25.

The **a**-Declension, corresponding to the Second or *o*-Declension of Latin and Greek, contains only (*a*) masculine and (*b*) neuter nouns. To this declension belong most of the O.E. masculine and neuter nouns of the Strong Declension. At a very early period, many of the nouns belonging properly to the **i**- and **u**-Declensions began to pass over to the **a**-Declension. This declension may therefore be considered the *normal declension* for all masculine and neuter nouns belonging to the Strong Declension.

26.

Paradigms of **sē mūð**, *mouth*; **sē fiscere**, *fisherman*; **sē hwæl**, *whale*; **sē mearh**, *horse*; **sē finger**, *finger*:

Sing. N.A.	mūð	fiscer-e	hwæl	mearh	finger
G.	mūð-es	fiscer-es	hwæl-es	mēar-es	fingr-es
D.I.	mūð-e	fiscer-e	hwæl-e	mēar-e	fingr-e
Plur N.A.	mūð-as	fiscer-as	hwal-as	mēar-as	fingr-as
G.	mūð-a	fiscer-a	hwal-a	mēar-a	fingr-a
D.I.	mūð-um	fiscer-um	hwal-um	mēar-um	fingr-um

NOTE.—For meanings of the cases, see § 12. The dative and instrumental are alike in all nouns.

27.

The student will observe (1) that nouns whose nominative ends in **-e** (**fiscere**) drop this letter before adding the case endings; (2) that **æ** before a consonant (**hwæl**) changes to **a** in the plural;1 (3) that **h**, preceded by **r** (**mearh**) or **l** (**seolh**, *seal*), is dropped before an inflectional vowel, the stem diphthong being then lengthened by way of compensation; (4) that dissyllables (**finger**) having the first syllable long, usually syncopate the vowel of the second syllable before adding the case endings.2

28.

Paradigm of the Definite Article3 **sē, sēo, ðæt** = *the*:

	Masculine.	Feminine.	Neuter.
Sing. N.	sē (se)	sēo	ðæt
G.	ðæs	ðǣre	ðæs
D.	ðǣm (ðām)	ðǣre	ðǣm (ðām)
A.	ðone	ðā	ðæt
I.	ðȳ, ðon	——	ðȳ, ðon

All Genders.

Plur. N.A.	ðā
G.	ðāra
D.	ðǣm (ðām)

29.

VOCABULARY.4

    sē bōcere, *scribe* [bōc].

    sē cyning, *king.*

    sē dæg, *day.*

    sē ęnde, *end.*

    sē ęngel, *angel* [angelus].

    sē frēodōm, *freedom.*

    sē fugol (G. sometimes **fugles**), *bird* [fowl].

sē **gār**, *spear* [gore, gar-fish].

sē **heofon**, *heaven.*

sē **hierde**, *herdsman* [shep-herd].

ǫnd (and), *and.*

sē **sęcg**, *man, warrior.*

sē **seolh**, *seal.*

sē **stān**, *stone.*

sē **wealh**, *foreigner, Welshman* [wal-nut].

sē **weall**, *wall.*

sē **wīsdōm**, *wisdom.*

sē **wulf**, *wolf.*

30.

EXERCISES.

I. 1. Ðāra wulfa mūðas. 2. Ðæs fisceres fingras. 3. Ðāra Wēala cyninge. 4. Ðǣm ęnglum ǫnd ðǣm hierdum. 5. Ðāra daga ęnde. 6. Ðǣm bōcerum ǫnd ðǣm sęcgum ðæs cyninges. 7. Ðǣm sēole ǫnd ðǣm fuglum. 8. Ðā stānas ǫnd ðā gāras. 9. Hwala ǫnd mēara. 10. Ðāra ęngla wīsdōm. 11. Ðæs cyninges bōceres frēodōm. 12. Ðāra hierda fuglum. 13. Ðȳ stāne. 14. Ðǣm wealle.

II. 1. For the horses and the seals. 2. For the Welshmen's freedom. 3. Of the king's birds. 4. By the wisdom of men and angels. 5. With the spear and the stone. 6. The herdsman's seal and the warriors' spears. 7. To the king of heaven. 8. By means of the scribe's wisdom. 9. The whale's mouth and the foreigner's spear. 10. For the bird belonging to (= of) the king's scribe. 11. Of that finger.

> 1. Adjectives usually retain **æ** in closed syllables, changing it to **a** in open syllables: **hwæt** (*active*), **glæd** (*glad*), **wær** (*wary*) have G. **hwates, glades, wares**; D. **hwatum, gladum, warum**; but A. **hwætne, glædne, wærne**. Nouns, however, change to **a** only in open syllables followed by a guttural vowel, **a** or **u**. The **æ** in the open syllables of the singular is doubtless due to the analogy of the N.A. singular, both being closed syllables.
>
> 2. *Cf.* Mn.E. *drizz'ling, rememb'ring, abysmal* (*abysm* = *abiz^{u}m*), *sick'ning*, in which the principle of syncopation is precisely the same.

3. This may mean four things: (1) *The*, (2) *That* (demonstrative), (3) *He, she, it*, (4) *Who, which, that* (relative pronoun). Mn.E. demonstrative *that* is, of course, the survival of O.E. neuter **ðæt** in its demonstrative sense. Professor Victor Henry (*Comparative Grammar of English and German*, § 160, 3) sees a survival of dative plural demonstrative **ðǣm** in such an expression as *in them days*. It seems more probable, however, that *them* so used has followed the lead of *this* and *these*, *that* and *those*, in their double function of pronoun and adjective. There was doubtless some such evolution as, *I saw them. Them what? Them boys.*

An unquestioned survival of the dative singular feminine of the article is seen in the *-ter* of *Atterbury* (= **æt ðǣre byrig**, *at the town*); and **ðǣm** survives in the *-ten* of *Attenborough*, the word *borough* having become an uninflected neuter. Skeat, *Principles*, First Series, § 185.

4. The brackets contain etymological hints that may help the student to discern relationships otherwise overlooked. The genitive is given only when not perfectly regular.

CHAPTER VII.

(*b*) **Neuter *a*-Stems.**

31.

The neuter nouns of the **a**-Declension differ from the masculines only in the N.A. plural.

32.

Paradigms of **ðæt hof**, *court, dwelling*; **ðæt bearn**, *child*; **ðæt bān**, *bone*; **ðæt rīce**, *kingdom*; **ðæt spere**, *spear*; **ðæt werod**, *band of men*; **ðæt tungol**, *star*.

Sing. N.A.	hof	bearn	bān	rīc-e	sper-e	werod	tungol
G.	hof-es	bearn-es	bān-es	rīc-es	sper-es	werod-es	tungl-es
D.I.	hof-e	bearn-e	bān-e	rīc-e	sper-e	werod-e	tungl-e

Plur N.A.	hof-u	bearn	bān	rīc-u	sper-u	werod	tungl-u
G.	hof-a	bearn-a	bān-a	rīc-a	sper-a	werod-a	tungl-a
D.I.	hof-um	bearn-um	bān-um	rīc-um	sper-um	werod-um	tungl-um

33.

The paradigms show (1) that monosyllables with short stems (**hof**) take **-u** in the N.A. plural; (2) that monosyllables with long stems (**bearn, bān**) do not distinguish the N.A. plural from the N.A. singular;1 (3) that dissyllables in **-e**, whether the stem be long or short (**rīce, spere**), have **-u** in the N.A. plural; (4) that dissyllables ending in a consonant and having the first syllable short2 (**werod**) do not usually distinguish the N.A. plural from the N.A. singular; (5) that dissyllables ending in a consonant and having the first syllable long (**tungol**) more frequently take **-u** in the N.A. plural.

NOTE.—Syncopation occurs as in the masculine **a**-stems. See § 27, (4).

34.

Present and Preterit Indicative of **habban**, *to have*:

PRESENT.

Sing. 1. **Ic hæbbe**, *I have*, or *shall have*.3

2. **ðū hæfst (hafast)**, *thou hast*, or *wilt have*.

3. **hē, hēo, hit hæfð (hafað)**, *he, she, it has*, or *will have*.

Plur. 1. **wē habbað**, *we have*, or *shall have*.

2. **gē habbað**, *ye have*, or *will have*.

3. **hīe habbað**, *they have*, or *will have*.

PRETERIT.

Sing. 1. **Ic hæfde** *I had*.

2. **ðū hæfdest**, *thou hadst*.

3. **hē, hēo, hit hæfde**, *he, she, it had*.

Plur. 1. **wē hæfdon**, *we had*.

2. **gē hæfdon**, *ye had*.

3. **hīe hæfdon**, *they had*.

NOTE.—The negative **ne**, *not*, which always precedes its verb, contracts with all the forms of **habban**. The negative loses its **e**, **habban** its **h**. Ne + habban = nabban; Ic ne hæbbe = Ic næbbe; Ic ne hæfde = Ic næfde, etc. The negative forms may be got, therefore, by simply substituting in each case **n** for **h**.

35.

Vocabulary.

    ðæt **dæl**, *dale.*

    ðæt **dēor**, *animal* [deer4].

    ðæt **dor**, *door.*

    ðæt **fæt**, *vessel* [vat].

    ðæt **fȳr**, *fire.*

    ðæt **gēar**, *year.*

    ðæt **geoc**, *yoke.*

    ðæt **geset**, *habitation* [settlement].

    ðæt **hēafod**, *head.*

    ðæt **hūs**, *house.*

    ðæt **līc**, *body* [lich-gate].

    ðæt **lim**, *limb.*

    on (with dat.) *in.*

    ðæt **spor**, *track.*

    ðæt **wǣpen**, *weapon.*

    ðæt **wīf**, *wife, woman.*

    ðæt **wīte**, *punishment.*

    ðæt **word**, *word.*

36.

EXERCISES.

I. 1. Hē hafað ðæs cyninges bearn. 2. Ðā Wēalas habbað ðā speru. 3. Ðā wīf habbað ðāra secga wǣpnu. 4. Ðū hæfst ðone fugol ǫnd ðæt hūs ðæs hierdes. 5. Hæfð5 hēo ðā fatu6? 6. Hæfde hē ðæs wīfes līc on ðǣm hofe? 7. Hē næfde ðæs wīfes līc; hē hæfde ðæs dēores hēafod. 8. Hæfð sē cyning gesetu on ðǣm dæle? 9. Sē bōcere hæfð ðā sēolas on ðǣm hūse. 10. Gē habbað frēodōm.

II. 1. They have yokes and spears. 2. We have not the vessels in the house. 3. He had fire in the vessel. 4. Did the woman have (= Had the woman) the children? 5. The animal has the body of the woman's child. 6. I shall have the heads of the wolves. 7. He and she have the king's houses. 8. Have not (= **Nabbað**) the children the warrior's weapons?

> 1. Note the many nouns in Mn.E. that are unchanged in the plural. These are either survivals of O.E. long stems, *swine, sheep, deer, folk*, or analogical forms, *fish, trout, mackerel, salmon*, etc.
>
> 2. Dissyllables whose first syllable is a prefix are, of course, excluded. They follow the declension of their last member: **gebed**, *prayer*, **gebedu**, *prayers*; **gefeoht**, *battle*, **gefeoht**, *battles*.
>
> 3. See § 17, Note 1. Note that (as in **hwæl**, § 27, (2)) **æ** changes to **a** when the following syllable contains **a**: **hæbbe**, but **hafast**.
>
> 4. The old meaning survives in Shakespeare's "Rats and mice and such small deer," *King Lear*, III, IV, 144.
>
> 5. See § 20, (2), (b).
>
> 6. See § 27, (2).

CHAPTER VIII.
THE ō-DECLENSION.

37.

The ō-Declension, corresponding to the First or *ā*-Declension of Latin and Greek, contains only feminine nouns. Many feminine **i**-stems and **u**-stems soon passed over to this Declension. The ō-Declension may, therefore, be considered the *normal declension* for all strong feminine nouns.

38.

Paradigms of **sēo giefu**, *gift*; **sēo wund**, *wound*; **sēo rōd**, *cross*; **sēo leornung**, *learning*; **sēo sāwol**, *soul*:

Sing. N.	gief-u	wund	rōd	leornung	sāwol
G.	gief-e	wund-e	rōd-e	leornung-a (e)	sāwl-e

D.I.	gief-e	wund-e	rōd-e	leornung-a(e)	sāwl-e
A.	gief-e	wund-e	rōd-e	leornung-a(e)	sāwl-e
Plur. N.A.	gief-a	wund-a	rōd-a	leornung-a	sāwl-a
G.	gief-a	wund-a	rōd-a	leornung-a	sāwl-a
D.I.	gief-um	wund-um	rōd-um	leornung-um	sāwl-um

39.

Note (1) that monosyllables with short stems (**giefu**) take **u** in the nominative singular; (2) that monosyllables with long stems (**wund, rōd**) present the unchanged stem in the nominative singular; (3) that dissyllables are declined as monosyllables, except that abstract nouns in **-ung** prefer **a** to **e** in the singular.

NOTE.—Syncopation occurs as in masculine and neuter **a**-stems. See § 27, (4).

40.

Present and Preterit Indicative of **bēon** (**wesan**) *to be*:

	PRESENT (first form).	PRESENT (second form).	PRETERIT.
Sing. 1.	Ic eom	1. Ic bēom	1. Ic wæs
2.	ðū eart	2. ðū bist	2. ðū wǣre
3.	hē is	3. hē bið	3. hē wæs
Plur. 1.	wē ⎫	1. wē ⎫	1. wē ⎫
2.	gē ⎬ sind(on), sint	2. gē ⎬ bēoð	2. gē ⎬ wǣron
3.	hīe ⎭	3. hīe ⎭	3. hīe ⎭

NOTE 1.—The forms **bēom, bist**, etc. are used chiefly as future tenses in O.E. They survive to-day only in dialects and in poetry. Farmer Dobson, for example, in Tennyson's *Promise of May*, uses *be* for all persons of the present indicative, both singular and plural; and *there be* is frequent in Shakespeare for *there are*. The Northern dialect employed **aron** as well as **sindon** and **sind** for the present plural; hence Mn.E. *are*.

NOTE 2.—Fusion with **ne** gives **neom, neart, nis** for the present; **næs, nǣre, nǣron** for the preterit.

NOTE 3.—The verb *to be* is followed by the nominative case, as in Mn.E.; but when the predicate noun is plural, and the subject a neuter pronoun in the singular, the verb agrees in number with the predicate noun. The neuter singular ðæt is frequently employed in this construction: **Ðæt wǣron eall Finnas,** *They were all Fins*; **Ðæt sind ęnglas,** *They are angels*; **Ðæt wǣron ęngla gāstas,** *They were angels' spirits*.

Notice, too, that O.E. writers do not say *It is I, It is thou*, but *I it am, Thou it art*: **Ic hit eom, ðū hit eart.** See § 21, (1), Note 1.

41.

Vocabulary.

    sēo brycg, *bridge.*

    sēo costnung, *temptation.*

    sēo cwalu, *death* [quail, quell].

    sēo fōr, *journey* [faran].

    sēo frōfor, *consolation, comfort.*

    sēo geoguð, *youth.*

    sēo glōf, *glove.*

    sēo hālignes[1], *holiness.*

    sēo heall, *hall.*

    hēr, *here.*

    hwā, *who?*

    hwǣr, *where?*

    sēo lufu, *love.*

    sēo mearc, *boundary* [mark, marches[2]].

sēo mēd, *meed, reward.*

sēo mildheortnes, *mild-heartedness, mercy.*

sēo stōw, *place* [stow away].

ðǣr, *there.*

sēo ðearf, *need.*

sēo wylf, *she wolf.*

42.

EXERCISES.

I. 1. Hwǣr is ðǣre brycge ęnde? 2. Hēr sind ðāra rīca mearca. 3. Hwā hæfð þā glōfa? 4. Ðǣr bið ðǣm cyninge frōfre ðearf. 5. Sēo wund is on ðǣre wylfe hēafde. 6. Wē habbað costnunga. 7. Hīe nǣron on ðǣre healle. 8. Ic hit neom. 9. Ðæt wǣron Wēalas. 10. Ðæt sind ðæs wīfes bearn.

II. 1. We shall have the women's gloves. 2. Where is the place? 3. He will be in the hall. 4. Those (**Ðæt**) were not the boundaries of the kingdom. 5. It was not I. 6. Ye are not the king's scribes. 7. The shepherd's words are full (**full + gen.**) of wisdom and comfort. 8. Where are the bodies of the children? 9. The gifts are not here. 10. Who has the seals and the birds?

> 1. All words ending in **-nes** double the **-s** before adding the case endings.
>
> 2. As in *warden of the marches.*

CHAPTER IX.
THE **i**-DECLENSION AND THE **u**-DECLENSION.

The *i*-Declension. (See § 58.)

43.

The **i**-Declension, corresponding to the group of *i*-stems in the classical Third Declension, contains chiefly (*a*) masculine and (*b*) feminine nouns. The N.A. plural of these nouns ended originally in **-e** (from older **i**).

(*a*) Masculine *i*-Stems.

44.

These stems have almost completely gone over to the **a**-Declension, so that **-as** is more common than **-e** as the N.A. plural ending, whether the stem is long or short. The short stems all have **-e** in the N.A. singular.

45.

Paradigms of **sē wyrm**, *worm*; **sē wine**, *friend.*

Sing. N.A.	wyrm	win-e
G.	wyrm-es	win-es
D.I.	wyrm-e	win-e
Plur N.A.	wyrm-as	win-as (e)
G.	wyrm-a	win-a
D.I.	wyrm-um	win-um

Names of Peoples.

46.

The only **i**-stems that regularly retain **-e** of the N.A. plural are certain names of tribes or peoples used only in the plural.

47.

Paradigms of **ðā Ęngle**, *Angles*; **ðā Norðymbre**, *Northumbrians*; **ðā lēode**, *people*:

Plur. N.A.	Ęngle	Norðymbre	lēode
G.	Ęngla	Norðymbra	lēoda
D.I.	Ęnglum	Norðymbrum	lēodum

(b) Feminine *i*-Stems.

48.

The short stems (**fręm-u**) conform entirely to the declension of short ō-stems; long stems (**cwēn, wyrt**) differ from long ō-stems in having no ending for the A. singular. They show, also, a preference for **-e** rather than **-a** in the N.A. plural.

49.

Paradigms of **sēo fręm-u**, *benefit*; **sēo cwēn**, *woman, queen* [quean]; **sēo wyrt**, *root* [wort]:

Sing. N.	fręm-u	cwēn	wyrt
G.	fręm-e	cwēn-e	wyrt-e
D.I.	fręm-e	cwēn-e	wyrt-e

A.	fręm-e	cwēn	wyrt
Plur N.A.	fręm-a	cwēn-e (a)	wyrt-e (a)
G.	fręm-a	cwēn-a	wyrt-a
D.I.	fręm-um	cwēn-um	wyrt-um

The *u*-Declension.

50.

The **u**-Declension, corresponding to the group of **u**-stems in the classical Third Declension, contains no neuters, and but few (*a*) masculines and (*b*) feminines. The short-stemmed nouns of both genders (**sun-u, dur-u**) retain the final **u** of the N.A. singular, while the long stems (**feld, họnd**) drop it. The influence of the masculine **a**-stems is most clearly seen in the long-stemmed masculines of the **u**-Declension (**feld, feld-es,** etc.).

NOTE.—Note the general aversion of all O.E. long stems to final **-u**: *cf.* N.A. plural **hof-u,** but **bearn, bān**; N. singular **gief-u,** but **wund, rōd**; N. singular **fręm-u,** but **cwēn, wyrt**; N.A. singular **sun-u, dur-u,** but **feld, họnd**.

(*a*) Masculine *u*-Stems.

51.

Paradigms of **sē sun-u,** *son*; **sē feld,** *field*:

Sing. N.A.	sun-u	feld
G.	sun-a	feld-a (es)
D.I.	sun-a	feld-a (e)
Plur N.A.	sun-a	feld-a (as)
G.	sun-a	feld-a
D.I.	sun-um	feld-um

(b) Feminine *u*-Stems.

52.

Paradigms of **sēo dur-u,** *door*; **sēo họnd,** *hand*:

Sing. N.A.	dur-u	họnd
G.	dur-a	họnd-a

D.I.	dur-a	hǫnd-a

Plur N.A.	dur-a	hǫnd-a
G.	dur-a	hǫnd-a
D.I.	dur-um	hǫnd-um

53.

Paradigm of the Third Personal Pronoun, **hē**, **hēo**, **hit** = *he, she, it*:

	Masculine.	Feminine.	Neuter.
Sing. N.	hē	hēo	hit
G.	his	hiere	his
D.	him	hiere	him
A.	hine, hiene	hīe	hit

All Genders.

Plur. N.A.	hīe
G.	hiera
D.	him

54.

Vocabulary.

(**i**-STEMS.)

sē cierr, *turn, time* [char, chare, chore].

sēo dǣd, *deed*.

sē dǣl, *part* [a great deal].

ðā Dęne, *Danes*.

sē frēondscipe, *friendship*.

sēo hȳd, *skin, hide*.

ðā lǫndlēode, *natives*.

ðā Mierce, *Mercians*.

ðā Rōmware, *Romans*.

ðā **Seaxe**, *Saxons.*

sē **stęde**, *place* [in-stead of].

(**u**-STEMS.)

sēo **flōr**, *floor.*

sēo **nosu**, *nose.*

sē **sumor** (*G.* **sumeres**, *D.* **sumera**), *summer.*

sē **winter** (*G.* **wintres**, *D.* **wintra**), *winter.*

sē **wudu**, *wood, forest.*

NOTE.—The numerous masculine nouns ending in **-hād**,—**cildhād** (*childhood*), **wīfhād** (*womanhood*),—belong to the **u**-stems historically; but they have all passed over to the **a**-Declension.

55.

Exercises.

I. 1. Ðā Seaxe habbað ðæs dēores hȳd on ðǣm wuda. 2. Hwā hæfð ðā giefa? 3. Ðā Mierce hīe1 habbað. 4. Hwǣr is ðæs Wēales fugol? 5. Ðā Dęne hiene habbað. 6. Hwǣr sindon hiera winas? 7. Hīe sindon on ðæs cyninges wuda. 8. Ðā Rōmware ǫnd ðā Seaxe hæfdon ðā gāras ǫnd ðā geocu. 9. Hēo is on ðǣm hūse on wintra, ǫnd on ðǣm feldum on sumera. 10. Hwǣr is ðæs hofes duru? 11. Hēo2 (= sēo duru) nis hēr.

II. 1. His friends have the bones of the seals and the bodies of the Danes. 2. Art thou the king's son? 3. Has she her3 gifts in her3 hands? 4. Here are the fields of the natives. 5. Who had the bird? 6. I had it.2 7. The child had the worm in his3 fingers. 8. The Mercians were here during (the) summer (**on** + dat.).

1. See § 21, (1).

2. Pronouns agree in gender with the nouns for which they stand. **Hit**, however, sometimes stands for inanimate things of both masculine and feminine genders. See Wülfing (*l.c.*) I, § 238.

3. See § 76 (last sentence).

CHAPTER X.
PRESENT INDICATIVE ENDINGS OF STRONG VERBS.

56.

The unchanged stem of the present indicative may always be found by dropping **-an** of the infinitive: **feall-an**, *to fall*; **cēos-an**, *to choose*; **bīd-an**, *to abide*.

57.

The personal endings are:

Sing. 1. **-e**   *Plur.* 1. ⎫
       2. **-est**   2. ⎬ **-að**
       3. **-eð**   3. ⎭

i-**Umlaut.**

58.

The 2d and 3d singular endings were originally not **-est** and **-eð**, but **-is** and **-ið**; and the **i** of these older endings has left its traces upon almost every page of Early West Saxon literature. This **i**, though unaccented and soon displaced, exerted a powerful back influence upon the vowel of the preceding accented syllable. This influence, a form of regressive assimilation, is known as **i**-umlaut (pronounced *oóm-lowt*). The vowel **i** or **j** (= *y*), being itself a palatal, succeeded in palatalizing every guttural vowel that preceded it, and in imposing still more of the **i**-quality upon diphthongs that were already palatal.1 The changes produced were these:

a	became	ę (æ):	**męnn** (< ***mann-iz**), *men*.
ā	"	ǣ	**ǣnig** (< ***ān-ig**), *any*.
u	"	y	**wyllen** (< ***wull-in**), *woollen*.
ū	"	ȳ	**mȳs** (< ***mūs-iz**), *mice*.
o	"	ę	**dęhter** (< ***dohtr-i**), *to or for the daughter*.
ō	"	ē	**fēt** (< ***fōt-iz**), *feet*.
ea	"	ie	**wiexð** (< ***weax-ið**), *he grows* (**weaxan** = *to grow*).
ēa	"	īe	**hīewð** (< ***hēaw-ið**), *he hews* (**hēawan** = to *hew*).
eo	"	ie	**wiercan** (< ***weorc-jan**), *to work*.
ēo	"	īe	**līehtan** (< ***lēoht-jan**), *to light*.

- 40 -

The Unchanged Present Indicative.

59.

In the Northumbrian and Mercian dialects, as well as in the dialect of Late West Saxon, the 2d and 3d singular endings were usually joined to the present stem without modification either of the stem itself or of the personal endings. The complete absence of umlauted forms in the present indicative of Mn.E. is thus accounted for.

In Early West Saxon, however, such forms as the following are comparatively rare in the 2d and 3d singular:

Sing. 1.   Ic feall-e (*I fall*)   cēos-e (*I choose*)   bīd-e (*I abide*)
2.   ðū feall-est   cēos-est   bīd-est
3.   hē feall-eð   cēos-eð   bīd-eð

Plur. 1.   wē
2.   gē } feall-að   cēos-að   bīd-að
3.   hīe

The Present Indicative with i-Umlaut and Contraction.

60.

The 2d and 3d persons singular are distinguished from the other forms of the present indicative in Early West Saxon by (1) **i**-umlaut of the vowel of the stem, (2) syncope of the vowel of the ending, giving **-st** and **-ð** for **-est** and **-eð**, and (3) contraction of **-st** and **-ð** with the final consonant or consonants of the stem.

Contraction.

61.

The changes produced by **i**-umlaut have been already discussed. By these changes, therefore, the stems of the 2d and 3d singular indicative of such verbs as (1) **stǫndan** (= **standan**), *to stand*, (2) **cuman**, *to come*, (3) **grōwan**, *to grow*, (4) **brūcan**, *to enjoy*, (5) **blāwan**, *to blow*, (6) **feallan**, *to fall*, (7) **hēawan**, *to hew*, (8) **weorpan**, *to throw*, and (9) **cēosan**, *to choose*, become respectively (1) **stęnd-**,2 (2) **cym-**, (3) **grēw-**, (4) **brȳc-**, (5) **blǣw-**, (6) **fiell-**, (7) **hīew-**, (8) **wierp-**, and (9) **cīes-**.

If the unchanged stem contains the vowel **e**, this is changed in the 2d and 3d singular to **i** (**ie**): **cweðan** *to say*, stem **cwið-**; **beran** *to bear*, stem **bier-**. But this mutation3 had taken place long before the period of O.E., and belongs to the Germanic languages in general. It is best, however, to class the change of **e** to **i** or **ie** with the changes due to umlaut, since it occurs consistently in the 2d and 3d singular stems of Early West Saxon, and outlasted almost all of the umlaut forms proper.

If, now, the syncopated endings **-st** and **-ð** are added directly to the umlauted stem, there will frequently result such a massing of consonants as almost to defy pronunciation: **cwið-st**, *thou sayest*; **stęnd-st**, *thou standest*, etc. Some sort of contraction, therefore, is demanded for the sake of euphony. The ear and eye will, by a little practice, become a sure guide in these contractions. The following rules, however, must be observed. They apply only to the 2d and 3d singular of the present indicative:

(1) If the stem ends in a double consonant, one of the consonants is dropped:

    1. feall-e (*I fall*)   1. winn-e (*I fight*)   1. swimm-e (*I swim*)

    2. fiel-st   2. win-st   2. swim-st

    3. fiel-ð   3. win-ð   3. swim-ð

(2) If the stem ends in **-ð**, this is dropped:

    1. cweð-e (*I say*)   1. weorð-e (*I become*)

    2. cwi-st   2. wier-st

    3. cwi-ð   3. wier-ð

(3) If the stem ends in **-d**, this is changed to **-t**. The **-ð** of the ending is then also changed to **-t**, and usually absorbed. Thus the stem of the 2d singular serves as stem and ending for the 3d singular:

    1. stǫnd-e (=   1. bind-e (*I*   1. bīd-e (*I*   1. rīd-e (*I*

        stand-e) (*I*   bind*)   abide*)   ride*)

                        stand*)

    2. stęnt-st   2. bint-st   2. bīt-st   2. rīt-st

    3. stęnt   3. bint   3. bīt (-t)   3. rīt (-t)

(4) If the stem ends already in **-t**, the endings are added as in (3), **-ð** being again changed to **-t** and absorbed:

    1. brēot-e (*I break*)   1. feoht-e (*I fight*)   1. bīt-e (*I bite*)

    2. brīet-st   2. fieht-st   2. bīt-st

    3. brīet (-t)   3. fieht   3. bīt (-t)

(5) If the stem ends in **-s**, this is dropped before **-st** (to avoid **-sst**), but is retained before **-ð**, the latter being changed to **-t**. Thus the 2d and 3d singulars are identical:4

1. cēos-e (*I choose*)   1. rīs-e (*I rise*)
2. cīe-st   2. rī-st
3. cīes-t   3. rīs-t

62.

Exercises.

I. 1. Sē cyning fielð. 2. Ðā wīf cēosað ðā giefa. 3. Ðū stęntst on ðǣm hūse. 4. Hē wierpð ðæt wǣpen. 5. Sē sęcg hīewð ðā līc. 6. Ðæt sǣd grēwð ǫnd wiexð (*Mark* iv. 27). 7. Ic stǫnde hēr, ǫnd ðū stęntst ðǣr. 8. "Ic hit eom," cwið hē. 9. Hīe berað ðæs wulfes bān. 10. Hē hīe bint, ǫnd ic hine binde. 11. Ne rītst ðū?

II. 1. We shall bind him. 2. Who chooses the child's gifts? 3. "He was not here," says she. 4. Wilt thou remain in the hall? 5. The wolves are biting (= bite) the fishermen. 6. He enjoys5 the love of his children. 7. Do you enjoy (= Enjoyest thou) the consolation and friendship of the scribe? 8. Will he come? 9. I shall throw the spear, and thou wilt bear the weapons. 10. The king's son will become king. 11. The army (**werod**) is breaking the doors and walls of the house.

> 1. The *palatal* vowels and diphthongs were long or short **æ, e, i, (ie), y, ea, eo**; the *guttural* vowels were long or short **a, o, u**.
>
> 2. The more common form for stems with **a** is **æ** rather than **ę**: **faran**, *to go*, 2d and 3d singular stem **fær-**; **sacan**, *to contend*, stem **sæc-**. Indeed, **a** changes to **ę** via **æ** (Cosijn, *Altwestsächsische Grammatik*, I, § 32).
>
> 3. Umlaut is frequently called Mutation. Metaphony is still another name for the same phenomenon. The term Metaphony has the advantage of easy adjectival formation (metaphonic). It was proposed by Professor Victor Henry (*Comparative Grammar of English and German*, Paris, 1894), but has not been naturalized.
>
> 4. This happens also when the infinitive stem ends in **st**:
>
>> 1. berst-e (*I burst*)
>>
>> 2. bier-st

3. bierst.

5. **Brūcan**, *to enjoy*, usually takes the genitive case, not the accusative. It means "to have joy of any thing."

CHAPTER XI.
The Consonant Declensions of Nouns.

The Weak or *n*-Declension.

63.

The **n**-Declension contains almost all of the O.E. nouns belonging to the Consonant Declensions. The stem characteristic **n** has been preserved in the oblique cases, so that there is no difficulty in distinguishing **n**-stems from the preceding vowel stems.

The **n**-Declension includes (*a*) masculines, (*b*) feminines, and (*c*) neuters. The masculines far outnumber the feminines, and the neuters contain only **ēage**, *eye* and **ēare**, *ear*. The masculines end in **-a**, the feminines and neuters in **-e**.

64.

Paradigms of (*a*) **sē hunta**, *hunter*; (*b*) **sēo tunge**, *tongue*; (*c*) **ðæt ēage**, *eye*:

Sing. N.	hunt-a	tung-e	ēag-e
G.D.I.	hunt-an	tung-an	ēag-an
A.	hunt-an	tung-an	ēag-e
Plur N.A.	hunt-an	tung-an	ēag-an
G.	hunt-ena	tung-ena	ēag-ena
D.I.	hunt-um	tung-um	ēag-um

65.

Vocabulary.

    sē adesa, *hatchet, adze*.

    sē ǣmetta, *leisure* [empt-iness].

    sē bǫna (bana), *murderer* [bane].

    sēo cirice, *church* [Scotch kirk].

    sē cnapa (later, **cnafa**), *boy* [knave].

sē cuma, *stranger* [comer].

ðæt ēare, *ear*.

sēo eorðe, *earth*.

sē gefēra, *companion* [co-farer].

sē guma, *man* [bride-groom1].

sēo heorte, *heart*.

sē mōna, *moon*.

sēo nǣdre, *adder* [a nadder > an adder2].

sē oxa, *ox*.

sē scēowyrhta, *shoe-maker* [shoe-wright].

sēo sunne, *sun*.

sē tēona, *injury* [teen].

biddan (with dat. of person and gen. of thing3), *to request, ask for*.

cwelan, *to die* [quail].

gescieppan, *to create* [shape, land-scape, friend-ship].

giefan (with dat. of indirect object), *to give*.

healdan, *to hold*.

helpan (with dat.), *to help*.

scęððan4 (with dat.), *to injure* [scathe].

wiðstǫndan (-standan) (with dat.), *to withstand*.

wrītan, *to write*.

66.

Exercises.

I. 1. Sē scēowyrhta brȳcð his ǣmettan. 2. Ðā guman biddað ðǣm cnapan ðæs adesan. 3. Hwā is sē cuma? 4. Hielpst ðū ðǣm bǫnan? 5. Ic him ne helpe. 6. Ðā bearn scęððað ðæs bǫnan ēagum ǫnd ēarum. 7. Sē cuma cwielð on ðǣre cirican. 8. Sē hunta wiðstęnt ðǣm wulfum. 9. Ðā oxan berað ðæs cnapan gefēran. 10. Sē mōna ǫnd ðā tunglu sind on ðǣm heofonum. 11. Ðā huntan healdað ðǣre nǣdran tungan. 12. Hē hiere giefð ðā giefa. 13. Ðā werod scęððað ðæs cyninges feldum.

II. 1. Who will bind the mouths of the oxen? 2. Who gives him the gifts? 3. Thou art helping him, and I am injuring him. 4. The boy's companion is dying. 5. His nephew does not enjoy his leisure. 6. The adder's tongue injures the king's companion. 7. The sun is the day's eye. 8. She asks the strangers for the spears. 9. The men's bodies are not here. 10. Is he not (**Nis hē**) the child's murderer? 11. Who creates the bodies and the souls of men? 12. Thou withstandest her. 13. He is not writing.

> 1. The *r* is intrusive in *-groom*, as it is in *cart-r-idge, part-r-idge, vag-r-ant,* and *hoa-r-se*.
>
> 2. The *n* has been appropriated by the article. Cf. *an apron* (< *a napron*), *an auger* (< *a nauger*), *an orange* (< *a norange*), *an umpire* (< *a numpire*).
>
> 3. In Mn.E. we say "I request a favor of you"; but in O.E. it was "I request you (dative) of a favor" (genitive). Cf. *Cymbeline*, III, VI, 92: "We'll mannerly demand thee of thy story." See Franz's *Shakespeare-Grammatik*, § 361 (1900).
>
> 4. **Scęððan** is conjugated through the present indicative like **fręmman**. See § 129.

CHAPTER XII.

Remnants of Other Consonant Declensions.

67.

The nouns belonging here are chiefly masculines and feminines. Their stem ended in a consonant other than **n**. The most important of them may be divided as follows: (1) The *foot* Declension, (2) **r**-Stems, and (3) **nd**-Stems. These declensions are all characterized by the prevalence, wherever possible, of **i**-umlaut in certain cases, the case ending being then dropped.

68.

(1) The nouns belonging to the *foot* Declension exhibit umlaut most consistently in the N.A. plural.

Sing. N.A.	sē fōt (*foot*)	sē mǫn (*man*)	sē tōð (*tooth*)	sēo cū (*cow*)
Plur N.A.	fēt	męn	tēð	cȳ

NOTE.—The dative singular usually has the same form as the N.A. plural. Here belong also **sēo bōc** (*book*), **sēo burg** (*borough*), **sēo gōs** (*goose*), **sēo lūs** (*louse*), and **sēo mūs** (*mouse*), all with umlauted plurals. Mn.E. preserves only six of the *foot* Declension plurals: *feet, men, teeth, geese, lice,* and *mice*. The *c* in the last two is an artificial spelling, intended to preserve the sound of voiceless *s*. Mn.E. *kine* (= *cy-en*) is a double plural formed after the analogy of weak stems; Burns in *The Twa Dogs* uses *kye*.

No umlaut is possible in **sēo niht** (*night*) and **sē mōnað** (*month*), plural **niht** and **mōnað** (preserved in Mn.E. *twelvemonth* and *fortnight*).

(2) The **r-Stems** contain nouns expressing kinship, and exhibit umlaut of the dative singular.

Sing.	sē	sē	sēo	sēo	sēo
N.A.	fæder	brōðor	mōdor	dohtor	swuster
	(*father*)	(*brother*)	(*mother*)	(*daughter*)	(*sister*)
D.	fæder	brēðer	mēder	dęhter	swyster

NOTE.—The N.A. plural is usually the same as the N.A. singular. These umlaut datives are all due to the presence of a former **i**. Cf. Lat. dative singular *patri, fratri, matri, sorori* (< *sosori*), and Greek θυγατρί.

(3) The **nd-Stems** show umlaut both in the N.A. plural and in the dative singular:

Sing. N.A.	sē frēond (*friend*)	sē fēond (*enemy*)
D.	frīend	fīend
Plur. N.A.	frīend	fīend

NOTE.—Mn.E. *friend* and *fiend* are interesting analogical spellings. When **s** had been added by analogy to the O.E. plurals **frīend** and **fīend**, thus giving the double plurals *friends* and *fiends*, a second singular was formed by dropping the **s**. Thus *friend* and *fiend* displaced the old singulars *frend* and *fend*, both of which occur in the M.E. *Ormulum*, written about the year 1200.

Summary of O.E. Declensions.

69.

A brief, working summary of the O.E. system of declensions may now be made on the basis of gender.

All O.E. nouns are (1) masculine, (2) feminine, or (3) neuter.

(1) The masculines follow the declension of **mūð** (§ 26), except those ending in **-a**, which are declined like **hunta** (§ 64):

Sing. N.A.	mūð	N.		hunta
G.	mūðes	G.D.A.		huntan
D.I.	mūðe	I.		huntan
Plur N.A.	mūðas			huntan
G.	mūða			huntena
D.I.	mūðum			huntum

(2) The short-stemmed neuters follow the declension of **hof** (§ 32); the long-stemmed, that of **bearn** (§ 32):

Sing. N.A.	hof	bearn
G.	hofes	bearnes
D.I.	hofe	bearne
Plur N.A.	hofu	bearn
G.	hofa	bearna
D.I.	hofum	bearnum

(3) The feminines follow the declensions of **giefu** and **wund** (§ 38) (the only difference being in the N. singular), except those ending in **-e**, which follow the declension of **tunge** (§ 64):

Sing. N.	giefu	wund	tunge
G.	giefe	wunde	tungan
D.I.	giefe	wunde	tungan
A.	giefe	wunde	tungan
Plur N.A.	giefa	wunda	tungan
G.	giefa	wunda	tungena
D.I.	giefum	wundum	tungum

70.

Vocabulary.

ac, *but.*

būtan (with dat.), *except, but, without.*

sē Crīst, *Christ.*

sē eorl, *earl, alderman, warrior.*

ðæt Ęnglalǫnd, *England* [Angles' land].

faran, *to go* [fare].

findan, *to find.*

sē God, *God.*

hātan, *to call, name.*

sē hlāford, *lord* [hlāf-weard].

mid (with dat.), *with.*

on (with acc.), *on, against, into.*

tō (with dat.), *to.*

uton (with infin.), *let us.*

NOTE.—O.E. **mǫn** (**man**) is frequently used in an indefinite sense for *one, people, they*. It thus takes the place of a passive construction proper: **And man nam þā gebrotu þe þār belifon, twęlf cȳpan fulle**, *And there were taken up of fragments that remained there twelve baskets full*; but more literally, *And one (or they) took the fragments*, etc.; **Ǫnd Hæstenes wīf ǫnd hīs suna twēgen mǫn brōhte tō ðǣm cyninge**, *And Hæsten's wife and his two sons were brought to the king.*

71.

EXERCISES.

I. 1. Mǫn hine hǣt Ælfred. 2. Uton faran on ðæt scip. 3. God is cyninga cyning ǫnd hlāforda hlāford. 4. Sē eorl ne giefð giefa his fīend. 5. Ic næs mid his frīend. 6. Sēo mōdor færð mid hiere dęhter on ðā burg. 7. Fintst ðū ðæs bōceres bēc? 8. Hē bint ealle (all) ðā dēor būtan ðǣm wulfum. 9. Ðū eart Crīst, Godes sunu. 10. "Uton bindan ðæs bǫnan fēt," cwið hē.

II. 1. Christ is the son of God. 2. Let us call him Cædmon. 3. He throws his spear against the door. 4. Thou art not the earl's brother. 5. He will go with his father to England, but I shall remain (abide) here. 6. Gifts are not given to murderers. 7. Who will find the tracks of the animals? 8. They ask their lord for his weapons (§ 65, Note 3).

CHAPTER XIII.
Pronouns.

(1) Personal Pronouns.

72.

Paradigms of **ic**, *I*; **ðū**, *thou*. For **hē, hēo, hit**, see § 53.

Sing. N.	ic	ðū
G.	mīn	ðīn
D.	mē	ðē
A.	mē (mec)	ðē (ðec)
Dual N.	wit (*we two*)	git (*ye two*)
G.	uncer (*of us two*)	incer (*of you two*)
D.	unc (*to* or *for us two*)	inc (*to* or *for you two*)
A.	unc (*us two*)	inc (*you two*)
Plur N.	wē	gē
G.	ūser (ūre)	ēower
D.	ūs	ēow
A.	ūs (ūsic)	ēow (ēowic)

NOTE 1.—The dual number was soon absorbed by the plural. No relic of it now remains. But when two and only two are referred to, the dual is consistently used in O.E. An example occurs in the case of the two blind men (*Matthew* ix. 27-31): **Gemiltsa unc, Davīdes sunu!** *Pity us, (thou) Son of David!* **Sīe inc æfter incrum gelēafan,** *Be it unto you according to your faith.*

NOTE 2.—Mn.E. *ye* (< **gē**), the nominative proper, is fast being displaced by *you* (< **ēow**), the old objective. The distinction is preserved in the King James's version of the Bible: *Ye in me, and I in you* (*John* xiv. 20); but not in Shakespeare and later writers.

(2) Demonstrative Pronouns.

73.

Paradigm of **ðēs, ðēos, ðis**, *this*. For the Definite Article as a demonstrative, meaning *that*, see § 28, Note 3.

	Masculine.	*Feminine.*	*Neuter.*
Sing. N.	ðēs	ðēos	ðis
G.	ðisses	ðisse	ðisses
D.	ðissum	ðisse	ðissum
A.	ðisne	ðās	ðis
I.	ðȳs	——	ðȳs

All Genders.

Plur. N.A.	ðās
G.	ðissa
D.	ðissum

(3) The Interrogative Pronoun.

74.

Paradigm of **hwā, hwæt**, *who, what?*

	Masculine.	*Neuter.*
Sing. N.	hwā	hwæt
G.	hwæs	hwæs
D.	hwǣm	hwǣm
A.	hwone	hwæt
I.	——	hwȳ

NOTE 1.—The derivative interrogatives, **hwæðer** (< **hwā-ðer*), *which of two?* and **hwilc** (< **hwā-līc*), *which?* are declined as strong adjectives (§§ 79-82).

NOTE 2.—The instrumental case of **hwā** survives in Mn.E. *why* = *on what account*; the instrumental of the definite article is seen in the adverbial *the*: *The sooner, the better* = *by how much sooner, by so much better*.

NOTE 3.—How were the Mn.E. relative pronouns, *who* and *which*, evolved from the O.E. interrogatives? The change began in early West Saxon with

hwæt used in indirect questions (Wülfing, *l.c.* § 310, β): **Nū ic wāt eall hwæt ðū woldest**, *Now I know all that thou desiredst.* The direct question was, **Hwæt woldest ðū?** But the presence of **eall** shows that in Alfred's mind **hwæt** was, in the indirect form, more relative than interrogative.

(4) Relative Pronouns.

75.

O.E. had no relative pronoun proper. It used instead (1) the Indeclinable Particle **ðe**, *who, whom, which, that*, (2) the Definite Article (§ 28), (3) the Definite Article with the Indeclinable Particle, (4) the Indeclinable Particle with a Personal Pronoun.

The Definite Article agrees in gender and number with the antecedent. The case depends upon the construction. *The bird which I have* may, therefore, be:—

(1) **Sē fugol ðe ic hæbbe**;

(2) **Sē fugol ðone ic hæbbe**;

(3) **Sē fugol ðone ðe** (= *the which*) **ic hæbbe**;

(4) **Sē fugol ðe hine ic hæbbe**.

NOTE.—O.E. **ðe** agrees closely in construction with Mn.E. relative *that*: (1) Both are indeclinable. (2) Both refer to animate or inanimate objects. (3) Both may be used with phrasal value: **ðȳ ylcan dæge ðe hī hine tō ðǣm āde beran wyllað**, *On the same day that* (= *on which*) *they intend to bear him to the funeral pile.* (4) Neither can be preceded by a preposition.

(5) Possessive Pronouns.

76.

The Possessive Pronouns are **mīn**, *mine*; **ðīn**, *thine*; **ūre**, *our*; **ēower**, *your*; [**sīn**, *his, her, its*]; **uncer**, *belonging to us two*; **incer**, *belonging to you two*. They are declined as strong adjectives. The genitives of the Third Personal Pronoun, **his**, *his*, **hiere**, *her*, **hiera**, *their*, are indeclinable.

(6) Indefinite Pronouns.

77.

These are **ǣlc**, *each, every*; **ān**, *a, an, one*; **ǣnig** (< ān-ig), *any*; **nǣnig** (< ne-ǣnig), *none*; **ōðer**, *other*; **sum**, *one, a certain one*; **swilc**, *such*. They are declined as strong adjectives.

NOTE.—O.E. had three established methods of converting an interrogative pronoun into an indefinite: (1) By prefixing **ge**, (2) by prefixing **ǣg**, (3) by interposing the interrogative between **swā ... swā**: (1) **gehwā**, *each*; **gehwæðer**, *either*; **gehwilc**, *each*; (2) **ǣghwā**, *each*; **ǣghwæðer**, *each*; **ǣghwilc**, *each*; (3) **swā hwā swā**, *whosoever*; **swā hwæðer swā**, *whichsoever of two*; **swā hwilc swā**, *whosoever*.

CHAPTER XIV.
ADJECTIVES, STRONG AND WEAK.

78.

The declension of adjectives conforms in general to the declension of nouns, though a few pronominal inflections have influenced certain cases. Adjectives belong either to (1) the Strong Declension or to (2) the Weak Declension. The Weak Declension is employed when the adjective is preceded by **sē** or **ðēs**, *the*, *that*, or *this*; otherwise, the Strong Declension is employed: **ðā gōdan cyningas**, *the good kings*; **ðēs gōda cyning**, *this good king*; but **gōde cyningas**, *good kings*.

NOTE.—The Weak Declension is also frequently used when the adjective is employed in direct address, or preceded by a possessive pronoun: **Dryhten, ælmihtiga God ... ic bidde ðē for ðīnre miclan mildheortnesse**, *Lord, almighty God, I pray thee, for thy great mercy.*

(1) Strong Declension of Adjectives.
(a) *Monosyllables.*

79.

The strong adjectives are chiefly monosyllabic with long stems: **gōd**, *good*; **eald**, *old*; **lǫng**, *long*; **swift**, *swift*. They are declined as follows.

80.

Paradigm of **gōd**, *good*:

	Masculine.	*Feminine.*	*Neuter.*
Sing. N.	gōd	gōd	gōd
G.	gōdes	gōdre	gōdes
D.	gōdum	gōdre	gōdum
A.	gōdne	gōde	gōd
I.	gōde	——	gōde

Plur N.A.	gōde	gōda	gōd
G.	gōdra	gōdra	gōdra
D.I.	gōdum	gōdum	gōdum

81.

If the stem is short, **-u** is retained as in **giefu** (§ 39, (1)) and **hofu** (§ 33, (1)). Thus **glæd** (§ 27, Note 1), *glad*, and **til**, *useful*, are inflected:

Masculine.   *Feminine.*   *Neuter.*

Sing. N. { glæd   gladu   glæd
             til   tilu   til

Plur N.A. { glade   glada   gladu
              tile   tila   tilu

(b) *Polysyllables.*

82.

Polysyllables follow the declension of short monosyllables. The most common terminations are **-en**, *-en*; **-fæst**, *-fast*; **-full**, *-ful*; **-lēas**, *-less*; **-līc**, *-ly*; **-ig**, *-y*: **hǣð-en** (**hǣð** = *heath*), *heathen*; **stęde-fæst** (**stęde** = *place*), *steadfast*; **sorg-full** (**sorg** = *sorrow*), *sorrowful*; **cyst-lēas** (**cyst** = *worth*), *worthless*; **eorð-līc** (**eorðe** = *earth*), *earthly*; **blōd-ig** (**blōd** = *blood*), *bloody*. The present and past participles, when inflected and not as weak adjectives, may be classed with the polysyllabic adjectives, their inflection being the same.

Syncopation occurs as in **a**-stems (§ 27, (4)). Thus **hālig**, *holy*, **blīðe**, *blithe*, **berende**, *bearing*, **geboren**, *born*, are thus inflected:

Masculine.   *Feminine.*   *Neuter.*

Sing. N. { hālig   hālgu   hālig
             blīðe   blīðu   blīðe
             berende   berende   berende
             geboren   geborenu   geboren

Plur N.A. { hālge   hālga   hālgu
              blīðe   blīða   blīðu
              berende   berenda   berendu
              geborene geborena   geborenu

- 54 -

(2) Weak Declension of Adjectives.

83.

The Weak Declension of adjectives, whether monosyllabic or polysyllabic, does not differ from the Weak Declension of nouns, except that **-ena** of the genitive plural is usually replaced by **-ra** of the strong adjectives.

84.

	Masculine.	Feminine.	Neuter.
Sing. N.	gōda	gōde	gōde
G.	gōdan	gōdan	gōdan
D.I.	gōdan	gōdan	gōdan
A.	gōdan	gōdan	gōde

All Genders.

Plur. N.A.	gōdan
G.	gōdra (gōdena)
D.I.	gōdum

85.

Rule of Syntax.

Adjectives agree with their nouns in gender, number, and case; but participles, when used predicatively, may remain uninflected (§ 139, § 140).

86.

Vocabulary.

    dēad, *dead.*

    eall, *all.*

    hāl,1 *whole, hale.*

    heard, *hard.*

    ðæt hors, *horse.*

    lēof, *dear* [as lief].

    lȳtel, *little.*

micel, *great, large.*

mǫnig, *many.*

niman, *to take* [nimble, numb].

nīwe, *new.*

rīce, *rich, powerful.*

sōð, *true* [sooth-sayer].

stælwierðe,2 *serviceable* [stalwart].

swīðe, *very.*

sē tūn, *town, village.*

sē ðegn, *servant, thane, warrior.*

ðæt ðing, *thing.*

sē weg, *way.*

wīs, *wise.*

wið (with acc.), *against*, in a hostile sense [with-stand].

sē ilca, *the same* [of that ilk].

87.

Exercises.

I. 1. Ðās scipu ne sind swīðe swift, ac hīe sind swīðe stælwierðu. 2. Sēo gōde cwēn giefð ǣlcum ðegne mǫniga giefa. 3. Ðēs wīsa cyning hæfð mǫnige micele tūnas on his rīce. 4. Nǣnig mǫn is wīs on eallum ðingum. 5. Ðȳ ilcan dæge (§ 98, (2)) mǫn fǫnd (found) ðone ðegn ðe mīnes wines bēc hæfde. 6. Ealle ðā sęcgas ðā ðe swift hors habbað rīdað wið ðone bǫnan. 7. Ðīne fīend sind mīne frīend. 8. Sē micela stān ðone ðe ic on mīnum hǫndum hæbbe is swīðe heard. 9. Hīe scęððað ðǣm ealdum horsum. 10. Uton niman ðās tilan giefa ǫnd hīe beran tō ūrum lēofum bearnum.

II. 1. These holy men are wise and good. 2. Are the little children very dear to the servants (dat. without **tō**)? 3. Gifts are not given (§ 70, Note 1) to rich men. 4. All the horses that are in the king's fields are swift. 5. These stones are very large and hard. 6. He takes the dead man's spear and fights against the large army. 7. This new house has many doors. 8. My ways are not your ways. 9. Whosoever chooses me, him I also (**ēac**) choose. 10. Every man has many friends that are not wise.

1. **Hālig**, *holy*, contains, of course, the same root. "I find," says Carlyle, "that you could not get any better definition of what 'holy' really is than 'healthy—completely healthy.'"

2. This word has been much discussed. The older etymologists explained it as meaning *worth stealing*. A more improbable conjecture is that it means *worth a stall* or *place*. It is used of ships in the *Anglo-Saxon Chronicle*. As applied to men, Skeat thinks it meant *good* or *worthy at stealing*; but the etymology is still unsettled.

CHAPTER XV.
Numerals.

88.

Numerals are either (*a*) Cardinal, expressing pure number, *one, two, three*; or (*b*) Ordinal, expressing rank or succession, *first, second, third*.

(*a*) Cardinals.

89.

The Cardinals fall into the three following syntactic groups:

Group I.

1. ān

2. twēgen [twain]

3. ðrīe

These numerals are inflected adjectives. **Ān**, *one, an, a*, being a long stemmed monosyllable, is declined like **gōd** (§ 80). The weak form, **āna**, means *alone*.

Twēgen and **ðrīe**, which have no singular, are thus declined:

	Masc.	*Fem.*	*Neut.*	*Masc.*	*Fem.*	*Neut.*
Plur. N.A.	twēgen	twā	twā (tū)	ðrīe	ðrēo	ðrēo
G.	twēgra	twēgra	twēgra	ðrēora	ðrēora	ðrēora
D.	twǣm (twām)	twǣm (twām)	twǣm (twām)	ðrīm	ðrīm	ðrīm

- 57 -

90.

Group II.

    4. fēower

    5. fīf

    6. siex

    7. seofon

    8. eahta

    9. nigon

    10. tīen

    11. ęndlefan

    12. twęlf

    13. ðrēotīene

    14. fēowertīene

    15. fīftīene

    16. siextīene

    17. seofontīene

    18. eahtatīene

    19. nigontīene

These words are used chiefly as uninflected adjectives: **on gewitscipe ðrēora oþþe fēower bisceopa**, *on testimony of three or four bishops*; **on siex dagum**, *in six days*; **ān nǣdre ðe hæfde nigon hēafdu**, *a serpent which had nine heads*; **æðeling eahtatīene wintra**, *a prince of eighteen winters*.

91.

Group III.

    20. twēntig

    21. ān ǫnd twēntig

    30. ðrītig

    40. fēowertig

    50. fīftig

    60. siextig

70.	hundseofontig
80.	hundeahtatig
90.	hundnigontig
100.	hund
200.	twā hund
1000.	ðūsend
2000.	twā ðūsend

All these numbers are employed as neuter singular nouns, and are followed by the genitive plural: **Næfde hē þēah mā ðonne twēntig hrȳðera, and twēntig scēapa, and twēntig swȳna,** *He did not have, however, more than twenty (of) cattle, and twenty (of) sheep, and twenty (of) swine;* **Hīe hæfdon hundeahtatig scipa,** *They had eighty ships;* **twā hund mīla brād,** *two hundred miles broad;* **ðǣr wǣron seofon hund gūðfanena genumen,** *there were seven hundred standards captured;* **ān ðūsend mǫnna,** *a thousand men;* **Hannibales folces wæs twā ðūsend ofslagen,** *Of Hannibal's men there were two thousand slain;* **Hīe ācuron ęndlefan ðūsend mǫnna,** *They chose eleven thousand men.*

NOTE 1.—Group III is rarely inflected. Almost the only inflectional endings that are added are (1) **-es**, a genitive singular termination for the numerals in **-tig**, and (2) **-e**, a dative singular for **hund**. (1) The first is confined to adjectives expressing extent of space or time, as, **eald**, *old;* **brād**, *broad;* **hēah**, *high;* and **lǫng**, *long.* **ðæt is ðrītiges mīla lǫng,** *that is thirty miles long;* **Hē wæs ðrītiges gēara eald,** *He was thirty years old.* (2) The second is employed after **mid**: **mid twǣm hunde scipa,** *with two hundred ships;* **mid ðrīm hunde mǫnna,** *with three hundred men;* **Ðǣr wearð ... Regulus gefangen mid V hunde mǫnna,** *There was Regulus captured with five hundred men.*

The statement made in nearly all the grammars that **hunde** occurs as a nominative and accusative plural is without foundation.

NOTE 2.—Many numerals, otherwise indeclinable, are used in the genitive plural with the indefinite pronoun **sum**, which then means *one of* a certain number. In this peculiar construction, the numeral always precedes **sum**: **fēowera sum,** *one of four* (= *with three others*); **Hē sǣde þæt hē syxa sum ofslōge syxtig,** *He said that he, with five others, slew sixty (whales);* **Hē wæs fēowertigra sum,** *He was one of forty.*

NOTE 3.—These are the most common constructions with the Cardinals. The forms in **-tig** have only recently been investigated. A study of Wülfing's citations shows that Alfred occasionally uses the forms in **-tig** (1) as adjectives with plural inflections: **mid XXXgum cyningum,** *with thirty kings;*

and (2) as nouns with plural inflections: **æfter siextigum daga**, *after sixty days*. But both constructions are rare.

(b) Ordinals.

92.

The Ordinals, except the first two, are formed from the Cardinals. They are:

1. forma, ǣresta, fyrsta
2. ōðer, æfterra
3. ðridda
4. fēorða
5. fīfta
6. siexta
7. seofoða
8. eahtoða
9. nigoða
10. tēoða
11. ęndlefta
12. twęlfta
13. ðrēotēoða
14. fēowertēoða
15. fīftēoða
    etc.
20. twēntigoða
21. ān ǫnd twēntigoða
30. ðrītigoða
    etc.

NOTE.—There are no Ordinals corresponding to **hund** and **ðūsend**.

With the exception of **ōðer** (§ 77), all the Ordinals are declined as Weak Adjectives; the article, however, as in Mn.E., is frequently omitted: **Brūtus wæs sē forma consul**, *Brutus was the first consul*; **Hēr ęndað sēo ǣreste bōc, ǫnd onginneð sēo ōðer**, *Here the first book ends, and the second begins*; **ðȳ fīftan**

dæge, *on the fifth day*; **on ðǣm tēoðan gēare hiera gewinnes**, *in the tenth year of their strife*; **Hēo wæs twęlfte**, *She was twelfth*; **Sē wæs fēorða frọm Agusto**, *He was fourth from Augustus*.

CHAPTER XVI.
Adverbs, Prepositions, and Conjunctions.

Adverbs.

93.

(1) Adverbs are formed by adding **-e** or **-līce** to the corresponding adjectives: **sōð**, *true*; **sōðe** or **sōðlīce**, *truly*; **earmlīc**, *wretched*; **earmlīce**, *wretchedly*; **wīd**, *wide*; **wīde**, *widely*; **micel**, *great*; **micle** (**micele**), *greatly, much*.

(2) The terminations **-e** and **-līce** are replaced in some adverbs by **-(l)unga** or **-(l)inga**: **eallunga**, *entirely*; **fǣringa**, *suddenly*; **grundlunga**, *from the ground, completely*.

NOTE 1.—In Mn.E. *headlong, darkling,* and *groveling,* originally adverbs, we have survivals of these endings.

(3) The genitive case is frequently used adverbially: **sūðeweardes**, *southwards*; **ealles**, *altogether, entirely*; **dæges**, *by day*; **nihtes**, *by night*; **ðæs**, *from that time, afterwards. Cf.* **hys** (= **his**) **weges** in **Ðonne rīdeð ǣlc hys weges**, *Then rides each his way*.

NOTE 2.—The adverbial genitive is abundantly preserved in Mn.E. *Always, crossways, sideways, needs* (= *necessarily*), *sometimes,* etc., are not plurals, but old genitive singulars. The same construction is seen in *of course, of a truth, of an evening, of old, of late,* and similar phrases.

(4) Dative and instrumental plurals may be used as adverbs: **hwīlum**, *at times, sometimes* [whilom]; **stundum** (**stund** = *period*), *from time to time*; **miclum**, *greatly*. Especially common is the suffix **-mǣlum** (**mǣl** = *time, measure* [meal]), preserved adverbially in Mn.E. *piecemeal:* **dropmǣlum**, *drop by drop*; **styccemǣlum** (**stycce** = *piece*), *piecemeal, here and there*.

(5) The suffix **-an** usually denotes motion from:

hēr, *here.*	**hider**, *hither.*	**heonan**, *hence.*
ðǣr, *there.*	**ðider**, *thither.*	**ðọnan**, *thence.*
hwǣr, *where?*	**hwider**, *whither?*	**hwọnan**, *whence?*
		norðan, *from the north.*

ēastan, *from the east.*

hindan, *from behind.*

feorran, *from far.*

ūtan, *from without.*

(6) The adverb **rihte** (**riht** = *right, straight*) denotes *motion toward* in **norðrihte**, *northward, due north*; **ēastrihte**, *due east*; **sūðrihte**, *due south*; **westrihte**, *due west.*

Prepositions.

94.

The nominative is the only case in O.E. that is never governed by a preposition. Of the other cases, the dative and accusative occur most frequently with prepositions.

(1) The prepositions that are most frequently found with the dative are:

æfter, *after.*

ǣt, *at.*

be (bī), *by, near, about.*

betwēonan (betuh), *between.*

būtan (būton), *except.*

for, *for.*

frǫm (fram), *from, by.*

mid, *with.*

of, *of, from.*

tō, *to.*

tōforan, *before.*

tōweard, *toward.*

(2) The following prepositions require the accusative:

geond, *throughout* [be-yond].

ofer, *over, upon.*

oð, *until, up to.*

ðurh, *through.*

- 62 -

ymbe, *about, around* [um-while, ember-days].

(3) The preposition **on** (rarely **in**), meaning *into*, is usually followed by the accusative; but meaning *in, on,* or *during,* it takes the dative or instrumental. The preposition **wið**, meaning *toward*, may be followed by the genitive, dative, or accusative; but meaning *against*, and implying *motion* or *hostility*, the accusative is more common.

(4) The following phrases are used prepositionally with the dative:

> **be norðan**, *north of.*
>
> **be ēastan**, *east of.*
>
> **be sūðan**, *south of.*
>
> **be westan**, *west of.*
>
> **tō ēacan**, *in addition to.*
>
> **on emnlange** (**efn-lang** = *evenly long*), *along.*
>
> **tō emnes**, *along.*

(5) Prepositions regularly precede the noun or pronoun that they introduce; but by their adverbial nature they are sometimes drawn in front of the verb: **And him wæs mycel męnegu tō gegaderod**, *And there was gathered unto him a great multitude.* In relative clauses introduced by **ðe**, the preceding position is very common: **sēo scīr ... ðe hē on būde**, *the district, ... which he dwelt in* (= *which he in-habited*); **Hē wæs swȳðe spēdig man on ðǣm ǣhtum ðe hiera spēda on bēoð**, *He was a very rich man in those possessions which their riches consist in*; **nȳhst ðǣm tūne ðe sē dēada man on līð**, *nearest the town that the dead man lies in.*

Conjunctions.

95.

(1) The most frequently occurring conjunctions are:

> **ac**, *but.*
>
> **ǣr**, *before, ere.*
>
> **būtan** (**būton**), *except that, unless.*
>
> **ēac**, *also* [eke].
>
> **for ðǣm**,   *because.*

- 63 -

for ðǣm ðe,

for ðon,

for ðon ðe,

for ðȳ, *therefore.*

gif, *if.*

hwæðer, *whether.*

ǫnd (and), *and.*

oððe, *or.*

ðæt, *that, so that.*

ðēah, *though, however.*

(2) The correlative conjunctions are:

ǣgðer ge	**ge,**	*both* .... *and.*
ǣgðer .... **ōðer**		*either* .... *or.*
oððe .... **oððe**		
nē	**nē,**	*neither* ..... *nor.*
sam	**sam,**	*whether* .... *or.*
swā	**swā**	*the* .... *the.*
		as .... *as.*
ðā .... **ðā**		*when* .... *then.*
ðonne .... **ðonne**		

CHAPTER XVII.
Comparison of Adjectives and Adverbs.

Adjectives.

96.

(1) Adjectives are regularly compared by adding **-ra** for the comparative, and **-ost** (rarely **-est**) for the superlative:

Positive.	*Comparative.*	*Superlative.*
earm, *poor*	**earmra**	**earmost**

- 64 -

rīce, *rich*	rīcra	rīcost
smæl, *narrow*	smælra	smalost
brād, *broad*	brādra (brǣdra)	brādost
swift, *swift*	swiftra	swiftost

(2) Forms with **i**-umlaut usually have superlative in **-est**:

Positive.	Comparative.	Superlative.
eald, *old*	**ieldra**	**ieldest**
lǫng, *long*	**lęngra**	**lęngest**
strǫng, *strong*	**stręngra**	**stręngest**
geong, *young*	**giengra**	**giengest**
hēah, *high*	**hīerra**	**hīehst**

(3) The following adjectives are compared irregularly:

Positive.	Comparative.	Superlative.
gōd, *good*	**bętra**	**bętst**
lȳtel, *little, small*	**lǣssa**	**lǣst**
micel, *great, much*	**māra**	**mǣst**
yfel, *bad*	**wiersa**	**wierst**

(4) The positive is sometimes supplied by an adverb:

Positive.	Comparative.	Superlative.
feor, *far*	**fierra**	**fierrest**
nēah, *near*	**nēarra**	**nīehst**
ǣr, *before*	**ǣrra**, *former*	**ǣrest**, *first*

(5) The comparatives all follow the Weak Declension. The superlatives, when preceded by the definite article, are weak; but when used predicatively they are frequently strong: **sē lǣsta dǣl**, *the least part*; **Ðonne cymeð sē man sē ðæt swiftoste hors hafað tō ðǣm ǣrestan dǣle and tō ðǣm mǣstan**, *Then comes the man that has the swiftest horse to the first part and to the largest.* But, **ðæt bȳne land is ēasteweard brādost** (not **brādoste**), *the cultivated land is broadest eastward;* **and (hit) bið ealra wyrta mǣst**, *and it is largest of all herbs;*

Ac hyra (= hiera) ār is mǣst on ðǣm gafole ðe ðā Finnas him gyldað, *But their income is greatest in the tribute that the Fins pay them.*

(6) The comparative is usually followed by **ðonne** and the nominative case: **Sē hwæl bið micle lǣssa ðonne ōðre hwalas,** *That whale is much smaller than other whales*; **Ðā wunda ðæs mōdes bēoð dīgelran ðonne ðā wunda ðæs līchaman.** *The wounds of the mind are more secret than the wounds of the body.*

But when **ðonne** is omitted, the comparative is followed by the dative: **Ūre Ālīesend, ðe māra is ǫnd mǣrra eallum gesceaftum,** *Our Redeemer, who is greater and more glorious than all created things*; **nē ongeat hē nō hiene selfne bętran ōðrum gōdum mǫnnum,** *nor did he consider himself better than other good men.*

Adverbs.

97.

(1) Adverbs are regularly compared by adding **-or** for the comparative and **-ost** (rarely **-est**) for the superlative:

Positive.	Comparative.	Superlative.
georne, *willingly*	**geornor**	**geornost**
swīðe, *very, severely*	**swīðor,** *more*	**swīðost,** *most, chiefly*
ǣr, *before*	**ǣror,** *formerly*	**ǣrest,** *first*
norð, *northwards*	**norðor**	**norðmest**1

(2) The comparatives of a few adverbs may be found by dropping **-ra** of the corresponding adjective form:

Positive.	Comparative.	Superlative.
lǫnge, *long*	**lęng**	**lęngest**
micle, *much*	**mā**	**mǣst**
wel, *well*	**bęt**	**bętst**

Expressions of Time.

98.

(1) Duration of time and extent of space are usually expressed by the accusative case: **Ealle ðā hwīle ðe ðæt līc bið inne,** *All the time that the body is within*; **twēgen dagas,** *for two days*; **ealne weg,** *all the way, always.*

(2) Time when is more often expressed by the instrumental case when no preposition is used: **ðȳ ilcan dæge**, *the same day*; **ǣlce gēare**, *each year*; **ðȳ gēare**, *that year*; **ǣlce dæge**, *each day*.

(3) Time or space within which is expressed by **on** and the dative: **on sumera**, *in summer*; **on wintra**, *in winter*; **on fīf dagum**, *in five days*; **on fīf mīlum**, *in five miles*; **on ðissum gēare**, *in this year*; **on ðǣm tīman**, *in those times*. Sometimes by the genitive without a preceding preposition: **ðæs gēares**, *in that year*.

99.

Vocabulary.

ðæt gefylce [folc], *troop, division.*

ðæt lǫnd (land), *land.*

sēo mīl, *mile.*

ōðer ... ōðer, *the one ... the other; the former ... the latter.*

sē sige, *victory.*

sige2 habban, *to win (the) victory.*

sprecan, *to speak.*

ðæt swīn (swȳn), *swine, hog.*

wēste, *waste.*

100.

Exercises.

I. 1. Hē hæfð ðrēo swīðe swift hors. 2. Ic hæbbe nigontīene scēap ǫnd mā ðonne twēntig swīna. 3. Sēo gōde cwēn cīest twā hund mǫnna. 4. Uton feohtan wið ðā Dęne mid ðrīm hunde scipa. 5. Ǫnd hīe wǣron on twǣm gefylcum: on ōðrum wæs3 Bāchsęcg ǫnd Halfdęne ðā hǣðnan cyningas, ǫnd on ōðrum wǣron ðā eorlas. 6. Ðū spricst sōðlīce. 7. Ðonne rīt ǣlc mǫn his weges. 8. Æfter mǫnigum dagum, hæfde Ælfred cyning4 sige. 9. Ðis lǫnd is wēste styccemǣlum. 10. Ðēs feld is fīftiges mīla brād. 11. Ælfred cyning hæfde mǫnige frīend, for ðǣm ðe hē wæs ǣgðer ge wīs ge gōd. 12. Ðā hwalas, ðe ðū ymbe spricst, sind micle lǣssan ōðrum hwalum. 13. Hēo is ieldre ðonne hiere swuster, ac mīn brōðor is ieldra ðonne hēo. 14. Wē cumað tō ðǣm tūne ǣlce gēare. 15. Ðā męn ðe ðā swiftostan hors hǣfdon wǣron mid ðǣm Dęnum fēower dagas.

II. 1. Our army (**werod**) was in two divisions: one was large, the other was small. 2. The richest men in the kingdom have more (**mā**) than thirty ships. 3. He was much wiser than his brother. 4. He fights against the Northumbrians with two ships. 5. After three years King Alfred gained the victory. 6. Whosoever chooses these gifts, chooses well. 7. This man's son is both wiser and better than his father. 8. When the king rides, then ride his thanes also. 9. The richest men are not always (**ā**) the wisest men.

1. This is really a double superlative, **m** being itself an old superlative suffix. *Cf.* Latin *opti-m-us*. In Mn.E. *northmost* and *hindmost*, *-m-est* has been confused with *-most*, with which etymologically it has nothing to do.

2. **Sige** usually, but not invariably, precedes **habban**.

3. See p. 100, note on **gefeaht**.

4. The proper noun comes first in appositive expressions: **Ælfred cyning**, **Sidroc eorl**, **Hēahmund bisceop**.

CHAPTER XVIII.
Strong Verbs: Class I. (See § 17.)

Syntax of Moods.

101.

Of the three hundred simple verbs belonging to the O.E. Strong Conjugation, it is estimated[1] that seventy-eight have preserved their strong inflections in Mn.E., that eighty-eight have become weak, and that the remaining one hundred and thirty-four have entirely disappeared, their places being taken in most cases by verbs of Latin origin introduced through the Norman-French.

Note.—Only the simple or primitive verbs, not the compound forms, are here taken into consideration. The proportionate loss, therefore, is really much greater. O.E. abounded in formative prefixes. "Thus from the Anglo-Saxon **flōwan**, *to flow*, ten new compounds were formed by the addition of various prefixes, of which ten, only one, **oferflōwan**, *to overflow*, survives with us. In a similar manner, from the verb **sittan**, *to sit*, thirteen new verbs were formed, of which not a single one is to be found to-day." Lounsbury, *ib.* Part I, p. 107.

102.

Class I: The "Drive" Conjugation.

Vowel Succession: ī, ā, i, i.

INFINITIVE.	PRETERIT SING.	PRETERIT PLUR.	Past Part.
Drīf-an	**drāf**	**drif-on**	**gedrif-en**, *to drive.*

Indicative. **Subjunctive.**

Present.   Present.

Sing. 1. Ic drīf-e   *Sing.* 1. Ic ⎫
2. ðū drīf-st (drīf-est)   2. ðū ⎬ drīf-e
3. hē drīf-ð (drīf-eð)   3. hē ⎭

Plur. 1. wē ⎫   *Plur.* 1. wē ⎫
2. gē ⎬ (drīf-að)   2. gē ⎬ drīf-en
3. hīe ⎭   3. hīe ⎭

PRETERIT.   PRETERIT.

Sing. 1. Ic drāf   *Sing.* 1. Ic ⎫
2. ðū drif-e   2. ðū ⎬ drif-e
3. hē drāf   3. hē ⎭

Plur. 1. wē ⎫   *Plur.* 1. wē ⎫
2. gē ⎬ drif-on   2. gē ⎬ drif-en
3. hīe ⎭   3. hīe ⎭

Imperative.   **Infinitive.**   **Present Participle.**

Sing. 2. drīf   drīf-an   drīf-ende
Plur. 1. drīf-an

2.   drīf-að   **Gerund.**   **Past Participle.**

tō drīf-anne (-enne)   gedrif-en

Tense Formation of Strong Verbs.

103.

(1) It will be seen from the conjugation of **drīfan** that the *present stem* in all strong verbs is used throughout the present indicative, the present subjunctive, the imperative, the infinitive, the gerund, and the present participle. More than half of the endings, therefore, of the Strong Conjugation are added directly to the present stem.

(2) That the *preterit singular stem* is used in only two forms of the verb, the 1st and 3d persons singular of the preterit indicative: **Ic drāf, hē drāf**.

(3) That the *preterit plural stem* is used in the preterit plural indicative, in the second person of the preterit singular indicative, and in the singular and plural of the preterit subjunctive.

(4) That the *stem of the past participle* (**gedrif-**) is used for no other form.

Syntax of the Verb.

104.

The Indicative Mood[2] represents the predicate *as a reality*. It is used both in independent and in dependent clauses, its function in O.E. corresponding with its function in Mn.E.

105.

The Subjunctive Mood represents the predicate *as an idea*.[3] It is of far more frequent occurrence in O.E. than in Mn.E.

1. When used in independent clauses it denotes desire, command, or entreaty, and usually precedes its subject: **Sīe ðīn nama gehālgod**, *Hallowed be Thy name*; **Ne swęrigen gē**, *Do not swear.*

2. In dependent clauses it denotes uncertainty, possibility, or mere futurity.[4] (*a*) Concessive clauses (introduced by **ðēah**, *though*) and (*b*) temporal clauses (introduced by **ǣr, ǣr ðǣm ðe**, *before*) are rarely found with any other mood than the subjunctive. The subjunctive is also regularly used in Alfredian prose (*c*) after verbs of saying, even when no suggestion of doubt or discredit attaches to the narration.[5] "Whether the statement refer to a fact or not, whether the subject-matter be vouched for by the reporter, as regards its

objective reality and truth, the subjunctive does not tell. It simply represents a statement as reported"6: **ðēah man āsętte twēgen fǣtels full ealað oððe wæteres**, *though one set two vessels full of ale or water*; **ǣr ðǣm ðe hit eall forhęrgod wǣre**, *before it was all ravaged*; **Hē sǣde ðæt Norðmanna land wǣre swȳðe lang and swȳðe smæl**, *He said that the Norwegians' land was very long and very narrow.*

106.

The Imperative is the mood of command or intercession: **Iōhannes, cum tō mē**, *John, come to me*; **And forgyf ūs ūre gyltas**, *And forgive us our trespasses*; **Ne drīf ūs fram ðē**, *Do not drive us from thee.*

107.

(1) The Infinitive and Participles are used chiefly in verb-phrases (§§ 138-141); but apart from this function, the Infinitive, being a neuter noun, may serve as the subject or direct object of a verb. **Hātan** (*to command, bid*), **lǣtan** (*to let, permit*), and **onginnan** (*to begin*) are regularly followed by the Infinitive: **Hine rīdan lyste**, *To ride pleased him*; **Hēt ðā bǣre sęttan**, *He bade set down the bier*;7 **Lǣtað ðā lȳtlingas tō mē cuman**, *Let the little ones come to me*; **ðā ongann hē sprecan**, *then began he to speak.*

(2) The Participles may be used independently in the dative absolute construction (an imitation of the Latin ablative absolute), usually for the expression of time:8 **Him ðā gȳt sprecendum**, *While he was yet speaking*; **gefylledum dagum**, *the days having been fulfilled.*

108.

The Gerund, or Gerundial Infinitive, is used:

(1) To express purpose: **Ūt ēode sē sāwere his sǣd tō sāwenne**, *Out went the sower his seed to sow.*

(2) To expand or determine the meaning of a noun or adjective: **Sȳmōn, ic hæbbe ðē tō sęcgenne sum ðing**, *Simon, I have something to say to thee*; **Hit is scǫndlīc ymb swelc tō sprecanne**, *It is shameful to speak about such things.*

(3) After **bēon (wesan)** to denote duty or necessity: **Hwæt is nū mā ymbe ðis tō sprecanne**, *What more is there now to say about this?* **ðonne is tō geðęncenne hwaet Crīst self cwæð**, *then it behooves to bethink what Christ himself said.*

NOTE.—The Gerund is simply the dative case of the Infinitive after **tō**. It began very early to supplant the simple Infinitive; hence the use of *to* with the Infinitive in Mn.E. As late as the Elizabethan age the Gerund sometimes replaced the Infinitive even after the auxiliary verbs:

"Some pagan shore,

Where these two Christian armies *might combine*

The blood of malice in a vein of league,

And not *to spend* it so unneighbourly."

—*King John*, V, II, 39.

NOTE.—The Gerund is simply the When *to* lost the meaning of purpose and came to be considered as a merely formal prefix, *for* was used to supplement the purpose element: *What went ye out for to see?*9

 1. Lounsbury, *English Language*, Part II, § 241.

 2. Usage sanctions *mood*, but the better spelling would be *mode*. It is from the Lat. *modus*, whereas *mood* (= *temper*) is O.E. *mōd*.

 3. Gildersleeve's *Latin Grammar*, § 255.

 4. Thus when Alfred writes that an event took place *before* the founding of Rome, he uses the subjunctive: **ǣr ðǣm ðe Rōmeburh getimbrod wǣre** = *before Rome were founded*; but, **æfter ðǣm ðe Rōmeburh getimbrod wæs** = *after Rome was founded*.

 5. "By the time of Ælfric, however, the levelling influence of the indicative [after verbs of saying] has made considerable progress."—Gorrell, *Indirect Discourse in Anglo-Saxon* (Dissertation, 1895), p. 101.

 6. Hotz, *On the Use of the Subjunctive Mood in Anglo-Saxon* (Zürich, 1882).

 7. Not, *He commanded the bier to be set down*. The Mn.E. passive in such sentences is a loss both in force and directness.

 8. Callaway, *The Absolute Participle in Anglo-Saxon* (Dissertation, 1889), p. 19.

 9. This is not the place to discuss the Gerund in Mn.E., the so-called "infinitive in *-ing*." The whole subject has been befogged for the lack of an accepted nomenclature, one that shall do violence neither to grammar nor to history.

CHAPTER XIX.
Strong Verbs: Classes II and III.

109.

Class II: The "Choose" Conjugation.

Vowel Succession: **ēo, ēa, u, o.**

Infinitive. 1	Pret. Sing.	Pret. Plur. 2	Past Part. 2
cēos-an,	**cēas,**	**cur-on**	**gecor-en,** *to choose.*

Indicative.   **Subjunctive.**

Present.   Present.

Sing. 1. Ic cēos-e   *Sing.* 1. Ic ⎫
2. ðū cīest (cēos-est)   2. ðū ⎬ cēos-e
3. hē cīest (cēos-eð)   3. hē ⎭

Plur. 1. wē ⎫   *Plur.* 1. wē ⎫
2. gē ⎬ cēos-að   2. gē ⎬ cēos-en
3. hīe ⎭   3. hīe ⎭

Preterit.   Preterit.

Sing. 1. Ic cēas   *Sing.* 1. Ic ⎫
2. ðū cur-e   2. ðū ⎬ cur-e
3. hē cēas   3. hē ⎭

Plur. 1. wē ⎫   *Plur.* 1. wē ⎫
2. gē ⎬ cur-on   2. gē ⎬ cur-en
3. hīe ⎭   3. hīe ⎭

Imperative.   **Infinitive.**   **Present Participle.**

Sing. 2. cēos   cēos-an   cēos-ende

Plur. 1. cēos-an

2.   cēos-að   **Gerund.**   **Past Participle.**

     tō cēos-anne (-enne)   gecor-en

110.

Class III: The "Bind" Conjugation.

Vowel Succession: $\left.\begin{array}{c}i\\e\end{array}\right\}$, a, u, $\left.\begin{array}{c}u\\o\end{array}\right\}$.

The present stem ends in **m, n, l, r,** or **h,** + one or more consonants:

m:	belimp-an,	belǫmp / belamp	belump-on,	belump-en,	*to belong.*
n:	bind-an,	bǫnd / band	bund-on,	gebund-en,	*to bind.*
l:	help-an,	healp,	hulp-on,	geholp-en,	*to help.*
r:	weorð-an,	wearð,	wurd-on,	geword-en,	*to become.*
h:	gefeoht-an,	gefeaht,	gefuht-on,	gefoht-en,	*to fight.*

NOTE 1.—If the present stem ends in a nasal (**m, n**) + a consonant, the past participle retains the **u** of the pret. plur.; but if the present stem ends in a liquid (**l, r**) or **h,** + a consonant, the past participle has **o** instead of **u**.

NOTE 2.—Why do we not find ***halp, *warð,** and ***faht** in the pret. sing.? Because **a** before **l, r,** or **h,** + a consonant, underwent "breaking" to **ea**. Breaking also changes every **e** followed by **r** or **h,** + a consonant, to **eo**: **weorðan** (< ***werðan**), feohtan (< ***fehtan**).

111.

Indicative.   **Subjunctive.**

Present.   Present.

Sing. 1.   Ic bind-e   *Sing.* 1.   Ic

      2.   ðū bintst (bind-est)   2.   ðū   bind-e

3.	hē bint (bind-eð)		3.	hē	

Plur. 1.	wē			*Plur.* 1.	wē		
2.	gē	}	bind-að	2.	gē	}	bind-en
3.	hīe			3.	hīe		

PRETERIT.   PRETERIT.

Sing. 1.	Ic bǫnd		*Sing.* 1.	Ic	
2.	ðū bund-e		2.	ðū	} bund-e
3.	hē bǫnd		3.	hē	

Plur. 1.	wē			*Plur.* 1.	wē		
2.	gē	}	bund-on	2.	gē	}	bund-en
3.	hīe			3.	hīe		

Imperative. **Infinitive.** **Present Participle.**

Sing. 2. bind   bind-an   bind-ende

Plur. 1. bind-an

2. bind-að **Gerund.**   **Past Participle.**

tō bind-anne (-enne) gebund-en

112.

Vocabulary.

    ðæt gefeoht, *fight, battle.*

    sēo geręcednes, *narration* [ręccan].

    ðæt gesceap, *creation* [scieppan].

    sēo hęrgung (§ 39, (3)), *harrying, plundering* [hęrgian].

    sē medu (medo) (§ 51), *mead.*

    sēo meolc, *milk.*

sē **middangeard**, *world* [middle-yard].

sē **munuc**, *monk* [monachus].

sēo **mȳre**, mare [**mearh**].

hē **sǣde**, *he said.*

hīe **sǣdon**, *they said.*

sēo **spēd**, *riches* [speed].

spēdig, *rich, prosperous* [speedy].

sēo **tīd**, *time* [tide].

unspēdig, *poor.*

sē **westanwind**, *west-wind.*

ðæt **wīn**, *wine.*

ārīsan,	ārās,	ārison,	ārisen,	*to arise.*
bīdan,	bād,	bidon,	gebiden,	*to remain, expect* (with gen.)
drēogan,3	drēag,	drugon,	gedrogen,	*to endure, suffer.*
drincan,	dronc,	druncon,	gedruncen,	*to drink.*
findan,	fond,	fundon,	gefunden,	*to find.*
geswīcan	geswāc,	geswicon,	geswicen,	*to cease, cease from* (with gen.)
iernan (yrnan),	orn,	urnon,	geurnen,	*to run.*
onginnan,	ongonn,	ongunnon,	ongunnen,	*to begin.*
rīdan,	rād,	ridon,	geriden,	*to ride.*
singan,	song,	sungon,	gesungen,	*to sing.*
wrītan,	wrāt,	writon,	gewriten,	*to write.*

113.

Exercises.

I. 1. Æfter ðissum wordum, sē munuc wrāt ealle ðā geręcednesse on ānre bēc. 2. Ðā eorlas ridon ūp ǣr ðǣm ðe ðā Dęne ðæs gefeohtes geswicen. 3. Cædmon song ǣrest be middangeardes gesceape. 4. Sē cyning ond ðā rīcostan męn drincað mȳran meolc, ond ðā unspēdigan drincað medu.

5. Ǫnd hē ārās ǫnd sē wind geswāc. 6. Hīe sǣdon ðæt hīe ðǣr westwindes biden. 7. Hwæt is nū mā ymbe ðās ðing tō sprecanne? 8. Ðā seċgas ongunnon geswīcan ðǣre hergunga. 9. Ðā bēag ðæt lǫnd ðǣr ēastryhte, oððe sēo sǣ in on ðæt lǫnd. 10. Ðās lǫnd belimpað tō, ðǣm Englum. 11. Ðēah ðā Dene ealne dæg gefuhten, ġīet hæfde Ælfred cyning sige. 12. Ǫnd ðæs (afterwards) ymbe ānne mōnað gefeaht Ælfred cyning wið ealne ðone here æt Wiltūne.

II. 1. The most prosperous men drank mare's milk and wine, but the poor men drank mead. 2. I suffered many things before you began to help me (dat.). 3. About two days afterwards (**Ðæs ymbe twēgen dagas**), the plundering ceased. 4. The king said that he fought against all the army (**here**). 5. Although the Danes remained one month (§ 98, (1)), they did not begin to fight. 6. These gifts belonged to my brother. 7. The earls were glad because their lord was (indicative) with them. 8. What did you find? 9. Then wrote he about (**be**) the wise man's deeds. 10. What more is there to endure?

1. A few verbs of Class II have **ū** instead of **ēo** in the infinitive:

    brūcan, brēac, brucon, gebrocen, *to enjoy* [brook].
    būgan, bēag, bugon, gebogen, *to bend, bow.*

2. By a law known as Grammatical Change, final **ð**, **s**, and **h** of strong verbs generally become **d**, **r**, and **g**, respectively, in the preterit plural and past participle.

3. *Cf.* the Scotch "to *dree* one's weird" = *to endure one's fate.*

CHAPTER XX.
Strong Verbs: Classes IV, V, VI, and VII.
Contract Verbs.

[The student can now complete the conjugation for himself (§ 103). Only the principal parts will be given.]

114.

Class IV: The "Bear" Conjugation.

Vowel Succession: **e, æ, ǣ, o**.

The present stem ends in **l**, **r**, or **m**, no consonant following:

    l: **hel-an, hæl, hǣl-on, gehol-en,** *to conceal.*
    r: **ber-an, bær, bǣr-on, gebor-en,** *to bear.*

The two following verbs are slightly irregular:

m: { nim-an, / cum-an, }   nōm (nam), c(w)ōm,   nōm-on (nām-on), c(w)ōm-on,   genum-en, gecum-en,   *to take.* *to come.*

115.

Class V: The "Give" Conjugation.

Succession of Vowels: **e (ie), æ, ǣ, e.**

The present stem ends in a single consonant, never a liquid or nasal:

    met-an, mæt, mǣton, gemet-en, *to measure, mete.*

    gief-an, geaf, gēaf-on, gegief-en, *to give.*

NOTE 1.—The palatal consonants, **g, c,** and **sc,** convert a following **e** into **ie, æ** into **ea,** and **ǣ** into **ēa.** Hence **giefan** (< *gefan), **geaf** (< *gæf), **gēafon** (< *gǣfon), **gegiefen** (< *gegefen). This change is known as Palatalization. See § 8.

NOTE 2.—The infinitives of the following important verbs are only apparently exceptional:

    biddan, bæd, bǣd-on, gebed-en, *to ask for* [bid].

    licgan, læg, lǣg-on, geleg-en, *to lie, extend.*

    sittan, sæt, sǣt-on, geset-en, *to sit.*

The original **e** reappears in the participial stems. It was changed to **i** in the present stems on account of a former **-jan** in the infinitive (**bid-jan,** etc.). See § 61. To the same cause is due the doubling of consonants in the infinitive. All simple consonants in O.E., with the exception of **r,** were doubled after a short vowel, when an original **j** followed.

116.

Class VI: The "Shake" Conjugation.

Succession of Vowels: **a, ō, ō, a.**

    scac-an, scōc, scōc-on, gescac-en, *to shake.*

    far-an, fōr, fōr-on, gefar-en, *to go* [fare].

117.

Class VII: The "Fall" Conjugation.

Vowel Succession:	$\left.\begin{array}{c}\bar{a}\\ \bar{æ}\end{array}\right\}$	$\bar{e},\ \bar{e},$	$\left.\begin{array}{c}\bar{a}\\ \bar{æ}\end{array}\right\}$; or	$\left.\begin{array}{c}ea\\ \bar{e}a\\ \bar{o}\end{array}\right\}$	$\bar{e}o,\ \bar{e}o,$	$\left.\begin{array}{c}ea\\ \bar{e}a\\ \bar{o}\end{array}\right\}$.
(1) hāt-an,	hēt,	hēt-on,	gehāt-en,		to call, name, command.	
lǣt-an,	lēt,	lēt-on,	gelǣt-en,	to let.		
(2) feall-an,	fēoll,	fēoll-on,	gefeall-en,	to fall.		
heald-an,	hēold,	hēold-on,	geheald-en,	to hold.		
hēaw-an,	hēow,	hēow-on,	gehēaw-en,	to hew.		
grōw-an,	grēow,	grēow-on,	gegrōw-en,	to grow.		

NOTE 1.—This class consists of the Reduplicating Verbs; that is, those verbs that originally formed their preterits not by internal vowel change (ablaut), but by prefixing to the present stem the initial consonant + **e** (*cf.* Gk. λέ-λοιπα and Lat. *dĕ-dī*). Contraction then took place between the syllabic prefix and the root, the fusion resulting in **ē** or **ēo**: **he-hat > heht > hēt*.

NOTE 2.—A peculiar interest attaches to **hātan**: the forms **hātte** and **hātton** are the sole remains in O.E. of the original Germanic passive. They are used both as presents and as preterits: **hātte** = *I am* or *was called, he is* or *was called*. No other verb in O.E. could have a passive sense without calling in the aid of the verb *to be* (§ 141).

Contract Verbs.

118.

The few Contract Verbs found in O.E. do not constitute a new class; they fall under Classes I, II, V, VI, and VII, already treated. The present stem ended originally in **h**. This was lost before **-an** of the infinitive, contraction and compensatory lengthening being the result. The following are the most important of these verbs:

Classes.

I.	ðēon	(< *ðīhan),	ðāh,	ðig-on,	geðig-en / geðung-en	, to thrive.
II.	tēon	(< *tēohan),	tēah,	tug-on,	getog-en,	to draw, go [tug].
V.	sēon	(< *sehwan),	seah,	sāw-on,	gesew-en,	to see.
VI.	slēan	(< *slahan),	slōh,	slōg-on,	geslæg-en,	to slay.
VII.	fōn	(< *fōhan),	fēng,	fēng-on,	gefǫng-en,	to seize [fang].

119.

The Present Indicative of these verbs runs as follows (see rules of **i**-umlaut, § 58):

Sing. 1.	Ic ðēo	tēo	sēo	slēa	fō
2.	ðū ðīhst	tīehst	siehst	sliehst	fēhst
3.	hē ðīhð	tīehð	siehð	sliehð	fēhð
Plur. 1.	wē				
2.	gē	ðēoð	tēoð	sēoð	slēað	fōð
3.	hīe				

The other tenses and moods are regularly formed from the given stems.

120.

Vocabulary.

    sēo ǣht, *property, possession* [**āgan**].

    aweg, *away* [**on weg**].

    sēo fierd, *English army* [**faran**].

    sē hęre, *Danish army* [**hęrgian**].

    on gehwæðre hǫnd, *on both sides*.

    sige niman (= **sige habban**), *to win (the) victory*.

    sēo sprǣc, *speech, language*.

tō rīce fōn, *to come to the throne.*1

ðæt wæl [Val-halla] ⎱ *slaughter, carnage.*
sē wælsliht,   ⎰

sē weall, *wall, rampart.*

ðæt wildor, *wild beast, reindeer.*

sē wīngeard, *vineyard.*

ābrecan,2	ābræc,	ābrǣcon,	ābrocen,	*to break down.*
cweðan,	cwæð,	cwǣdon,	gecweden,	*to say* [quoth].
gesēon,	geseah,	gesāwon,	gesewen,	*to see.*
grōwan,	grēow,	grēowon,	gegrōwen,	*to grow.*
ofslēan,	ofslōh,	ofslōgon,	ofslægen,	*to slay.*
sprecan,	spræc,	sprǣcon,	gesprecen,	*to speak.*
stelan,	stæl,	stǣlon,	gestolen,	*to steal.*
stǫndan,	stōd,	stōdon,	gestǫnden,	*to stand.*
weaxan,	wēox,	wēoxon,	geweaxen,	*to grow, increase* [wax].

121.

EXERCISES.

I. 1. Æfter ðǣm sōðlīce (indeed) ealle męn sprǣcon āne (one) sprǣce. 2. Ǫnd hē cwæð: "Ðis is ān folc, ǫnd ealle hīe sprecað āne sprǣce." 3. On sumum stōwum wīngeardas grōwað. 4. Hē hēt ðā nædran ofslēan. 5. Ðā Ęngle ābrǣcon ðone lǫngan weall, ǫnd sige nōmon. 6. Ǫnd ðæt sǣd grēow ǫnd wēox. 7. Ic ne geseah ðone mǫn sē ðe ðæs cnapan adesan stæl. 8. Hē wæs swȳðe spēdig man on ðǣm ǣhtum ðe hiera spēda on3 bēoð, ðæt is, on wildrum. 9. Ǫnd ðǣr wearð (was) micel wælsliht on gehwæðre hǫnd. 10. Ǫnd æfter ðissum gefeohte cōm Ælfred cyning mid his fierde, ǫnd gefeaht wið ealne ðone hęre, ǫnd sige nōm. 11. Ðēos burg hātte4 Æscesdūn (Ashdown). 12. Ðǣre cwēne līc læg on ðǣm hūse. 13. Ǫnd sē dǣl ðe ðǣr aweg cōm wæs swȳðe lȳtel. 14. Ǫnd ðæs ðrēotīene dagas Æðered tō rīce fēng.

II. 1. The men stood in the ships and fought against the Danes. 2. Before the thanes came, the king rode away. 3. They said (**sǣdon**) that all the men spoke one language. 4. They bore the queen's body to Wilton. 5. Alfred gave many gifts to his army (dat. without **tō**) before he went away. 6. These men are called earls. 7. God sees all things. 8. The boy held the reindeer with (**mid**) his hands. 9. About six months afterwards, Alfred gained the victory, and came to the throne. 10. He said that there was very great slaughter on both sides.

>1. Literally, *to take to (the) kingdom. Cf.* "Have you anything to take to?" (*Two Gentlemen of Verona*, IV, I, 42).
>
>2. **Brecan** belongs properly in Class V, but it has been drawn into Class IV possibly through the influence of the **r** in the root.
>
>3. See § **94**, (5).
>
>4. See § **117**, Note 2.

CHAPTER XXI.
WEAK VERBS (§ **18**).

122.

The verbs belonging to the Weak Conjugation are generally of more recent origin than the strong verbs, being frequently formed from the roots of strong verbs. The Weak Conjugation was the growing conjugation in O.E. as it is in Mn.E. We instinctively put our newly coined or borrowed words into this conjugation (*telegraphed, boycotted*); and children, by the analogy of weak verbs, say *runned* for *ran*, *seed* for *saw*, *teared* for *tore*, *drawed* for *drew*, and *growed* for *grew*. So, for example, when Latin *dictāre* and *breviāre* came into O.E., they came as weak verbs, **dihtian** and **brēfian**.

The Three Classes of Weak Verbs.

123.

There is no difficulty in telling, from the infinitive alone, to which of the three classes a weak verb belongs. Class III has been so invaded by Class II that but three important verbs remain to it: **habban**, *to have*; **libban**, *to live*; and **sęcgan**, *to say*. Distinction is to be made, therefore, only between Classes II and I. Class II contains the verbs with infinitive in **-ian** not preceded by **r**. Class I contains the remaining weak verbs; that is, those with infinitive in **-r-ian** and those with infinitive in **-an** (not **-ian**).

Class I.

124.

The preterit singular and past participle of Class I end in **-ede** and **-ed**, or **-de** and **-ed** respectively.

NOTE.—The infinitives of this class ended originally in **-jan** (= **-ian**). This accounts for the prevalence of **i**-umlaut in these verbs, and also for the large number of short-voweled stems ending in a double consonant (§ 115, Note 2). The weak verb is frequently the causative of the corresponding strong verb. In such cases, the root of the weak verb corresponds in form to the preterit singular of the strong verb: Mn.E. *drench* (= *to make drink*), *lay* (= *to make lie*), *rear* (= *to make rise*), and *set* (= *to make sit*), are the umlauted forms of **drǫnc** (preterit singular of **drincan**), **læg** (preterit singular of **licgan**), **rās** (preterit singular of **rīsan**), and **sæt** (preterit singular of **sittan**).

Preterit and Past Participle in -ede and -ed.

125.

Verbs with infinitive in **-an** preceded by **ri-** or the double consonants **mm, nn, ss, bb, cg** (= **gg**), add **-ede** for the preterit, and **-ed** for the past participle, the double consonant being always made single:

ri:	nęri-an,	nęr-ede,	genęr-ed,	*to save.*
mm:	fręmm-an,	fręm-ede,	gefręm-ed,	*to perform* [frame].
nn:	ðęnn-an,	ðęn-ede,	geðęn-ed,	*to extend.*
ss:	cnyss-an,	cnys-ede,	gecnys-ed,	*to beat.*
bb:	swębb-an,	swęf-ede,	geswęf-ed,	*to put to sleep.*
cg:	węcg-an,	węg-ede,	geweg-ed,	*to agitate.*

NOTE.—**Lęcgan,** *to lay,* is the only one of these verbs that syncopates the **e**: **lęcgan, lęgde (lēde), gelęgd (gelēd),** instead of **lęgede, gelęged.**

Preterit and Past Participle in -de and -ed.

126.

All the other verbs belonging to Class I. add **-de** for the preterit and **-ed** for the past participle. This division includes, therefore, all stems long by nature (§ 10, (3), (*a*)):

dǣl-an,	dǣl-de,	gedǣl-ed,	*to deal out, divide* [**dǣl**].
dēm-an,	dēm-de,	gedēm-ed,	*to judge* [**dōm**].

grēt-an,	grēt-te,	gegrēt-ed,	*to greet.*
hīer-an,	hīer-de,	gehīer-ed,	*to hear.*
lǣd-an,	lǣd-de,	gelǣd-ed,	*to lead.*

NOTE 1.—A preceding voiceless consonant (§ 9, Note) changes **-de** into **-te**: ***grēt-de > grēt-te; *mēt-de > mēt-te; *īec-de > īec-te**. Syncope and contraction are also frequent in the participles: **gegrēt-ed > *gegrēt-d > gegrēt(t); gelǣd-ed > gelǣd(d)**.

NOTE 2.—**Būan**, *to dwell, cultivate*, has an admixture of strong forms in the past participle: **būan, būde, gebūd (bȳn, gebūn)**. The present participle survives in Mn.E. *husband* = *house-dweller*.

127.

It includes, also, all stems long by position (§ 10, (3), (*b*)) except those in **mm, nn, ss, bb**, and **cg** (§ 125):

sęnd-an,	sęnd-e,	gesęnd-ed,	*to send.*
sętt-an,	sęt-te,	gesęt-ed,	*to set* [sittan].
sigl-an,	sigl-de,	gesigl-ed,	*to sail.*
spęnd-an,	spęnd-e,	gespęnd-ed,	*to spend.*
trędd-an,	tręd-de,	getręd-ed,	*to tread.*

NOTE.—The participles frequently undergo syncope and contraction: **gesęnded > gesęnd; gesęted > gesęt(t); gespęnded > gespęnd; getręded > getręd(d)**.

Irregular Verbs of Class I.

128.

There are about twenty verbs belonging to Class I that are irregular in having no umlaut in the preterit and past participle. The preterit ends in **-de**, the past participle in **-d**; but, through the influence of a preceding voiceless consonant (§ 9, Note), **-ed** is generally unvoiced to **-te**, and **-d** to **-t**. The most important of these verbs are as follows:

bring-an,	brōh-te,	gebrōh-t,	*to bring.*
byc-gan,	boh-te,	geboh-t,	*to buy.*
sēc-an,	sōh-te,	gesōh-t,	*to seek.*
sęll-an,	seal-de,	geseal-d,	*to give, sell* [hand-sel].

tǣc-an,	tǣh-te,	getǣh-t,	*to teach.*
tęll-an,	teal-de,	geteal-d,	*to count* [tell].
ðęnc-an,	ðōh-te,	geðōh-t,	*to think.*
ðync-an,	ðūh-te,	geðūh-t,	*to seem* [methinks].
wyrc-an,	worh-te,	geworh-t,	*to work.*

NOTE.—Such of these verbs as have stems in **c** or **g** are frequently written with an inserted **e**: **bycgean, sēcean, tǣcean,** etc. This **e** indicates that **c** and **g** have palatal value; that is, are to be followed with a vanishing **y**-sound. In such cases, O.E. **c** usually passes into Mn.E. *ch*: **tǣc(e)an** > *to teach*; **rǣc(e)an** > *to reach*; **stręcc(e)an** > *to stretch*. **Sēc(e)an** gives *beseech* as well as *seek*. See § 8.

Conjugation of Class I.

129.

Paradigms of **nęrian,** *to save;* **fręmman,** *to perform;* **dǣlan,** *to divide*:

Indicative.

PRESENT.

Sing. 1.	Ic nęrie	fręmme	dǣle
2.	ðū nęrest	fręmest	dǣlst
3.	hē nęreð	fręmeð	dǣlð

Plur. 1.	wē ⎫			
2.	gē ⎬ nęriað	fręmmað	dǣlað
3.	hīe ⎭			

PRETERIT.

Sing. 1.	Ic nęrede	fręmede	dǣlde
2.	ðū nęredest	fręmedest	dǣldest
3.	hē nęrede	fręmede	dǣlde

Plur. 1. wē
2. gē } nęredon   fręmedon   dǣldon
3. hīe

Subjunctive.

PRESENT.

Sing. 1. Ic
2. ðū } nęrie   fręmme   dǣle
3. hē

Plur. 1. wē
2. gē } nęrien   fręmmen   dǣlen
3. hīe

PRETERIT.

Sing. 1. Ic
2. ðū } nęrede   fręmede   dǣlde
3. hē

Plur. 1. wē
2. gē } nęreden   fręmeden   dǣlden
3. hīe

Imperative.

Sing. 2.   nęre   fręme   dǣl
Plur. 1.   nęrian   fręmman   dǣlan
2.   nęriað   fręmmað   dǣlað

Infinitive.

nęrian   fręmman   dǣlan

Gerund.

tō nęrianne (-enne)   tō fręmmanne (-enne)   tō dǣlanne (-enne)

Present Participle.

nęriende   fręmmende   dǣlende

Past Participle.

genęred   gefręmed   gedǣled

NOTE.—The endings of the preterit present no difficulties; in the 2d and 3d singular present, however, the student will observe (*a*) that double consonants in the stem are made single: **fręmest, fręmeð** (not ***freęmmest, *freęmmeð**); **ðęnest, ðęneð**; **sętest (sętst), sęęteð (sętt); fylst, fylð**, from **fyllan**, *to fill*; (*b*) that syncope is the rule in stems long by nature: **dǣlst** (< **dǣlest**), **dǣlð** (< **dǣleð**); **dēmst** (< **dēmest**), **dēmð** (< **dēmeð**); **hīerst** (< **hīerest**), **hīerð** (< **hīereð**). Double consonants are also made single in the imperative 2d singular and in the past participle. Stems long by nature take no final **-e** in the imperative: **dǣl, hīer, dēm**.

Class II.

130.

The infinitive of verbs belonging to this class ends in **-ian** (not **-r-ian**), the preterit singular in **-ode**, the past participle in **-od**. The preterit plural usually has **-edon**, however, instead of **-odon**:

eard-ian,	**eard-ode,**	**geeard-od,**	*to dwell* [**eorðe**].
luf-ian,	**luf-ode,**	**geluf-od,**	*to love* [**lufu**].
rīcs-ian,	**rīcs-ode,**	**gerīcs-od,**	*to rule* [**rīce**].
sealf-ian,	**sealf-ode,**	**gesealf-od,**	*to anoint* [salve].
segl-ian,	**segl-ode,**	**gesegl-od,**	*to sail* [**segel**].

NOTE.—These verbs have no trace of original umlaut, since their **-ian** was once **-ōjan**. Hence, the vowel of the stem was shielded from the influence of the **j** (= **i**) by the interposition of **ō**.

Conjugation of Class II.
131.

Paradigm of **lufian**, *to love*:

Indicative.		**Subjunctive.**	
PRESENT.		PRESENT.	

Sing. 1. Ic lufie
2. ðu lufast
3. hē lufað

Sing. 1. Ic
2. ðū } lufie
3. hē

Plur. 1. wē
2. gē } lufiað
3. hīe

Plur. 1. wē
2. gē } lufien
3. hīe

PRETERIT. PRETERIT.

Sing. 1. Ic lufode
2. ðū lufodest
3. hē lufode

Sing. 1. Ic
2. ðū } lufode
3. hē

Plur. 1. wē
2. gē } lufedon (-odon)
3. hīe

Plur. 1. wē
2. gē } lufeden (-oden)
3. hīe

Imperative.   **Infinitive.**   **Present Participle.**

Sing. 2. lufa   lufian   lufiende
Plur. 1. lufian
2.   lufiað   **Gerund.**   **Past Participle.**

tō lufianne (-enne)   gelufod

NOTE 1.—The **-ie** (**-ien**) occurring in the present must be pronounced as a dissyllable. The **y**-sound thus interposed between the **i** and **e** is frequently indicated by the letter **g**: **lufie**, or **lufige**; **lufien**, or **lufigen**. So also for **ia**: **lufiað**, or **lufigað**; **lufian**, or **lufig(e)an**.

NOTE 2.—In the preterit singular, **-ade**, **-ude**, and **-ede** are not infrequent for **-ode**.

Class III.

132.

The few verbs belonging here show a blending of Classes I and II. Like certain verbs of Class I (§ 128), the preterit and past participle are formed by adding **-de** and **-d**; like Class II, the 2d and 3d present indicative singular end in **-ast** and **-að**, the imperative 2d singular in **-a**:

habb-an,	**hæf-de,**	**gehæf-d,**	*to have.*
libb-an,	**lif-de,**	**gelif-d,**	*to live.*
sęcg-an,	**sǣd-e (sæg-de),**	**gesǣd (gesæg-d),**	*to say.*

Conjugation of Class III.

133.

Paradigms of **habban**, *to have*; **libban**, *to live*; **sęcgan**, *to say*.

Indicative.

PRESENT.

Sing. 1.	Ic hæbbe	libbe		sęcge
2.	ðū hæfst (hafast)	lifast		sægst (sagast)
3.	hē hæfð (hafað)	lifað		sægð (sagað)

Plur. 1.	wē			
2.	gē	habbað	libbað	sęcgað
3.	hīe			

PRETERIT.

Sing. 1.	Ic hæfde	lifde	sǣde
2.	ðū hæfdest	lifdest	sǣdest

3. hē hæfde lifde sǣde

Plur. 1. wē
2. gē } hæfdon lifdon sǣdon
3. hīe

Subjunctive.

PRESENT.

Sing. 1. Ic
2. ðū } hæbbe libbe sęcge
3. hē

Plur. 1. wē
2. gē } hæbben libben sęcgen
3. hīe

PRETERIT.

Sing. 1. Ic
2. ðū } hæfde lifde sǣde
3. hē

Plur. 1. wē
2. gē } hæfden lifden sǣden
3. hīe

Imperative.

Sing. 2. hafa lifa saga
Plur. 1. habban libban sęcgan
2. habbað libbað sęcgað

Infinitive.

habban   libban   sęcgan

Gerund.

tō habbanne (-enne)   tō libbanne (-enne)   tō sęcganne (-enne)

Present Participle.

hæbbende   libbende   sęcgende

Past Participle.

gehæfd   gelifd   gesǣd

CHAPTER XXII.

REMAINING VERBS; VERB-PHRASES WITH **habban, bēon,** AND **weorðan**.

Anomalous Verbs. (See § 19.)

134.

These are:

bēon (wesan),	**wæs,**	**wǣron,**	——,	*to be.*
willan,	**wolde,**	**woldon,**	——,	*to will, intend.*
dōn,	**dyde,**	**dydon,**	**gedōn,**	*to do, cause.*
gān,	**ēode,**	**ēodon,**	**gegān,**	*to go.*

NOTE.—In the original Indo-Germanic language, the first person of the present indicative singular ended in (1) **ō** or (2) **mi**. *Cf.* Gk. λύ-ω, εἰ-μί, Lat. *am-ō, su-m*. The Strong and Weak Conjugations of O.E. are survivals of the **ō**-class. The four Anomalous Verbs mentioned above are the sole remains in O.E. of the **mi**-class. Note the surviving **m** in **eom** *I am*, and **dōm** *I do* (Northumbrian form). These **mi**-verbs are sometimes called non-Thematic to distinguish them from the Thematic or **ō**-verbs.

Conjugation of Anomalous Verbs.

135.

Only the present indicative and subjunctive are at all irregular:

Indicative.

PRESENT.

Sing. 1.	Ic eom (bēom)	wille	dō	gā
2.	ðū eart (bist)	wilt	dēst	gǣst
3.	hē is (bið)	wille	dēð	gǣð

Plur. 1.	wē ⎫				
2.	gē ⎬ sind(on)	willað	dōð	gāð
3.	hīe ⎭				

Subjunctive.

PRESENT.

Sing. 1.	Ic ⎫				
2.	ðū ⎬ sīe	wille	dō	gā
3.	hē ⎭				

Plur. 1.	wē ⎫				
2.	gē ⎬ sīen	willen	dōn	gān
3.	hīe ⎭				

NOTE.—The preterit subjunctive of **bēon** is formed, of course, not from **wæs**, but from **wǣron**. See § 103, (3).

Preterit-Present Verbs. (See § 19.)

136.

These verbs are called Preterit-Present because the present tense (indicative and subjunctive) of each of them is, in form, a strong preterit, the old present having been displaced by the new. They all have weak preterits. Most of the Mn.E. Auxiliary Verbs belong to this class.

witan,	wiste, / wisse,	wiston,	gewiten,	to know [to wit, wot].
āgan,	āhte,	āhton,	āgen (adj.),	to possess [owe].
cunnan,	cūðe,	cūðon,	gecunnen, / cūð (adj.),	to know, can [uncouth, cunning].
durran,	dorste,	dorston,	——	to dare.
sculan,	sceolde,	sceoldon,	——	shall.
magan,	meahte, / mihte,	meahton, / mihton,	——	to be able, may.
mōtan,	mōste,	mōston,	——	may, must.

NOTE.—The change in meaning from preterit to present, with retention of the preterit form, is not uncommon in other languages. Several examples are found in Latin and Greek (cf. *nōvi* and οἶδα, *I know*). Mn.E. has gone further still: **āhte** and **mōste**, which had already suffered the loss of their old preterits (**āh, mōt**), have been forced back again into the present (*ought, must*). Having exhausted, therefore, the only means of preterit formation known to Germanic, the strong and the weak, it is not likely that either *ought* or *must* will ever develop distinct preterit forms.

Conjugation of Preterit-Present Verbs.

137.

The irregularities occur in the present indicative and subjunctive:

Indicative.

PRESENT.

Sing. 1.	Ic wāt	āh	cǫn (can)	dear	sceal	mæg	mōt
2.	ðū wāst	āhst	cǫnst (canst)	dearst	scealt	meaht	mōst
3.	hē wāt	āh	cǫn (can)	dear	sceal	mæg	mōt

Plur. 1. wē
2. gē } witon   āgon   cunnon   durron   sculon   magon   mōton
3. hīe

Subjunctive.

PRESENT.

Sing. 1. Ic
2. ðū } wite   āge   cunne   durre   scule   mæge   mōte
                                      (scyle)
3. hē

Plur. 1. wē
2. gē } witen   āgen   cunnen   durren   sculen   mægen   mōten
                                       (scylen)
3. hīe

NOTE 1.—**Willan** and **sculan** do not often connote simple futurity in Early West Saxon, yet they were fast drifting that way. The Mn.E. use of *shall* only with the 1st person and *will* only with the 2d and 3d, to express simple futurity, was wholly unknown even in Shakespeare's day. The elaborate distinctions drawn between these words by modern grammarians are not only cumbersome and foreign to the genius of English, but equally lacking in psychological basis.

NOTE 2.—**Sculan** originally implied the idea of (1) *duty*, or *compulsion* (= *ought to*, or *must*), and this conception lurks with more or less prominence in almost every function of **sculan** in O.E.: **Dryhten bebēad Moyse hū hē sceolde beran ðā earce**, *The Lord instructed Moses how he ought to bear the ark*; **Ǣlc mann sceal be his andgietes mǣðe ... sprecan ðæt he spricð, and dōn ðæt ðæt hē dēð**, *Every man must, according to the measure of his intelligence, speak what he speaks, and do what he does*. Its next most frequent use is to express (2) *custom*, the transition from the obligatory to the customary being an easy one: **Sē byrdesta sceall gyldan fīftȳne mearðes fell**, *The man of highest rank pays fifteen marten skins*.

NOTE 3.—**Willan** expressed originally (1) *pure volition*, and this is its most frequent use in O.E. It may occur without the infinitive: **Nylle ic ðæs synfullan dēað, ac ic wille ðæt hē gecyrre and lybbe,** *I do not desire the sinner's death, but I desire that he return and live.* The wish being father to the intention, **willan** soon came to express (2) *purpose*: **Hē sǣde ðæt hē at sumum cirre wolde fandian hū longe ðæt land norðryhte lǣge,** *He said that he intended, at some time, to investigate how far that land extended northward.*

Verb-Phrases with *habban*, *bēon* (*wesan*), and *weorðan*.
Verb-Phrases in the Active Voice.

138.

The present and preterit of **habban**, combined with a past participle, are used in O.E., as in Mn.E., to form the present perfect and past perfect tenses:

PRESENT PERFECT.   PAST PERFECT.

Sing. 1. Ic hæbbe gedrifen   *Sing.* 1. Ic hæfde gedrifen
2.   ðū hæfst gedrifen   2.   ðū hæfdest gedrifen
3.   hē hæfð gedrifen   3.   hē hæfde gedrifen

Plur. 1. wē ⎫   *Plur.* 1. wē ⎫
2.   gē ⎬ habbað gedrifen   2.   gē ⎬ hæfdon gedrifen
3.   hīe ⎭   3.   hīe ⎭

The past participle is not usually inflected to agree with the direct object: **Norðymbre ǫnd Ēastęngle hæfdon Ælfrede cyninge āðas geseald** (not **gesealde**, § 82), *The Northumbrians and East Anglians had given king Alfred oaths*; **ǫnd hæfdon miclne dǣl ðāra horsa freten** (not **fretenne**), *and (they) had devoured a large part of the horses.*

NOTE.—Many sentences might be quoted in which the participle does agree with the direct object, but there seems to be no clear line of demarcation between them and the sentences just cited. Originally, the participle expressed a *resultant state*, and belonged in sense more to the object than to **habban**; but in Early West Saxon **habban** had already, in the majority of cases, become a pure auxiliary when used with the past participle. This is conclusively proved by the use of **habban** with intransitive verbs. In such a clause, therefore, as **oð ðæt hīe hine ofslægenne hæfdon**, there is no occasion to translate *until they had him slain* (= *resultant state*); the agreement here is more probably due to the proximity of **ofslægenne** to **hine**. So also

ac hī hæfdon þā hiera stemn gesętenne, *but they had already served out (sat out) their military term.*

139.

If the verb is intransitive, and denotes *a change of condition, a departure or arrival*, **bēon (wesan)** usually replaces **habban**. The past participle, in such cases, partakes of the nature of an adjective, and generally agrees with the subject: **Mīne welan þe ic īo hæfde syndon ealle gewitene ǫnd gedrorene**, *My possessions which I once had are all departed and fallen away;* **wǣron þā męn uppe on lǫnde of āgāne,** *the men had gone up ashore;* **ǫnd þā ōþre wǣron hungre ācwolen**, *and the others had perished of hunger;* **ǫnd ēac sē micla hęre wæs þā þǣr tō cumen**, *and also the large army had then arrived there.*

140.

A progressive present and preterit (not always, however, with distinctively progressive meanings) are formed by combining a present participle with the present and preterit of **bēon (wesan)**. The participle remains uninflected: **ǫnd hīe alle on ðone cyning wǣrun feohtende,** *and they all were fighting against the king;* **Symle hē bið lōciende, nē slǣpð hē nǣfre,** *He is always looking, nor does He ever sleep.*

NOTE.—In most sentences of this sort, the subject is masculine (singular or plural); hence no inference can be made as to agreement, since **-e** is the participial ending for both numbers of the nominative masculine (§ 82). By analogy, therefore, the other genders usually conform in inflection to the masculine: **wǣron þā ealle þā dēoflu clypigende ānre stefne,** *then were all the devils crying with one voice.*

Verb-Phrases in the Passive Voice.

141.

Passive constructions are formed by combining **bēon (wesan)** or **weorðan** with a past participle. The participle agrees regularly with the subject: **hīe wǣron benumene ǣgðer ge þæs cēapes ge þæs cornes**, *they were deprived both of the cattle and the corn;* **hī bēoð āblęnde mid ðǣm þīostrum heora scylda**, *they are blinded with the darkness of their sins;* **and sē wælhrēowa Domiciānus on ðām ylcan gēare wearð ācweald**, *and the murderous Domitian was killed in the same year;* **ǫnd Æþelwulf aldormǫn wearð ofslægen**, *and Æthelwulf, alderman, was slain.*

NOTE 1.—To express agency, Mn.E. employs *by*, rarely *of*; M.E. *of*, rarely *by*; O.E. **frǫm (fram)**, rarely **of: Sē ðe Godes bebodu ne gecnǣwð, ne bið hē oncnāwen frǫm Gode**, *He who does not recognise God's commands, will not be* *recognized by God*; **Betwux þǣm wearð ofslagen Ēadwine ... fram Brytta cyninge**, *Meanwhile, Edwin was slain by the king of the Britons.*

NOTE 2.—O.E. had no progressive forms for the passive, and could not, therefore, distinguish between *He is being wounded* and *He is wounded.* It was not until more than a hundred years after Shakespeare's death that *being* assumed this function. **Weorðan**, which originally denoted *a passage from one state to another*, was ultimately driven out by **bēon** (**wesan**), and survives now only in *Woe worth* (= *be to*).

142.

Vocabulary.

ðā Beormas, *Permians.*

ðā Dęniscan, *the Danish (men), Danes.*

ðā Finnas, *Fins.*

ðæt gewald, *control* [wealdan].

sēo sǣ, *sea.*

sēo scīr, *shire, district.*

sēo wælstōw, *battle-field.*

āgan wælstōwe gewald, *to maintain possession of the battle-field.*

sē wealdend, *ruler, wielder.*

geflīeman,   geflīemde,   geflīemed, *to put to flight.*

gestaðelian, gestaðelode, gestaðelod, *to establish, restore.*

gewissian, gewissode, gewissod, *to guide, direct.*

wīcian,   wīcode,   gewīcod, *to dwell* [**wīc** = village].

143.

EXERCISES.

I. 1. Ǫnd ðǣr wæs micel wæl geslægen on gehwæþre hǫnd, ǫnd Æþelwulf ealdormǫn wearþ ofslægen; ǫnd þā Dęniscan āhton wælstōwe gewald. 2. Ǫnd þæs ymb ānne mōnaþ gefeaht Ælfred cyning wiþ ealne þone hęre ond hine geflīemde. 3. Hē sǣde þēah þæt þæt land sīe swīþe lang norþ þǫnan. 4. Þā Beormas hæfdon swīþe wel gebūd (§ 126, Note 2) hiera land. 5. Ohthęre sǣde þæt sēo scīr hātte (§ 117, Note 2) Hālgoland, þe hē on (§ 94, (5)) būde. 6. Þā Finnas wīcedon be þǣre sǣ. 7. Dryhten, ælmihtiga (§ 78, Note) God, Wyrhta and Wealdend ealra gesceafta, ic bidde ðē for ðīnre miclan mildheortnesse ðæt ðū mē gewissie tō ðīnum willan; and gestaðela mīn mōd tō ðīnum willan and tō mīnre sāwle ðearfe. 8. Þā sceolde hē ðǣr bīdan ryhtnorþanwindes, for ðǣm þæt land bēag þǣr sūðryhte, oþþe sēo sǣ in on ðæt land, hē nysse hwæðer. 9. For ðȳ, mē ðyncð bętre, gif ēow swā ðyncð, ðæt wē ēac ðās bēc on ðæt geðēode węnden ðe wē ealle gecnāwan mægen.

II. 1. When the king heard that, he went (= then went he) westward with his army to Ashdown. 2. Lovest thou me more than these? 3. The men said that the shire which they lived in was called Halgoland. 4. All things were made (**wyrcan**) by God. 5. They were fighting for two days with (= against) the Danes. 6. King Alfred fought with the Danes, and gained the victory; but the Danes retained possession of the battle-field. 7. These men dwelt in England before they came hither. 8. I have not seen the book of (**ymbe**) which you speak (**sprecan**).

PART III.

SELECTIONS FOR READING.

PROSE.
INTRODUCTORY.

I. The Anglo-Saxon Chronicle.

THIS famous work, a series of progressive annals by unknown hands, embraces a period extending from Cæsar's invasion of England to 1154. It is not known when or where these annals began to be recorded in English.

"The annals from the year 866—that of Ethelred's ascent of the throne—to the year 887 seem to be the work of one mind. Not a single year is passed over, and to several is granted considerable space, especially to the years 871, 878, and 885. The whole has gained a certain roundness and fulness, because the events—nearly all of them episodes in the ever-recurring conflict with the Danes—are taken in their connection, and the thread dropped in one year is resumed in the next. Not only is the style in itself concise; it has a sort of nervous severity and pithy rigor. The construction is often antiquated, and suggests at times the freedom of poetry; though this purely historical prose is far removed from poetry in profusion of language." (Ten Brink, *Early Eng. Lit.*, I.)

II. The Translations of Alfred.

Alfred's reign (871-901) may be divided into four periods. The *first*, the period of Danish invasion, extends from 871 to 881; the *second*, the period of comparative quiet, from 881 to 893; the *third*, the period of renewed strife (beginning with the incursions of Hasting), from 893 to 897; the *fourth*, the period of peace, from 897 to 901. His literary work probably falls in the second period.*

The works translated by Alfred from Latin into the vernacular were (1) *Consolation of Philosophy (De Consolatione Philosophiae)* by Boëthius (475-525), (2) *Compendious History of the World (Historiarum Libri VII)* by Orosius (c. 418), (3) *Ecclesiastical History of the English (Historia Ecclesiastica Gentis Anglorum)* by Bede (672-735), and (4) *Pastoral Care (De Cura Pastorali)* by Pope Gregory the Great (540-604).

The chronological sequence of these works is wholly unknown. That given is supported by Turner, Arend, Morley, Grein, and Pauli. Wülker argues for an exact reversal of this order. According to Ten Brink, the order was more probably (1) *Orosius*, (2) *Bede*, (3) *Boëthius*, and (4) *Pastoral Care*. The most recent contribution to the subject is from Wülfing, who contends for (1) *Bede*, (2) *Orosius*, (3) *Pastoral Care*, and (4) *Boëthius*.

* There is something inexpressibly touching in this clause from the great king's pen: gif wē ðā stilnesse habbað. He is speaking of how much he hopes to do, by his translations, for the enlightenment of his people.

I. THE BATTLE OF ASHDOWN.

[From the *Chronicle*, Parker MS. The event and date are significant. The Danes had for the first time invaded Wessex. Alfred's older brother, Ethelred, was king; but to Alfred belongs the glory of the victory at Ashdown (Berkshire). Asser (*Life of Alfred*) tells us that for a long time Ethelred remained praying in his tent, while Alfred and his followers went forth "like a wild boar against the hounds."]

1 871. Hēr cuōm1 sē here tō Rēadingum on Westseaxe,

2 ǫnd þæs ymb iii niht ridon ii eorlas ūp. Þa gemētte hīe

1 Æþelwulf aldorman2 on Ęnglafelda, ǫnd him þǣr wiþ gefeaht,

2 ǫnd sige nam. Þæs ymb iiii niht Æþered cyning

3 ǫnd Ælfred his brōþur3 þǣr micle fierd tō Rēadingum

4 gelǣddon, ǫnd wiþ þone here gefuhton; ǫnd þǣr wæs

5 micel wæl geslægen on gehwæþre hǫnd, ǫnd Æþelwulf

6 aldormǫn wearþ ofslægen; ǫnd þa Dęniscan āhton wælstōwe

7 gewald.

8 Ǫnd þæs ymb iiii niht gefeaht Æþered cyning ǫnd

9 Ælfred his brōþur wiþ alne4 þone here on Æscesdūne.

10 Ǫnd hīe wǣrun5 on twǣm gefylcum: on ōþrum wæs

11 Bāchsęcg ǫnd Halfdęne þā hǣþnan cyningas, ǫnd on

12 ōþrum wǣron þā eorlas. Ǫnd þā gefeaht sē cyning

13 Æþered wiþ þāra cyninga getruman, ǫnd þǣr wearþ sē

14 cyning Bāgsęcg ofslægen; ǫnd Ælfred his brōþur wiþ

15 þāra eorla getruman, ǫnd þǣr wearþ Sidroc eorl ofslægen

16 sē alda,6 ǫnd Sidroc eorl sē gioncga,7 ǫnd Ōsbearn eorl,

17 ǫnd Fræ̆na eorl, ǫnd Hareld eorl; ǫnd þā hęrgas8 bēgen
18 geflīemde, ǫnd fela þūsenda ofslægenra, ǫnd onfeohtende
19 wæ̆ron oþ niht.
20 Ǫnd þæs ymb xiiii niht gefeaht Æþered cyning ǫnd
21 Ælfred his brōður wiþ þone hęre æt Basengum, ǫnd þæ̆r
22 þa Dęniscan sige nāmon.
23 Ǫnd þæs ymb ii mōnaþ gefeaht Æþered cyning ǫnd
24 Ælfred his brōþur wiþ þone hęre æt Męretūne, ǫnd hīe
25 wæ̆run on tuæ̆m9 gefylcium, ǫnd hīe būtū geflīemdon, ǫnd
26 lǫnge on dæg sige āhton; ǫnd þæ̆r wearþ micel wælsliht
27 on gehwæþere hǫnd; ǫnd þā Dęniscan āhton wælstōwe

1 gewald; ǫnd þær wearþ Hēahmund bisceop ofslægen,
2 ǫnd fela gōdra mǫnna. Ǫnd æfter þissum gefeohte cuōm1
3 micel sumorlida.
4 Ǫnd þæs ofer Ēastron gefōr Æþered cyning; ǫnd hē
5 rīcsode v gēar; ǫnd his līc līþ æt Wīnburnan.
6 Þā fēng Ælfred Æþelwulfing his brōþur tō Wesseaxna
7 rīce. Ǫnd þæs ymb ānne mōnaþ gefeaht Ælfred cyning
8 wiþ alne4 þone hęre lȳtle werede10 æt Wiltūne, ǫnd hine
9 lǫnge on dæg geflīemde, ǫnd þā Dęniscan āhton wælstōwe
10 gewald.
11 Ǫnd þæs gēares wurdon viiii folcgefeoht gefohten wiþ
12 þone hęre on þȳ cynerīce be sūþan Tęmese, būtan þām þe
13 him Ælfred þæs cyninges brōþur ǫnd ānlīpig aldormǫn2 ǫnd
14 cyninges þegnas oft rāde onridon þe mǫn nā ne rīmde;
15 ǫnd þæs gēares wæ̆run5 ofslægene viiii eorlas ǫnd ān cyning.
16 Ǫnd þȳ gēare nāmon Westseaxe friþ wiþ þone hęre.

100.8. **gefeaht**. Notice that the singular is used. This is the more common construction in O.E. when a compound subject, composed of singular members, follows its predicate. Cf. *For thine is the kingdom, and the power, and the glory.* See also p. 107, note on **wæs**.

100.18. **ǫnd fela þūsenda ofslægenra**, *and there were many thousands of slain* (§ 91).

101.12. **būtan þām þe**, etc., *besides which, Alfred ... made raids against them* (**him**), *which were not counted.* See § 70, Note.

Consult Glossary and Paradigms under Forms given below.

No note is made of such variants as **y** (**ȳ**) or **i** (**ī**) for **ie** (**īe**). See Glossary under **ie** (**īe**); occurrences, also, of **and** for **ǫnd**, **land** for **lǫnd**, are found on almost every page of Early West Saxon. Such words should be sought for under the more common forms, **ǫnd, lǫnd**.

      1 = cwōm.

      2 = ealdormǫn.

      3 = brōþor.

      4 = ealne.

      5 = wǣron.

      6 = ealda.

      7 = geonga.

      8 = hęras.

      9 = twǣm.

     10 = werode.

II. A PRAYER OF KING ALFRED.

[With this characteristic prayer, Alfred concludes his translation of Boëthius's *Consolation of Philosophy*. Unfortunately, the only extant MS. (Bodleian 180) is Late West Saxon. I follow, therefore, Prof. A. S. Cook's normalization on an Early West Saxon basis. See Cook's *First Book in Old English*, p. 163.]

1 Dryhten, ælmihtiga God, Wyrhta and Wealdend ealra

2 gesceafta, ic bidde ðē for ðīnre miclan mildheortnesse,

3 and for ðǣre hālgan rōde tācne, and for Sanctæ Marian

4 mægðhāde, and for Sancti Michaeles gehīersumnesse, and

5 for ealra ðīnra hālgena lufan and hīera earnungum, ðæt

6 ðū mē gewissie bet ðonne ic āworhte tō ðē; and gewissa

7 mē tō ðīnum willan, and tō mīnre sāwle ðearfe, bet ðonne

8 ic self cunne; and gestaðela mīn mōd tō ðinum willan and

9 tō mīnre sāwle ðearfe; and gestranga mē wið ðæs dēofles

10 costnungum; and āfierr fram mē ðā fūlan gālnesse and

11 ǣlce unrihtwīsnesse; and gescield mē wið mīnum wiðerwinnum,

12 gesewenlīcum and ungesewenlīcum; and tǣc mē

13 ðīnne willan tō wyrceanne; ðæt ic mæge ðē inweardlīce

14 lufian tōforan eallum ðingum, mid clǣnum geðance and

15 mid clǣnum līchaman. For ðon ðe ðū eart mīn Scieppend,

16 and mīn Alīesend, mīn Fultum, mīn Frōfor, mīn Trēownes,

17 and mīn Tōhopa. Sīe ðē lof and wuldor nū and

18 ā ā ā, tō worulde būtan ǣghwilcum ende. Amen.

> 102.3-4. **Marian ... Michaeles**. O.E. is inconsistent in the treatment of foreign names. They are sometimes naturalized, and sometimes retain in part their original inflections. **Marian**, an original accusative, is here used as a genitive; while **Michaeles** has the O.E. genitive ending.
>
> 102.17. **Sīe ðē lof**. See § **105**, 1.

III. THE VOYAGES OF OHTHERE AND WULFSTAN.

[Lauderdale and Cottonian MSS. These voyages are an original insertion by Alfred into his translation of Orosius's *Compendious History of the World.*

"They consist," says Ten Brink, "of a complete description of all the countries in which the Teutonic tongue prevailed at Alfred's time, and a full narrative of the travels of two voyagers, which the king wrote down from their own lips. One of these, a Norwegian named Ohthere, had quite circumnavigated the coast of Scandinavia in his travels, and had even penetrated to the White Sea; the other, named Wulfstan, had sailed from Schleswig to Frische Haff. The geographical and ethnographical details of both accounts are exceedingly interesting, and their style is attractive, clear, and concrete."

Ohthere made two voyages. Sailing first northward along the western coast of Norway, he rounded the North Cape, passed into the White Sea, and entered the Dwina River (**ān micel ēa**). On his second voyage he sailed southward along the western coast of Norway, entered the Skager Rack (**wīdsǣ**), passed through the Cattegat, and anchored at the Danish port of Haddeby (**æt Hǣþum**), modern Schleswig.

Wulfstan sailed only in the Baltic Sea. His voyage of seven days from Schleswig brought him to Drausen (**Trūsō**) on the shore of the Drausensea.]

Ohthere's First Voyage.

1 Ōthẹre sǣde his hlāforde, Ælfrede cyninge, þæt hē

2 ealra Norðmọnna norþmest būde. Hē cwæð þæt hē būde

3 on þǣm lande norþweardum wiþ þā Westsǣ. Hē sǣde

4 þēah þæt þæt land sīe swīþe lang norþ þonan; ac hit is

5 eal wēste, būton on fēawum stōwum styccemǣlum wīciað

6 Finnas, on huntoðe on wintra, ọnd on sumera on fiscaþe

7 be þǣre sǣ. Hē sǣde þæt hē æt sumum cirre wolde

8 fandian hū lọnge þæt land norþryhte lǣge, oþþe hwæðer

9 ǣnig mọn be norðan þǣm wēstenne būde. Þā fōr hē

10 norþryhte be þǣm lande: lēt him ealne weg þæt wēste

11 land on ðæt stēorbord, ọnd þā wīdsǣ on ðæt bæcbord þrīe

12 dagas. Þā wæs hē swā feor norþ swā þā hwælhuntan

13 firrest faraþ. Þā fōr hē þā gīet norþryhte swā feor swā

14 hē meahte on þǣm ōþrum þrīm dagum gesiglan. Þā bēag

15 þæt land þǣr ēastryhte, oþþe sēo sǣ in on ðæt lọnd, hē

16 nysse hwæðer, būton hē wisse ðæt hē ðǣr bād westanwindes

17 ọnd hwōn norþan, ọnd siglde ðā ēast be lande

18 swā swā hē meahte on fēower dagum gesiglan. Þā

19 sceolde hē ðǣr bīdan ryhtnorþanwindes, for ðǣm þæt
20 land bēag þǣr sūþryhte, oþþe sēo sǣ in on ðæt land, hē
21 nysse hwæþer. Þā siglde hē þǫnan sūðryhte be lande

1 swā swā hē męhte1 on fīf dagum gesiglan. Ðā læg þǣr
2 ān micel ēa ūp in on þæt land. Þā cirdon hīe ūp in on
3 ðā ēa, for þǣm hīe ne dorston forþ bī þǣre ēa siglan for
4 unfriþe; for þǣm ðæt land wæs eall gebūn on ōþre healfe
5 þǣre ēas. Ne mētte hē ǣr nān gebūn land, siþþan hē
6 frǫm his āgnum hām fōr; ac him wæs ealne weg wēste
7 land on þæt stēorbord, būtan fiscerum ǫnd fugelerum ōnd
8 huntum, ǫnd þæt wǣron eall Finnas; ǫnd him wæs ā
9 wīdsǣ on ðæt bæcbord. Þā Beormas hæfdon swīþe wel
10 gebūd hira land: ac hīe ne dorston þǣr on cuman. Ac
11 þāra Terfinna land wæs eal wēste, būton ðǣr huntan
12 gewīcodon, oþþe fisceras, oþþe fugeleras.
13 Fela spella him sǣdon þā Beormas ǣgþer ge of hiera
14 āgnum lande ge of þǣm landum þe ymb hīe ūtan wǣron;
15 ac hē nyste hwæt þæs sōþes wæs, for þǣm hē hit self ne
16 geseah. Þā Finnas, him þūhte, ǫnd þā Beormas sprǣcon
17 nēah ān geþēode. Swīþost hē fōr ðider, tō ēacan þæs
18 landes scēawunge, for þǣm horshwælum, for ðǣm hīe
19 habbað swīþe æþele bān on hiora2 tōþum—þā tēð hīe brōhton
20 sume þǣm cyninge—ǫnd hiora hȳd bið swīðe gōd tō
21 sciprāpum. Sē hwæl bið micle lǣssa þonne ōðre hwalas:
22 ne bið hē lęngra ðonne syfan3 ęlna lang; ac on his āgnum
23 lande is sē bętsta hwælhuntað: þā bēoð eahta and fēowertiges
24 ęlna lange, and þā mǣstan fīftiges ęlna lange;

25 þāra hē sǣde þæt hē syxa sum ofslōge syxtig on twām
26 dagum.

1 Hē wæs swȳðe spēdig man on þǣm ǣhtum þe heora2
2 spēda on bēoð, þæt is, on wildrum. Hē hæfde þā gȳt, ðā
3 hē þone cyningc5 sōhte, tamra dēora unbebohtra syx hund.
4 Þā dēor hī hātað 'hrānas'; þāra wǣron syx stælhrānas;
5 ðā bēoð swȳðe dȳre mid Finnum, for ðǣm hȳ fōð þā
6 wildan hrānas mid. Hē wæs mid þǣm fyrstum mannum
7 on þǣm lande: næfde hē þēah mā ðonne twēntig hrȳðera,
8 and twēntig scēapa, and twēntig swȳna; and þæt lȳtle
9 þæt hē ęrede, hē ęrede mid horsan.4 Ac hyra ār is mǣst
10 on þǣm gafole þe ðā Finnas him gyldað. Þæt gafol bið
11 on dēora fellum, and on fugela feðerum, and hwales bāne,
12 and on þǣm sciprāpum þe bēoð of hwæles hȳde geworht
13 and of sēoles. Ǣghwilc gylt be hys gebyrdum. Sē byrdesta
14 sceall gyldan fīftȳne mearðes fell, and fīf hrānes,
15 and ān beren fel, and tȳn ambra feðra, and berenne kyrtel
16 oððe yterenne, and twēgen sciprāpas; ǣgþer sȳ syxtig
17 ęlna lang, ōþer sȳ of hwæles hȳde geworht, ōþer of sīoles.6
18 Hē sǣde ðæt Norðmanna land wǣre swȳþe lang and
19 swȳðe smæl. Eal þæt his man āðer oððe ęttan oððe ęrian
20 mæg, þæt līð wið ðā sǣ; and þæt is þēah on sumum
21 stōwum swȳðe clūdig; and licgað wilde mōras wið ēastan
22 and wið ūpp on emnlange þǣm bȳnum lande. On þǣm
23 mōrum eardiað Finnas. And þæt bȳne land is ēasteweard
24 brādost, and symle swā norðor swā smælre. Ēastewęrd7
25 hit mæg bīon8 syxtig mīla brād, oþþe hwēne brǣdre;

26 and middeweard þrītig oððe brādre; and norðeweard hē

27 cwæð, þǣr hit smalost wǣre, þæt hit mihte bēon þrēora

28 mīla brād tō þǣm mōre; and sē mōr syðþan,9 on sumum

1 stōwum, swā brād swā man mæg on twām wucum oferfēran;

2 and on sumum stōwum swā brād swā man mæg

3 on syx dagum oferfēran.

4 Đonne is tōemnes þǣm lande sūðeweardum, on ōðre

5 healfe þæs mōres, Swēoland, oþ þæt land norðeweard;

6 and tōemnes þǣm lande norðeweardum, Cwēna land. Þā

7 Cwēnas hęrgiað hwīlum on ðā Norðmęn ofer ðone mōr,

8 hwīlum þā Norðmęn on hȳ. And þǣr sint swīðe micle

9 męras fersce geond þā mōras; and berað þā Cwēnas hyra

10 scypu ofer land on ðā męras, and þanon hęrgiað on ðā

11 Norðmęn; hȳ habbað swȳðe lȳtle scypa and swȳðe

12 leohte.

> 104.6. **fṛọm his āgnum hām.** An adverbial dative singular without an inflectional ending is found with **hām, dæg, morgen,** and **ǣfen.**
>
> 104.8. **ọnd þæt wǣron.** See § 40, Note 3.
>
> 104.15. **hwæt þæs sōþes wæs.** Sweet errs in explaining **sōþes** as attracted into the genitive by **þæs.** It is not a predicate adjective, but a partitive genitive after **hwæt.**
>
> 104.25. **syxa sum.** See § 91, Note 2.
>
> 105.2. **on bēoð.** See § 94, (5).
>
> 105.19. **Eal þæt his man.** Pronominal genitives are not always possessive in O.E.; **his** is here the partitive genitive of **hit,** the succeeding relative pronoun being omitted: *All that (portion) of it that may, either-of-the-two, either be grazed or plowed,* etc. (§ 70, Note).

106.11-12. **scypa ... leohte**. These words exhibit inflections more frequent in Late than in Early West Saxon. The normal forms would be **scypu, leoht**; but in Late West Saxon the **-u** of short-stemmed neuters is generally replaced by **-a**; and the nominative accusative plural neuter of adjectives takes, by analogy, the masculine endings; **hwate, gōde, hālge**, instead of **hwatu, gōd, hālgu**.

1 = meahte, mihte.

2 = hiera.

3 = seofon.

4 = horsum.

5 = cyning.

6 = sēoles.

7 = -weard.

8 = bēon.

9 = siððan.

Ohthere's Second Voyage.

13 Ōhthẹre sǣde þæt sīo1 scīr hātte Hālgoland, þe hē on

14 būde. Hē cwæð þæt nān man ne būde be norðan him.

15 Þonne is ān port on sūðeweardum þǣm lande, þone man

16 hǣt Sciringeshēal. Þyder hē cwæð þæt man ne mihte

17 geseglian on ānum mōnðe, gyf man on niht wīcode, and

18 ǣlce dæge hæfde ambyrne wind; and ealle ðā hwīle hē

19 sceal seglian be lande. And on þæt stēorbord him bið

20 ǣrest Īraland, and þonne ðā īgland þe synd betux Īralande

21 and þissum lande. Þonne is þis land, oð hē cymð

22 tō Scirincgeshēale, and ealne weg on þæt bæcbord Norðweg.

1 Wið sūðan þone Sciringeshēal fylð swȳðe mycel

2 sǣ ūp in on ðæt land; sēo is brādre þonne ǣnig man ofer
3 sēon mæge. And is Gotland on ōðre healfe ongēan, and
4 siððan Sillende. Sēo sǣ līð mænig2 hund mīla ūp in on
5 þæt land.

6 And of Sciringeshēale hē cwæð ðæt hē seglode on fīf
7 dagan3 tō þǣm porte þe mon hǣt æt Hǣþum; sē stent
8 betuh Winedum, and Seaxum, and Angle, and hȳrð in
9 on Dene. Ðā hē þiderweard seglode fram Sciringeshēale,
10 þā wæs him on þæt bæcbord Denamearc and on
11 þæt stēorbord wīdsǣ þrȳ dagas; and þā, twēgen dagas ǣr
12 hē tō Hǣþum cōme, him wæs on þæt stēorbord Gotland,
13 and Sillende, and īglanda fela. On þǣm landum eardodon
14 Engle, ǣr hī hider on land cōman.4 And hym wæs
15 ðā twēgen dagas on ðæt bæcbord þā īgland þe in on
16 Denemearce hȳrað.

> 107.7. **æt Hǣþum**. "This pleonastic use of *æt* with names of places occurs elsewhere in the older writings, as in the Chronicle (552), 'in þǣre stōwe þe is genemned æt Searobyrg,' where the *æt* has been erased by some later hand, showing that the idiom had become obsolete. *Cp*. the German 'Gasthaus zur Krone,' Stamboul = *es tān pólin*." (Sweet.) See, also, *Atterbury*, § 28, Note 3.
>
> 107.14-15. **wæs ... þā īgland**. The singular predicate is due again to inversion (p. 100, note on **gefeaht**). The construction is comparatively rare in O.E., but frequent in Shakespeare and in the popular speech of to-day. Cf. *There is, Here is, There has been*, etc., with a (single) plural subject following.
>
> 1 = sēo.
>
> 2 = monig.
>
> 3 = dagum.

4 = cōmen.

Wulfstan's Voyage.

17 Wulfstān sǣde þæt hē gefōre of Hǣðum, þæt hē wǣre
18 on Trūsō on syfan dagum and nihtum, þæt þæt scip wæs
19 ealne weg yrnende under segle. Weonoðland him wæs

1 on stēorbord, and on bæcbord him wæs Langaland, and
2 Lǣland, and Falster, and Scōnēg; and þās land eall
3 hȳrað tō Dęnemearcan. And þonne Burgenda land wæs
4 ūs on bæcbord, and þā habbað him sylfe1 cyning. Þonne
5 æfter Burgenda lande wǣron ūs þās land, þā synd hātene
6 ǣrest Blēcinga-ēg, and Mēore, and Ēowland, and Gotland
7 on bæcbord; and þās land hȳrað tō Swēom. And Weonodland
8 wæs ūs ealne weg on stēorbord oð Wīslemūðan.
9 Sēo Wīsle is swȳðe mycel ēa, and hīo2 tōlīð Wītland and
10 Weonodland; and þæt Wītland belimpeð tō Estum; and
11 sēo Wīsle līð ūt of Weonodlande, and līð in Estmęre;
12 and sē Estmęre is hūru fīftēne3 mīla brād. Þonne cymeð
13 Ilfing ēastan in Estmęre of ðām męre, ðe Trūsō standeð
14 in stæðe; and cumað ūt samod in Estmęre, Ilfing ēastan
15 of Estlande, and Wīsle sūðan of Winodlande. And
16 þonne benimð Wīsle Ilfing hire naman, and ligeð of þǣm
17 męre west and norð on sǣ; for ðȳ hit man hǣt
18 Wīslemūða.
19 Þæt Estland is swȳðe mycel, and þǣr bið swȳðe manig
20 burh, and on ǣlcere byrig bið cyning. And þǣr bið
21 swȳðe mycel hunig, and fiscnað; and sē cyning and þā
22 rīcostan męn drincað mȳran meolc, and þā unspēdigan

23 and þā þēowan drincað medo.4 Þǣr bið swȳðe mycel
24 gewinn betwēonan him. And ne bið ðǣr nǣnig ealo5
25 gebrowen mid Estum, ac þǣr bið medo genōh. And þǣr
26 is mid Estum ðēaw, þonne þǣr bið man dēad, þæt hē līð
27 inne unforbærned mid his māgum and frēondum mōnað,
28 ge hwīlum twēgen; and þā cyningas, and þā ōðre hēahðungene
29 mẹn, swā micle lẹncg6 swā hī māran spēda
30 habbað, hwīlum healf gēar þæt hī bēoð unforbærned, and

1 licgað bufan eorðan on hyra hūsum. And ealle þā hwīle
2 þe þæt līc bið inne, þǣr sceal bēon gedrync and plega,
3 oð ðone dæg þe hī hine forbærnað. Þonne þȳ ylcan dæge
4 þe hī hine tō þǣm āde beran wyllað, þonne tōdǣlað hī
5 his feoh, þæt þǣr tō lāfe bið æfter þǣm gedrynce and þǣm
6 plegan, on fīf oððe syx, hwȳlum on mā, swā swā þæs fēos
7 andēfn bið. Ālẹcgað hit ðonne forhwæga on ānre mīle
8 þone mǣstan dǣl fram þǣm tūne, þonne ōðerne, ðonne
9 þone þriddan, oþ þe hyt eall ālēd bið on þǣre ānre mīle;
10 and sceall bēon sē lǣsta dǣl nȳhst þǣm tūne ðe sē dēada
11 man on līð. Ðonne sceolon7 bēon gesamnode ealle ðā
12 mẹnn ðe swyftoste hors habbað on þǣm lande, forhwæga
13 on fīf mīlum oððe on syx mīlum fram þǣm fēo. Þonne
14 ærnað hȳ ealle tōweard þǣm fēo: ðonne cymeð sē man
15 sē þæt swiftoste hors hafað tō þǣm ǣrestan dǣle and tō
16 þǣm mǣstan, and swā ǣlc æfter ōðrum, oþ hit bið eall
17 genumen; and sē nimð þone lǣstan dǣl sē nȳhst þǣm
18 tūne þæt feoh geærneð. And þonne rīdeð ǣlc hys weges
19 mid ðǣm fēo, and hyt mōtan8 habban eall; and for ðȳ

20 þǣr bēoð þā swiftan hors ungefōge dȳre. And þonne his
21 gestrēon bēoð þus eall āspęnded, þonne byrð man hine ūt,
22 and forbærneð mid his wǣpnum and hrægle; and swīðost

1 ealle hys spēda hȳ forspęndað mid þǣm langan legere
2 þæs dēadan mannes inne, and þæs þe hȳ be þǣm wegum
3 ālęcgað, þe ðā fręmdan tō ærnað, and nimað. And þæt
4 is mid Estum þēaw þæt þǣr sceal ǣlces geðēodes man
5 bēon forbærned; and gyf þār9 man ān bān findeð unforbærned,
6 hī hit sceolan7 miclum gebētan. And þǣr is mid
7 Estum ān mǣgð þæt hī magon cyle gewyrcan; and þȳ
8 þǣr licgað þā dēadan męn swā lange, and ne fūliað, þæt
9 hȳ wyrcað þone cyle him on. And þēah man āsętte
10 twēgen fǣtels full ealað oððe wæteres, hȳ gedōð þæt
11 ǣgþer bið oferfroren, sam hit sȳ sumor sam winter.

 108.1-4. **him ... ūs**. Note the characteristic change of person, the transition from *indirect* to *direct discourse*.

 109.2. **sceal**. See § **137**, Note 2 (2).

 109.7. **Ālęcgað hit**. Bosworth illustrates thus:

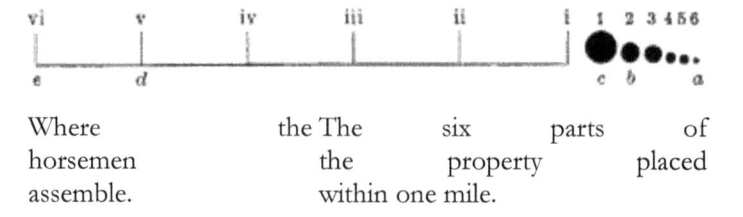

```
vi         v         iv        iii        ii         i   1 2 3 4 5 6
|          |         |          |          |          |  ● ● ● . . .
     e          d                                        c   b      a
```

| Where the horsemen assemble. | The property | six parts of the placed within one mile. |

"The horsemen assemble five or six miles from the property, at *d* or *e*, and run towards *c*; the man who has the swiftest horse, coming first to 1 or *c*, takes the first and largest part. The man who has the horse coming second takes part 2 or *b*, and so, in succession, till the least part, 6 or *a*, is taken."

110.5-6. **man ... hī**. Here the plural **hī** refers to the singular **man**. *Cf.* p. 109, ll. 18-19, **ǣlc ... mōtan**. In *Exodus* xxxii, 24, we find "*Whosoever* hath any gold, let *them* break it off"; and Addison writes, "I do not mean that I think *anyone* to blame for taking due care of *their* health." The construction, though outlawed now, has been common in all periods of our language. Paul remarks (*Prinzipien der Sprachgeschichte*, 3d ed., § 186) that "When a word is used as an indefinite [one, man, somebody, etc.] it is, strictly speaking, incapable of any distinction of number. Since, however, in respect of the external form, a particular number has to be chosen, it is a matter of indifference which this is.... Hence a change of numbers is common in the different languages." Paul fails to observe that the change is always from singular to plural, not from plural to singular. See *Note on the Concord of Collectives and Indefinites* (Anglia XI, 1901). See p. 119, note on ll. 19-21.

1 = selfe.

2 = hēo.

3 = fīftīene.

4 = medu.

5 = ealu.

6 = lęng.

7 = sculon.

8 = mōton.

9 = ðǣr.

IV. THE STORY OF CÆDMON.

[From the so-called Alfredian version of Bede's *Ecclesiastical History*. The text generally followed is that of MS. Bodley, Tanner 10. Miller (*Early English Text Society*, No. 95, *Introd.*) argues, chiefly from the use of the prepositions, that the original O.E. MS. was Mercian, composed possibly in Lichfield

(Staffordshire). At any rate, O.E. idiom is frequently sacrificed to the Latin original.

"Cædmon, as he is called, is the first Englishman whose name we know who wrote poetry in our island of England; and the first to embody in verse the new passions and ideas which Christianity had brought into England.... Undisturbed by any previous making of lighter poetry, he came fresh to the work of Christianising English song. It was a great step to make. He built the chariot in which all the new religious emotions of England could now drive along." (Brooke, *The History of Early English Literature*, cap. XV.) There is no reason to doubt the historical existence of Cædmon; for Bede, who relates the story, lived near Whitby, and was seven years old when Cædmon died (A.D. 680)].

1 In ðysse abbudissan mynstre wæs sum brōðor syndriglīce

2 mid godcundre gife gemǣred ǫnd geweorðad, for þon

3 he gewunade gerisenlīce lēoð wyrcan, þā ðe tō ǣfęstnisse1

4 ǫnd tō ārfæstnisse belumpon; swā ðætte swā hwæt swā

5 hē of godcundum stafum þurh bōceras geleornode, þæt hē

6 æfter medmiclum fæce in scopgereorde mid þā mǣstan

7 swētnisse ǫnd inbryrdnisse geglęngde, ǫnd in Ęngliscgereorde

8 wel geworht forþ brōhte. Ǫnd for his lēoþsǫngum

1 mǫnigra mǫnna mōd oft to worulde forhogdnisse ǫnd tō

2 geþēodnisse þæs heofonlīcan līfes onbærnde wǣron. Ǫnd

3 ēac swelce2 mǫnige ōðre æfter him in Ǫngelþēode ongunnon

4 ǣfęste lēoð wyrcan, ac nǣnig hwæðre him þæt gelīce

5 dōn ne meahte; for þon hē nālæs frǫm mǫnnum nē ðurh

6 mǫn gelǣred wæs þæt hē ðone lēoðcræft leornade, ac hē

7 wæs godcundlīce gefultumod, ǫnd þurh Godes gife þone

8 sǫngcræft onfēng; ǫnd hē for ðon nǣfre nōht lēasunge,

9 nē īdles lēoþes wyrcan ne meahte, ac efne þā ān ðā ðē tō

10 ǣfęstnisse1 belumpon ǫnd his þā ǣfęstan tungan gedafenode

11 singan.

12 Wæs hē, sē mọn, in weoruldhāde3 gesẹted oð þā tīde þe
13 hē wæs gelȳfdre ylde, ọnd nǣfre nǣnig lēoð geleornade.
14 Ọnd hē for þon oft in gebēorscipe, þonne þǣr wæs blisse
15 intinga gedēmed, þæt hēo4 ealle sceolden þurh ẹndebyrdnesse
16 be hearpan singan, þonne hē geseah þā hearpan him
17 nēalēcan, þonne ārās hē for scọme frọm þǣm symble,
18 ọnd hām ēode tō his hūse. Þā hē þæt þā sumre tīde
19 dyde, þæt hē forlēt þæt hūs þæs gebēorscipes, ọnd ūt wæs

1 gọngende tō nēata scipene, þāra heord him wæs þǣre
2 nihte beboden; þā hē ðā þǣr on gelimplīcre tīde his
3 leomu5 on rẹste gesẹtte ọnd onslēpte, þa stōd him sum
4 mọn æt þurh swefn, ọnd hine hālette ọnd grētte, ọnd hine
5 be his nọman nẹmnde: "Cædmọn, sing mē hwæthwugu."
6 Þā ọndswarede hē, ọnd cwæð: "Ne cọn ic nōht singan;
7 ọnd ic for þon of þyssum gebēorscipe ūt ēode ọnd hider
8 gewāt, for þon ic nāht singan ne cūðe." Eft hē cwæð sē ðe
9 wið hine sprecende wæs: "Hwæðre þū meaht mē singan."
10 Þā cwæð hē: "Hwæt sceal ic singan?" Cwæð hē: "Sing
11 mē frumsceaft." Þā hē ðā þās andsware onfēng, þā
12 ongọn hē sōna singan, in hẹrenesse Godes Scyppendes,
13 þā fers ọnd þā word þe hē nǣfre ne gehȳrde, þāra ẹndebyrdnes
14 þis is:
15 Nū sculon hẹrigean6   heofonrīces Weard,
16 Metodes meahte   ọnd his mōdgeþanc,
17 weorc Wuldorfæder,   swā hē wundra gehwæs,
18 ēce Drihten   ōr onstealde.

1 Hē ǣrest scēop   eorðan bearnum
2 heofon tō hrōfe,   hālig Scyppend;
3 þā middangeard   monncynnes Weard,
4 ēce Drihten,   æfter tēode
5 fīrum foldan,   Frēa ælmihtig.
6 Þā ārās hē from þǣm slǣpe, ond eal þā þe hē slǣpende
7 song fæste in gemynde hæfde; ond þǣm wordum sōna
8 monig word in þæt ilce gemet Gode wyrðes songes
9 tōgeþēodde. Þā cōm hē on morgenne tō þǣm tūngerēfan,
10 sē þe his ealdormon wæs: sægde him hwylce gife hē
11 onfēng; ond hē hine sōna tō þǣre abbudissan gelǣdde,
12 ond hire þæt cȳðde ond sægde. Þā heht hēo gesomnian
13 ealle þā gelǣredestan men ond þā leorneras, ond him
14 ondweardum hēt secgan þæt swefn, ond þæt lēoð singan,
15 þæt ealra heora7 dōme gecoren wǣre, hwæt oððe hwonan
16 þæt cumen wǣre. Þā wæs him eallum gesewen, swā swā
17 hit wæs, þæt him wǣre from Drihtne sylfum heofonlīc

1 gifu forgifen. Þā rehton heo4 him ond sægdon sum hālig
2 spell ond godcundre lāre word: bebudon him þā, gif hē
3 meahte, þæt hē in swīnsunge lēoþsonges þæt gehwyrfde.
4 Þā hē ðā hæfde þā wīsan onfongne, þā ēode hē hām tō
5 his hūse, ond cwōm eft on morgenne, ond þȳ betstan
6 lēoðe geglenged him āsong ond āgeaf þæt him beboden
7 wæs.
8 Ðā ongan sēo abbudisse clyppan ond lufigean8 þā Godes
9 gife in þǣm men, ond hēo hine þā monade ond lǣrde
10 þæt hē woruldhād forlēte ond munuchād onfēnge: ond

11 hē þæt wel þafode. Ǫnd hēo hine in þæt mynster onfēng
12 mid his gōdum, ǫnd hine geþēodde tō gesǫmnunge þāra
13 Godes þēowa, ǫnd heht hine lǣran þæt getæl þæs hālgan
14 stǣres ǫnd spelles. Ǫnd hē eal þā hē in gehȳrnesse
15 geleornian meahte, mid hine gemyndgade, ǫnd swā swā
16 clǣne nēten9 eodorcende in þæt swēteste lēoð gehwyrfde.
17 Ǫnd his sǫng ǫnd his lēoð wǣron swā wynsumu tō gehȳranne,
18 þætte þā seolfan10 his lārēowas æt his mūðe writon
19 ǫnd leornodon. Sǫng hē ǣrest be middangeardes gesceape,
20 ǫnd bī fruman mǫncynnes, ǫnd eal þæt stǣr Genesis (þæt
21 is sēo ǣreste Moyses bōc); ǫnd eft bī ūtgǫnge Israhēla
22 folces of Ǣgypta lǫnde, ǫnd bī ingǫnge þæs gehātlandes;
23 ǫnd bī ōðrum mǫnegum spellum þæs hālgan gewrites

1 canōnes bōca; ǫnd bī Crīstes męnniscnesse, ǫnd bī his
2 þrōwunge, ǫnd bī his ūpāstīgnesse in heofonas; ǫnd bī
3 þæs Hālgan Gāstes cyme, ǫnd þāra apostola lāre; ǫnd eft
4 bī þǣm dæge þæs tōweardan dōmes, ǫnd bī fyrhtu þæs
5 tintreglīcan wītes, ǫnd bī swētnesse þæs heofonlīcan rīces,
6 hē monig lēoð geworhte; ǫnd swelce2 ēac ōðer mǫnig be
7 þǣm godcundan fręmsumnessum ǫnd dōmum hē geworhte.
8 In eallum þǣm hē geornlīce gēmde11 þæt hē męn ātuge
9 frǫm synna lufan ǫnd māndǣda, ǫnd tō lufan ǫnd tō
10 geornfulnesse āwęhte gōdra dǣda, for þon hē wæs, sē
11 mǫn, swīþe ǣfęst ǫnd regollīcum þēodscipum ēaðmōdlīce
12 underþēoded; ǫnd wið þǣm þā ðe in ōðre wīsan dōn woldon,
13 hē wæs mid welme12 micelre ęllenwōdnisse onbærned.
14 Ǫnd hē for ðon fægre ęnde his līf betȳnde ǫnd geęndade.

111.1. **ðysse abbudissan.** The abbess referred to is the famous Hild, or Hilda, then living in the monastery at Streones-halh, which, according to Bede, means "Bay of the Beacon." The Danes afterward gave it the name Whitby, or "White Town." The surroundings were eminently fitted to nurture England's first poet. "The natural scenery which surrounded him, the valley of the Esk, on whose sides he probably lived, the great cliffs, the billowy sea, the vast sky seen from the heights over the ocean, played incessantly upon him." (Brooke.)

Note, also, in this connection, the numerous Latin words that the introduction of Christianity (A.D. 597) brought into the vocabulary of O.E.: **abbudisse, mynster, bisceop, Læden, prēost, æstel, mancus.**

112.4-5. The more usual order of words would be **ac nǣnig, hwæðre, ne meahte ðæt dōn gelīce him.**

112.10-11. **ǫnd his ... singan,** *and which it became his (the) pious tongue to sing.*

112.14-15. **blisse intinga,** *for the sake of joy*; but the translator has confused *laetitiae causā* (ablative) and *laetitiae causa* (nominative). The proper form would be **for blisse** with omission of **intingan,** just as *for my sake* is usually **for mē**; *for his (or their) sake,* **for him.** *Cf.* Mark vi, 26: "Yet *for his oath's sake, and for their sakes which sat with him,* he would not reject her," **for ðǣm āðe, ǫnd for ðǣm þe him mid sǣton.** *For his sake* is frequently **for his ðingon (ðingum),** rarely **for his intingan. Þingon** is regularly used when the preceding genitive is a noun denoting a person: *for my wife's sake,* **for mīnes wīfes ðingon** (*Genesis* xx, 11), etc.

112.18-19. **þæt ... þæt hē forlēt.** The substantival clause introduced by the second **þæt** amplifies by apposition the first **þæt**: *When he then, at a certain time* (instrumental case, § 98, (2)), *did that, namely, when he left the house.* The better Mn.E. would be *this ... that*: "Added yet *this* above all, *that* he shut up John in prison" (*Luke* iv, 20).

113.1-2. **þāra ... beboden**. This does not mean that Cædmon was a herdsman, but that he served in turn as did the other secular attendants at the monastery.

113.13-14. **þāra ęndebyrdnes þis is**. Bede writes *Hic est sensus, non autem ordo ipse verborum*, and gives in Latin prose a translation of the hymn from the Northumbrian dialect, in which Cædmon wrote. The O.E. version given above is, of course, not the Northumbrian original (which, however, with some variations is preserved in several of the Latin MSS. of Bede's *History*), but a West Saxon version made also from the Northumbrian, not from the Latin.

113.15. **Nū sculon hęrigean**, *Now ought we to praise*. The subject **wē** is omitted in the best MSS. Note the characteristic use of synonyms, or epithets, in this bit of O.E. poetry. Observe that it is not the *thought* that is repeated, but rather the *idea*, the *concept*, God. See p. 124.

113.17. **wundra gehwæs**. See p. 140, note on **cēnra gehwylcum**.

114.7-9. **ǫnd þǣm wordum ... tōgeþēodde**, *and to those words he soon joined, in the same meter, many (other) words of song worthy of God*. But the translator has not only blundered over Bede's Latin (*eis mox plura in eundem modum verba Deo digna carminis adjunxit*), but sacrificed still more the idiom of O.E. The predicate should not come at the end; **in** should be followed by the dative; and for **Gode wyrðes sǫnges** the better O.E. would be **sǫnges Godes wyrðes**. When used with the dative **wyrð** (**weorð**) usually means *dear* (= *of worth*) *to*.

114.16. **þā ... gesewen**. We should expect **frǫm him eallum**; but the translator has again closely followed the Latin (*visumque est omnibus*), as later (in the *Conversion of Edwin*) he renders *Talis mihi videtur* by **þyslīc mē is gesewen**. *Talis* (**þyslīc**) agreeing with a following *vita* (**līf**). Ælfric, however, with no Latin before him, writes that John **wearð ðā him** [= **frǫm Drihtene**] **inweardlīce gelufod**. It would seem that in proportion as a past participle has the force of an adjective, the *to* relation may supplant the *by* relation; just as we say *unknown to* instead of *unknown by*, *unknown* being more adjectival than participial. **Gesewen**, therefore, may here be translated *visible, evident, patent* (= **gesynelīc, sweotol**); and **gelufod**, *dear* (= **weorð, lēof**).

A survival of adjectival **gesewen** is found in Wycliffe's *New Testament* (1 *Cor.* xv, 5-8): "He was *seyn to* Cephas, and aftir these thingis *to* enleuene; aftirward he was *seyn to* mo than fyue hundrid britheren togidere ... aftirward he was *seyn to* James, and aftirward *to* alle the apostlis. And last of alle he was *seyn to* me, as *to* a deed borun child." The construction is frequent in Chaucer.

115.9-10. **ǫnd hēo hine þā mǫnade ... munuchād onfēnge**. Hild's advice has in it the suggestion of a personal experience, for she herself had lived half of her life (thirty-three years) "before," says Bede, "she dedicated the remaining half to our Lord in a monastic life."

116.6. **hē mǫnig lēoð geworhte**. The opinion is now gaining ground that of these "many poems" only the short hymn, already given, has come down to us. Of other poems claimed for Cædmon, the strongest arguments are advanced in favor of a part of the fragmentary poetical paraphrase of *Genesis*.

1 = ǣfæstnesse.

2 = swilce.

3 = woruldhāde.

4 = hīe.

5 = limu.

6 = hęrian.

7 = hiera.

8 = lufian.

9 = nīeten.

10 = selfan.

11 = gīemde.

12 = wielme.

V. ALFRED'S PREFACE TO THE PASTORAL CARE.

[Based on the Hatton MS. Of the year 597, the *Chronicle* says: "In this year, Gregory the Pope sent into Britain Augustine with very many monks, who gospelled [preached] God's word to the English folk." Gregory I, surnamed "The Great," has ever since been considered the apostle of English Christianity, and his *Pastoral Care*, which contains instruction in conduct and doctrine for all bishops, was a work that Alfred could not afford to leave untranslated. For this translation Alfred wrote a *Preface*, the historical value of which it would be hard to overrate. In it he describes vividly the intellectual ruin that the Danes had wrought, and develops at the same time his plan for repairing that ruin.

This *Preface* and the *Battle of Ashdown* (p. 99) show the great king in his twofold character of warrior and statesman, and justify the inscription on the base of the statue erected to him in 1877, at Wantage (Berkshire), his birth-place: "Ælfred found Learning dead, and he restored it; Education neglected, and he revived it; the laws powerless, and he gave them force; the Church debased, and he raised it; the Land ravaged by a fearful Enemy, from which he delivered it. Ælfred's name will live as long as mankind shall respect the Past."]

1 Ælfred kyning hāteð grētan Wærferð biscep1 his wordum

2 luflīce ǫnd frēondlīce; ǫnd ðē cȳðan hāte ðæt mē cōm

3 swīðe oft on gemynd, hwelce2 witan īu3 wǣron giond4

4 Angelcynn, ǣgðer ge godcundra hāda ge woruldcundra;

5 ǫnd hū gesǣliglīca tīda ðā wǣron giond Angelcynn; ǫnd

6 hū ðā kyningas ðe ðone onwald hæfdon ðæs folces on

7 ðām dagum Gode ǫnd his ǣrendwrecum hērsumedon5;

8 ǫnd hū hīe ǣgðer ge hiora sibbe ge hiora siodo6 ge hiora

9 onweald innanbordes gehīoldon,4 ǫnd ēac ūt hiora ēðel

10 gerȳmdon; ǫnd hū him ðā spēow ǣgðer ge mid wīge ge

11 mid wīsdōme; ǫnd ēac ða godcundan hādas hū giorne

12 hīe wǣron ǣgðer ge ymb lāre ge ymb liornunga, ge ymb
13 ealle ðā ðīowotdōmas ðe hīe Gode dōn scoldon; ǫnd hū
14 man ūtanbordes wīsdōm ǫnd lāre hieder on lǫnd sōhte,
15 ǫnd hū wē hīe nū sceoldon ūte begietan, gif wē hīe habban
16 sceoldon. Swǣ7 clǣne hīo wæs oðfeallenu on Angelcynne
17 ðæt swīðe fēawa wǣron behionan Humbre ðe hiora ðēninga
18 cūðen understǫndan on Ęnglisc oððe furðum ān ǣrendgewrit
19 of Lǣdene on Ęnglisc āręccean; ǫnd ic wēne ðætte
20 nōht mǫnige begiondan Humbre nǣren. Swǣ7 fēawa
21 hiora wǣron ðæt ic furðum ānne ānlēpne8 ne mæg geðencean

1 be sūðan Tęmese, ðā ðā ic tō rīce fēng. Gode ælmihtegum
2 sīe ðǫnc ðætte wē nū ǣnigne onstāl habbað
3 lārēowa. Ǫnd for ðon ic ðē bebīode ðæt ðū dō swǣ7 ic
4 gelīefe ðæt ðū wille, ðæt ðū ðē ðissa worulddinga tō ðǣm
5 geǣmetige, swǣ ðū oftost mæge, ðæt ðū ðone wīsdōm ðe
6 ðē God sealde ðǣr ðǣr ðū hiene befæstan mæge, befæste.
7 Geðęnc hwelc9 wītu ūs ðā becōmon for ðisse worulde, ðā
8 ðā wē hit nōhwæðer nē selfe ne lufodon, nē ēac ōðrum
9 mǫnnum ne lēfdon10: ðone naman ānne wē lufodon ðætte
10 wē Crīstne wǣren, ǫnd swīðe fēawe ðā ðēawas.
11 Ðā ic ðā ðis eall gemunde, ðā gemunde ic ēac hū ic
12 geseah, ǣr ðǣm ðe hit eall forhęrgod wǣre ǫnd forbærned,
13 hū ðā ciricean giond eall Angelcynn stōdon
14 māðma ǫnd bōca gefylda, ǫnd ēac micel męnigeo11 Godes
15 ðīowa; ǫnd ðā swīðe lȳtle fiorme ðāra bōca wiston, for
16 ðǣm ðe hīe hiora nānwuht12 ongietan ne meahton, for
17 ðǣm ðe hīe nǣron on hiora āgen geðīode awritene.

- 122 -

18 Swelce13 hīe cwǣden: "Ure ieldran, ðā ðe ðās stōwa ǣr
19 hīoldon, hīe lufodon wīsdōm, ǫnd ðurh ðone hīe begēaton
20 welan, ǫnd ūs lǣfdon. Hēr mǫn mæg gīet gesīon hiora
21 swæð, ac wē him ne cunnon æfter spyrigean,14 ǫnd for
22 ðǣm wē habbað nū ǣgðer forlǣten ge ðone welan ge ðone
23 wīsdōm, for ðǣm ðe wē noldon tō ðǣm spore mid ūre
24 mōde onlūtan."
25 Ðā ic ðā ðis eall gemunde, ðā wundrade ic swīðe swīðe
26 ðāra gōdena wiotona15 ðe gīu wǣron giond Angelcynn, ǫnd
27 ðā bēc ealla be fullan geliornod hæfdon, ðæt hīe hiora ðā

1 nǣnne dǣl noldon on hiora āgen geðīode węndan. Ac
2 ic ðā sōna eft mē selfum andwyrde, ǫnd cwæð: "Hīe ne
3 wēndon þætte ǣfre męnn sceolden swǣ7 reccelēase weorðan,
4 ǫnd sīo lār swǣ oðfeallan; for ðǣre wilnunga hīe
5 hit forlēton, ǫnd woldon ðæt hēr ðȳ māra wīsdōm on
6 lǫnde wǣre ðȳ wē mā geðēoda cūðon."
7 Ðā gemunde ic hū sīo ǣ wæs ǣrest on Ebrēisc geðīode
8 funden, ǫnd eft, ðā hīe Crēacas geliornodon, ðā węndon
9 hīe hīe on hiora āgen geðīode ealle, ǫnd ēac ealle ōðre
10 bēc. Ǫnd eft Lǣdenware swǣ same, siððan hīe hīe geliornodon,
11 hīe hīe węndon ealla ðurh wīse wealhstōdas
12 on hiora āgen geðīode. Ǫnd ēac ealla ōðra Crīstena
13 ðīoda sumne dǣl hiora on hiora āgen geðīode węndon.
14 For ðȳ mē ðyncð bętre, gif īow swǣ ðyncð, ðæt wē ēac
15 suma bēc, ðā ðe nīedbeðearfosta sīen eallum mǫnnum
16 tō wiotonne,16 ðæt wē ðā on ðæt geðīode węnden ðe wē

17 ealle gecnāwan mægen, ǫnd gedōn swǣ wē swīðe ēaðe

18 magon mid Godes fultume, gif wē ðā stilnesse habbað,

19 ðætte eall sīo gioguð ðe nū is on Angelcynne friora

20 mǫnna, ðāra ðe ðā spēda hæbben ðæt hīe ðǣm befēolan

21 mægen, sīen tō liornunga oðfæste, ðā hwīle ðe hīe tō

1 nānre ōðerre note ne mægen, oð ðone first ðe hīe wel

2 cunnen Ęnglisc gewrit ārǣdan: lǣre mǫn siððan furður

3 on Lǣdengeðīode ðā ðe mǫn furðor lǣran wille, ǫnd tō

4 hīerran hāde dōn wille. Ðā ic ðā gemunde hū sīo lār

5 Lǣdengeðīodes ǣr ðissum āfeallen wæs giond Angelcynn,

6 ǫnd ðeah mǫnige cūðon Ęnglisc gewrit ārǣdan, ðā

7 ongan ic ongemang oðrum mislīcum ǫnd manigfealdum

8 bisgum ðisses kynerīces ðā bōc węndan on Ęnglisc ðe is

9 genęmned on Lǣden "Pastoralis," ǫnd on Ęnglisc "Hierdebōc,"

10 hwīlum word be worde, hwīlum andgit of andgiete,

11 swǣ swǣ ic hīe geliornode æt Plegmunde mīnum

12 ærcebiscepe, ǫnd æt Assere mīnum biscepe, ǫnd æt Grimbolde

13 mīnum mæssepriōste, ǫnd æt Iōhanne mīnum mæsseprēoste.

14 Siððan ic hīe ðā geliornod hæfde, swǣ swǣ

15 ic hīe forstōd, ǫnd swǣ ic hīe andgitfullīcost āręccean

16 meahte, ic hīe on Ęnglisc āwęnde; ǫnd tō ǣlcum biscepstōle

17 on mīnum rīce wille āne onsęndan; ǫnd on ǣlcre

18 bið ān æstel, sē bið on fīftegum mancessa. Ǫnd ic bebīode

19 on Godes naman ðæt nān mǫn ðone æstel frǫm

20 ðǣre bēc ne dō, nē ðā bōc frǫm ðǣm mynstre; uncūð hū

21 lǫnge ðǣr swǣ gelǣrede biscepas sīen, swǣ swǣ nū, Gode

22 ðonc, wel hwǣr siendon. For ðȳ ic wolde ðætte hīe ealneg

1 æt ðǣre stōwe wǣren, būton sē biscep hīe mid him

2 habban wille, oððe hīo hwǣr tō lǣne sīe, oððe hwā ōðre

3 bī wrīte.

> 117.1-2. **Ælfred kyning hāteð ... hāte**. Note the change from the formal and official third person (**hāteð**) to the more familiar first person (**hāte**). So Ælfric, in his *Preface to Genesis*, writes **Ælfric munuc grēt Æðelwærd ealdormann ēadmōdlīce. Þū bǣde mē, lēof, þæt ic**, etc.: *Ælfric, monk, greets Æthelweard, alderman, humbly. Thou, beloved, didst bid me that I*, etc.

> 118.5. Notice that **mæge** (l. 5) and **mæge** (l. 6) are not in the subjunctive because the sense requires it, but because they have been attracted by **gǣmetige** and **befæste**. **Sīen** (p. 119, l. 15) and **hæbben** (p. 119, l. 20) illustrate the same construction.

> 118.9-10. *We liked only the reputation of being Christians, very few (of us) the Christian virtues.*

> 119.14. Alfred is here addressing the bishops collectively, and hence uses the plural **īow** (= **ēow**), not **þē**.

> 119.16. **ðæt wē ðā**. These three words are not necessary to the sense. They constitute the figure known as epanalepsis, in which "the same word or phrase is repeated after one or more intervening words." **Þā** is the pronominal substitute for **suma bēc**.

> 119.17. **Gedōn** is the first person plural subjunctive (from infinitive **gedōn**). It and **wenden** are in the same construction. Two things seem "better" to Alfred: (1) *that we translate*, etc., (2) *that we cause*, etc.

> 119.19-21. **sīo gioguð ... is ... hīe ... sīen**. Notice how the collective noun, **gioguð**, singular at first both in form and function, gradually loses its oneness before the close of the sentence is reached, and becomes plural. The construction is entirely legitimate

in Mn.E. Spanish is the only modern language known to me that condemns such an idiom: "Spanish ideas of congruity do not permit a collective noun, though denoting a plurality, to be accompanied by a plural verb or adjective in the same clause" (Ramsey, *Text-Book of Modern Spanish*, § 1452).

120.2. **lǣre mǫn**. See § 105, 1.

120.11-13. That none of these advisers of the king, except Plegmond, a Mercian, were natives, bears out what Alfred says about the scarcity of learned men in England when he began to reign. Asser, to whose Latin *Life of Alfred*, in spite of its mutilations, we owe almost all of our knowledge of the king, came from St. David's (in Wales), and was made Bishop of Sherborne.

121.1. Translate **æt ðǣre stōwe** by *each in its place*. The change from plural **hīe** (in **hīe ... wǣren**) to singular **hīe** (in the clauses that follow) will thus be prepared for.

121.2-3. **oððe hwā ōðre bī wrīte**, *or unless some one wish to copy a new one (write thereby another)*.

1 = bisceop.

2 = hwilce.

3 = gīu.

4 = For all words with *io* (*īo*), consult Glossary under *eo* (*ēo*).

5 = hīersumedon.

6 = sidu (siodu).

7 = swā.

8 = ānlīpigne.

9 = hwilc.

10 = līefdon.

11 = męnigu.

12 = nānwiht.

13 = swilce.

14 = spyrian.

15 = witena.

16 = witanne.

POETRY.

INTRODUCTORY.

In Section II., Structure, the stress markers ´ and ` are intended to display above the macron – or (rarely) breve ˘:

´ × `

Some computers will instead show them after (to the right of) the macron. "Resolved stress" (two short syllables acting as one long) is shown with a double breve below the syllables:

´
×
◡

If your computer does not have this character, it will probably display a box or question mark between the two syllables.

I. HISTORY.

(a) Old English Poetry as a Whole.

NORTHUMBRIA was the home of Old English poetry. Beginning with Cædmon and his school A.D. 670, Northumbria maintained her poetical supremacy till A.D. 800, seven years before which date the ravages of the Danes had begun. When Alfred ascended the throne of Wessex (871), the Danes had destroyed the seats of learning throughout the whole of Northumbria. As Whitby had been "the cradle of English poetry," Winchester (Alfred's capital) became now the cradle of English prose; and the older poems that had survived the fire and sword of the Vikings were translated from the original Northumbrian dialect into the West Saxon dialect. It is, therefore, in the West Saxon dialect that these poems1 have come down to us.

Old English poetry contains in all only about thirty thousand lines; but it includes epic, lyric, didactic, elegiac, and allegorical poems, together with war-ballads, paraphrases, riddles, and charms. Of the five elegiac poems (*Wanderer, Seafarer, Ruin, Wife's Complaint,* and *Husband's Message*), the *Wanderer* is the most artistic, and best portrays the gloomy contrast between past happiness and present grief so characteristic of the Old English lyric.

Old English literature has no love poems. The central themes of its poets are battle and bereavement, with a certain grim resignation on the part of the hero to the issues of either. The movement of the thought is usually abrupt, there being a noticeable poverty of transitional particles, or connectives, "which," says Ten Brink, "are the cement of sentence-structure."

(b) Beowulf.

The greatest of all Old English poems is the epic, *Beowulf*.2 It consists of more than three thousand lines, and probably assumed approximately its present form in Northumbria about A.D. 700. It is a crystallization of continental myths; and, though nothing is said of England, the story is an invaluable index to the social, political, and ethical ideals of our Germanic ancestors before and after they settled along the English coast. It is most poetical, and its testimony is historically most valuable, in the character-portraits that it contains. The fatalism that runs through it, instead of making the characters weak and less human, serves at times rather to dignify and elevate them. "Fate," says Beowulf (l. 572), recounting his battle with the sea-monsters, "often saves an undoomed man *if his courage hold out.*"

"The ethical essence of this poetry," says Ten Brink, "lies principally in the conception of manly virtue, undismayed courage, the stoical encounter with death, silent submission to fate, in the readiness to help others, in the clemency and liberality of the prince toward his thanes, and the self-sacrificing loyalty with which they reward him."

NOTE 1.—Many different interpretations have been put upon the story of *Beowulf* (for argument of story, see texts). Thus Müllenhoff sees in Grendel the giant-god of the storm-tossed equinoctial sea, while Beowulf is the Scandinavian god Freyr, who in the spring drives back the sea and restores the land. Laistner finds the prototype of Grendel in the noxious exhalations that rise from the Frisian coast-marshes during the summer months; Beowulf is the wind-hero, the autumnal storm-god, who dissipates the effluvia.

> 1. This does not, of course, include the few short poems in the *Chronicle*, or that portion of *Genesis* (*Genesis B*) supposed to have been put directly into West Saxon from an Old Saxon original. There still remain in Northumbrian the version of *Cædmon's Hymn*, fragments of the *Ruthwell Cross*, *Bede's Death-Song*, and the *Leiden Riddle*.

> 2. The word *bēowulf*, says Grimm, meant originally *bee-wolf*, or *bee-enemy*, one of the names of the woodpecker. Sweet thinks the bear was meant. But the word is almost certainly a compound of *Bēow* (cf. O.E. **bēow** = grain), a Danish demigod, and *wulf* used as a mere suffix.

II. STRUCTURE.

(a) Style.

In the structure of Old English poetry the most characteristic feature is the constant repetition of the idea (sometimes of the thought) with a corresponding variation of phrase, or epithet. When, for example, the Queen passes into the banquet hall in *Beowulf*, she is designated at first by her name, **Wealhþēow**; she is then described in turn as **cwēn Hrōðgāres** (*Hrothgar's queen*), **gold-hroden** (*the gold-adorned*), **frēolīc wīf** (*the noble woman*), **ides Helminga** (*the Helmings' lady*), **bēag-hroden cwēn** (*the ring-adorned queen*), **mōde geþungen** (*the high-spirited*), and **gold-hroden frēolīcu folc-cwēn** (*the gold-adorned, noble folk-queen*).

And whenever the sea enters largely into the poet's verse, not content with simple (uncompounded) words (such as **sǣ**, **lagu**, **holm**, **strēam**, **męre**, etc.), he will use numerous other equivalents (phrases or compounds), such as **waþema gebind** (*the commingling of waves*), **lagu-flōd** (*the sea-flood*), **lagu-strǣt** (*the sea-street*), **swan-rād** (*the swan-road*), etc. These compounds are usually nouns, or adjectives and participles used in a sense more appositive than attributive.

It is evident, therefore, that this abundant use of compounds, or periphrastic synonyms, grows out of the desire to repeat the idea in varying language. It is to be observed, also, that the Old English poets rarely make any studied attempt to balance phrase against phrase or clause against clause. Theirs is a repetition of idea, rather than a parallelism of structure.

NOTE 1.—It is impossible to tell how many of these synonymous expressions had already become stereotyped, and were used, like many of the epithets in the *Iliad* and *Odyssey*, purely as padding. When, for example, the poet tells us that at the most critical moment Beowulf's sword failed him, adding in the same breath, **īren ǣr-gōd** (*matchless blade*), we conclude that the bard is either nodding or parroting.

(b) Meter.

[Re-read § 10, (3).]

Primary Stress.

Old English poetry is composed of certain rhythmically ordered combinations of accented and unaccented syllables. The accented syllable (the arsis) is usually long, and will be indicated by the macron with the acute accent over it (–́); when short, by the breve with the same accent (˘́). The unaccented syllable or syllables (the thesis) may be long or short, and will be indicated by the oblique cross (×).

Secondary Stress.

A secondary accent, or stress, is usually put upon the second member of compound and derivative nouns, adjectives, and adverbs. This will be indicated by the macron with the grave accent, if the secondary stress falls on a long syllable (-̀); by the breve with the same accent, if the secondary stress falls on a short syllable (̆̀). Nouns:

Hrōðgāres (´—̀×), **fēondgrāpum** (´—̀×), **frēomǣgum** (´—̀×), **Ēast-Dęna** (´–̆̀×), **Helminga** (´—̀×), **Scyldinga** (´—̀×), **ānhaga** (´–̆̀×), **Ecgþēowes** (´—̀×), **sinc-fato** (´–̆̀×).

Adjectives:1

ǣghwylcne (´—̀×), **þrīsthȳdig** (´—̀×), **gold-hroden** (´–̆̀×), **drēorigne** (´—̀×), **gyldenne** (´—̀×), **ōðerne** (´—̀×), **gǣstlīcum** (´—̀×), **wynsume** (´–̆̀×), **ǣnigne** (´—̀×).

Adverbs:2

unsōfte (´—̀×), **heardlīce** (´—̀×), **sęmninga** (´—̀×).

The Old English poets place also a secondary accent upon the ending of present participles (**-ende**), and upon the penultimate of weak verbs of the second class (§ 130), provided the root-syllable is long.3 Present participles:

slǣpendne (´—̀×), **wīs-hycgende** (´—´—̀×), **flēotendra** (´—̀×), **hrēosende** (´–—̀×).

Weak verbs:

swynsode (´–̆̀×), **þancode** (´–̆̀×), **wānigean** (´–̆̀×), **scēawian** (´–̆̀×), **scēawige** (´–̆̀×), **hlīfian** (´–̆̀×).

Resolved Stress.

A short accented syllable followed in the same word by an unaccented syllable (usually short also) is equivalent to one long accented syllable (´̆× = –´). This is known as a resolved stress, and will be indicated thus, ´x̱;

hæleða (´x̱×), **guman** (´x̱), **Gode** (´x̱), **sęle-ful** (´x̱×), **ides** (´x̱), **fyrena** (´x̱×), **maðelode** (´x̱ ̆̀×), **hogode** (´x̱×), **mægen-ęllen** (´x̱–̀), **hige-þihtigne** (´x̱—̀×), **Metudes** (´x̱×), **lagulāde** (´x̱–̀×), **unlyfigendes** (–´x̱–̀×), **biforan** (×´x̱), **forþolian** (×´x̱×), **baðian** (´x̱×), **worolde** (´x̱–̀×).

Resolution of stress may also attend secondary stresses:

sinc-fato (–´x̱), **dryht-sęle** (–´x̱), **ferðloca** (–´x̱), **forðwege** (–´x̱).

The Normal Line.

Every normal line of Old English poetry has four primary accents, two in the first half-line and two in the second half-line. These half-lines are separated by the cesura and united by alliteration, the alliterative letter being found in the first stressed syllable of the second half-line. This syllable, therefore, gives the cue to the scansion of the whole line. It is also the only alliterating syllable in the second half-line. The first half-line, however, usually has two alliterating syllables, but frequently only one (the ratio being about three to two in the following selections). When the first half-line contains but one alliterating syllable, that syllable marks the first stress, rarely the second. The following lines are given in the order of their frequency:

(1) **þǽr wæs *h*ǽleða *h*léahtor; *h*lýn swýnsode.**

(2) ***m*ṓde geþúngen, *m*édo-ful ætbǽr.**

(3) **s*ṓ*na þæt on*f*únde *f*ýrena hýrde.**

Any initial vowel or diphthong may alliterate with any other initial vowel or diphthong; but a consonant requires the same consonant, except **st**, **sp**, and **sc**, each of which alliterates only with itself.

Remembering, now, that either half-line (especially the second) may begin with several unaccented syllables (these syllables being known in types A, D, and E as the *anacrusis*), but that neither half-line can end with more than one unaccented syllable, the student may begin at once to read and properly accentuate Old English poetry. It will be found that the alliterative principle does not operate mechanically, but that the poet employs it for the purpose of emphasizing the words that are really most important. Sound is made subservient to sense.

When, from the lack of alliteration, the student is in doubt as to what word to stress, let him first get the exact meaning of the line, and then put the emphasis on the word or words that seem to bear the chief burden of the poet's thought.

NOTE 1.—A few lines, rare or abnormal in their alliteration or lack of alliteration, may here be noted. In the texts to be read, there is one line with no alliteration: *Wanderer* 58; three of the type $a \cdots b \mid a \cdots b$: *Beowulf* 654, 830, 2746; one of the type $a \cdots a \mid b \cdots a$: *Beowulf* 2744; one of the type $a \cdots a \mid b \cdots c$: *Beowulf* 2718; and one of the type $a \cdots b \mid c \cdots a$: *Beowulf* 2738.

The Five Types.

By an exhaustive comparative study of the metrical unit in Old English verse, the half-line, Professor Eduard Sievers,[4] of the University of Leipzig, has shown that there are only five types, or varieties, employed. These he classifies as follows, the perpendicular line serving to separate the so-called feet, or measures:

1. A $\acute{-} \times \mid \acute{-} \times$

2. B $\times \acute{-} \mid \times \acute{-}$

3. C $\times \acute{-} \mid \acute{-} \times$

4. D $\begin{cases} D^1 \acute{-} \mid \acute{-} \grave{-} \times \\ D^2 \acute{-} \mid \acute{-} \times \grave{-} \end{cases}$

5. E $\begin{cases} E^1 \acute{-} \grave{-} \times \mid \acute{-} \\ E^2 \acute{-} \times \grave{-} \mid \acute{-} \end{cases}$

It will be seen (1) that each half-line contains two, and only two, feet; (2) that each foot contains one, and only one, primary stress; (3) that A is trochaic, B iambic; (4) that C is iambic-trochaic; (5) that D and E consist of the same feet but in inverse order.

The Five Types Illustrated.

[All the illustrations, as hitherto, are taken from the texts to be read. The figures prefixed indicate whether first or second half-line is cited. B = *Beowulf*; W = *Wanderer*.]

1. TYPE A, $\acute{-} \times \mid \acute{-} \times$

Two or more unaccented syllables (instead of one) may intervene between the two stresses, but only one may follow the last stress. If the thesis in either foot is the second part of a compound it receives, of course, a secondary stress.

(2)	**ful gesealde**, B. 616,	$\acute{-} \times$	$\mid \acute{-} \times$
(1)	**wīdre gewindan**, B. 764,	$\acute{-} \times \times$	$\mid \acute{-} \times$
(1)5	**Gemunde þā sē gōda**, B. 759,	$\times \mid \acute{-} \times \times \mid \acute{-} \times$ ×	
(1)5	**swylce hē on ealder-dagum**, B. 758,	$\times \times \times \times$	$\mid \acute{-} \times \mid \grave{\cdot} \times$
(1)	**ȳþde swā þisne eardgeard**, W. 85,	$\acute{-} \times \times \times \times$	$\mid \acute{-} \grave{-}$
(1)	**wīs-fæst wordum**, B. 627,	$\acute{-} \grave{-}$	$\mid \acute{-} \times$
(1)	**gryre-lēoð galan**, B. 787,	$\grave{\cdot}\underline{\times} \acute{-}$	$\mid \grave{\cdot} \times$
(2)	**somod ætgædre**, W. 39,	$\grave{\cdot}\underline{\times} \times$	$\mid \acute{-} \times$

- 133 -

(1)	**duguðe ǫnd geogoðe**, B. 622,		´x̱ × ×	| ´x̱ ×
(1)	**fǣger fold-bold**, B. 774,		´– ×	| ´– ` –
(1)	**atelīc ęgesa**, B. 785,		´x̱ ` –	| ´x̱ ×
(2)	**goldwine mīnne**, W. 22,		´– ` x̱	| ´– ×
(1)	**ęgesan þēon** [> *þīhan: § 118], B. 2737,		´x̱ ×	| ´– ×

NOTE.—Rare forms of A are ´– ` – × | ´– × (does not occur in texts), ´– ` – × | ´– ` – (occurs once, B. 781 (1)), and ´– × ` – | ´– × (once, B. 2743 (1)).

2. TYPE B, × ´– | × ´–

Two, but not more than two, unaccented syllables may intervene between the stresses. The type of B most frequently occurring is × × ´– | × ´–.

(1)	**ǫnd þā frēolīc wīf**, B. 616,	× × ´–	| × ´–
(2)	**hē on lust geþeah**, B. 619,	× × ´–	| × ´–
(2)	**þā se æðeling gīong**, B. 2716,	× × ´x̱	| × ´–
(2)	**seah on ęnta geweorc**, B. 2718,	× × ´–	| × × ´–
(1)	**ofer flōda genipu**, B. 2809,	× × ´–	| × × ´x̱
(1)	**forþam mē wītan ne þearf**, B. 2742,	× × × ´–	| × × ´–
(2)	**þaes þe hire se willa gelamp**, B. 627,	× × × × × ´–	| × × ´–
(1)	**forþon ne mæg weorþan wīs**, W. 64,	× × × × ´–	| × ´–
(1)	**Nǣfre ic ǣnegum** [= **ǣn'gum**] **męn**, B. 656,	× × × ´–	| × ´–

NOTE.—In the last half-line Sievers substitutes the older form **ǣngum**, and supposes elision of the **e** in **Nǣfre** (= **Nǣfr-ic**: ××´– | ×´–).

3. TYPE C, × ´– | ´– ×

The conditions of this type are usually satisfied by compound and derivative words, and the second stress (not so strong as the first) is frequently on a short syllable. The two arses rarely alliterate. As in B, two unaccented syllables in the first thesis are more common than one.

(1) þæt hēo on ǣnigne, B. 628,   × × × ´– | ´– ×

(1) þæt ic ānunga, B. 635,   × × ´– | ´– ×

(2) ēode gold-hroden, B. 641,   × × ´– | ˘– ×

(1) gemyne mǣrðo, B. 660,   × ˘–̲ | ´– ×

(1) on þisse meodu-healle, B. 639,   × × × ˘–̲ | ´– ×

(2) æt brimes nosan, B. 2804,   × ˘–̲ | ˘– ×

(2) æt Wealhþéon [= -þēowan], B. 630,   × ´– | ´– ×

(1) geond lagulāde, W. 3,   × ˘–̲ | ´– ×

(1) Swā cwæð eardstapa, W. 6,   × × ´– | ˘– ×

(2) ēalā byrnwiga, W. 94,   × × ´– | ˘– ×

(2) nō þǣr fela bringeð, W. 54,   × × ˘–̲ | ´– ×

4. Type D, $\begin{cases} D^1 \; \acute{-} \; | \; \acute{-}\grave{-} \times \\ D^2 \; \acute{-} \; | \; \acute{-} \times \grave{-} \end{cases}$

Both types of D may take one unaccented syllable between the two primary stresses (´– × | ´– `– ×, ´– × | ´– × `–). The secondary stress in D[1] falls usually on the second syllable of a compound or derivative word, and this syllable (as in C) is frequently short.

(a) D[1] ´– | ´– `– ×

    (1) cwēn Hrōðgāres, B. 614,   ´– | ´– `– ×

    (2) dǣl ǣghwylcne, B. 622,   ´– | ´– `– ×

    (1) Bēowulf maðelode, B. 632,   ´– × | ˘–̲ ˘ ×

    (2) slāt unwearnum, B. 742,   ´– | ´– `– ×

    (1) wrāþra wælsleahta, W. 7,   ´– × | ´– `– ×

    (1) wōd wintercearig [= wint'rcearig], W. 24,   ´– | ´– ˘ ×

    (1) sōhte sęle drēorig, W. 25,   ´– × | ˘–̲ ´– ×

    (1) ne sōhte searo-nīðas, B. 2739, × | ´– × | ˘–̲ ´– ×

NOTE.—There is one instance in the texts (B. 613, (1)) of apparent ´– × × | ´– ˘ ×: **word wǣron wynsume**. (The triple alliteration has no significance.

- 135 -

The sense, besides, precludes our stressing **wǣron**.) The difficulty is avoided by bringing the line under the A type: $\acute{-} \times \times \mid \acute{-} \overset{\smile}{\times}$.

(b) D² $\acute{-} \mid \acute{-} \times \grave{-}$

(2)	**Forð nēar ætstōp**, B. 746,	$\acute{-} \quad \mid \acute{-} \times \grave{-}$
(2)	**eorl furður stōp**, B. 762,	$\acute{-} \quad \mid \acute{-} \times \grave{-}$
(2)	**Denum eallum wearð**, B. 768,	$\overset{\smile}{\times} \quad \mid \acute{-} \times \grave{-}$
(1)	**grētte Gēata lēod**, B. 626,	$\acute{-} \times \mid \acute{-} \times \grave{-}$
(1)	**ǣnig yrfe-weard**, B. 2732,	$\acute{-} \times \mid \acute{-} \times \grave{-}$
(1)	**hrēosan hrīm and snāw**, W. 48,	$\acute{-} \times \mid \acute{-} \times \grave{-}$
(2)	**swimmað eft on weg**, W. 53,	$\acute{-} \times \mid \acute{-} \times \grave{-}$

Very rarely is the thesis in the second foot expanded.

(2)	**þegn ungemete till**, B. 2722,	$\acute{-} \quad \mid \acute{-} \times \times \times \grave{-}$
(1)	**hrūsan heolster biwrāh**, W. 23,	$\acute{-} \times \mid \acute{-} \times \times \times \grave{-}$

5. Type E, $\begin{cases} E^1 \; \acute{-} \grave{-} \times \mid \acute{-} \\ E^2 \; \acute{-} \times \grave{-} \mid \acute{-} \end{cases}$

The secondary stress in E¹ falls frequently on a short syllable, as in D¹.

(a) E¹ $\acute{-} \grave{-} \times \mid \acute{-}$

(1)	**wyrmlīcum fāh**, W. 98,	$\acute{-} \grave{-} \times \mid \acute{-}$
(2)	**medo-ful ætbær**, B. 625,	$\overset{\smile}{\times} \overset{\smile}{} \times \mid \acute{-}$
(1)	**sǣ-bāt gesæt**, B. 634,	$\acute{-} \grave{-} \times \mid \acute{-}$
(1)	**sige-folca swēg**, B. 645,	$\overset{\smile}{\times} \grave{-} \times \mid \acute{-}$
(2)	**Norð-Denum stōd**, B. 784,	$\acute{-} \overset{\smile}{} \times \mid \acute{-}$
(1)	**fēond-grāpum fæst**, B. 637,	$\acute{-} \grave{-} \times \mid \acute{-}$
(2)	**wyn eal gedrēas**, W. 36,	$\acute{-} \grave{-} \times \mid \acute{-}$
(2)	**feor oft gemǫn**, W. 90,	$\acute{-} \grave{-} \times \mid \acute{-}$

As in D², the thesis in the first foot is very rarely expanded.

(1) **wīn-ærnes geweald**, B. 655, $\acute{-}\grave{-}\times\times\ |\ \acute{-}$

(1) **Hafa nū ǫnd geheald**, B. 659, $\acute{\underline{\times}}\grave{-}\times\times\ |\ \acute{-}$

(1) **searo-þǫncum besmiðod**, B. 776, $\acute{\underline{\times}}\grave{-}\times\times\ |\ \acute{\underline{\times}}$

NOTE.—Our ignorance of Old English sentence-stress makes it impossible for us to draw a hard-and-fast line in all cases between D^2 and E^1. For example, in these half-lines (already cited),

>**wyn eal gedrēas**
>
>**feor oft gemǫn**
>
>**Forð nēar ætstōp**

if we throw a strong stress on the adverbs that precede their verbs, the type is D^2. Lessen the stress on the adverbs and increase it on the verbs, and we have E^1. The position of the adverbs furnishes no clue; for the order of words in Old English was governed not only by considerations of relative emphasis, but by syntactic and euphonic considerations as well.

(*b*) $E^2\ \acute{-}\times\grave{-}\ |\ \acute{-}$

This is the rarest of all types. It does not occur in the texts, there being but one instance of this type (l. 2437 (2)), and that doubtful, in the whole of *Beowulf*.

Abnormal Lines.

The lines that fall under none of the five types enumerated are comparatively few. They may be divided into two classes, (1) hypermetrical lines, and (2) defective lines.

(1) Hypermetrical Lines.

Each hypermetrical half-line has usually three stresses, thus giving six stresses to the whole line instead of two. These lines occur chiefly in groups, and mark increased range and dignity in the thought. Whether the half-line be first or second, it is usually of the A type without anacrusis. To this type belong the last five lines of the *Wanderer*. Lines 92 and 93 are also unusually long, but not hypermetrical. The first half-line of 65 is hypermetrical, a fusion of A and C, consisting of ($\acute{-}\times\times\times\acute{\underline{-}}\ |\ \acute{-}\times$).

(2) Defective Lines.

The only defective lines in the texts are B. 748 and 2715 (the second half-line in each). As they stand, these half-lines would have to be scanned thus:

- 137 -

ræhte ongēan   ´− × | × −´

bealo-nīð wēoll   ´×⏜ `− | −´

Sievers emends as follows:

ræhte tōgēanes   ´− × × | ´− × = A

bealo-nīðe wēoll   ´×⏜ ´− × | ´− = E[1]

These defective half-lines are made up of syntactic combinations found on almost every page of Old English prose. That they occur so rarely in poetry is strong presumptive evidence, if further evidence were needed, in favor of the adequacy of Sievers' five-fold classification.

NOTE.—All the lines that could possibly occasion any difficulty to the student have been purposely cited as illustrations under the different types. If these are mastered, the student will find it an easy matter to scan the lines that remain.

1. It will be seen that the adjectives are chiefly derivatives in **-ig, -en, -er, -līc,** and **-sum**.

2. Most of the adverbs belonging here end in **-līce, -unga,** and **-inga,** § 93, (1), (2): such words as **æt-gǽdere, on-gḗan, on-wég, tō-gḗanes, tō-míddes,** etc., are invariably accented as here indicated.

3. It will save the student some trouble to remember that this means long by nature (**līcodon**), or long by position (**swynsode**), or long by resolution of stress (**maðelode**),—see next paragraph.

4. Sievers' two articles appeared in the *Beiträge zur Geschichte der deutschen Sprache und Literatur,* Vols. X (1885) and XII (1887). A brief summary, with slight modifications, is found in the same author's *Altgermanische Metrik,* pp. 120-144 (1893).

Before attempting to employ Sievers' types, the student would do well to read several pages of Old English poetry, taking care to accentuate according to the principles already laid down. In this way his ear will become accustomed to the rhythm of the line, and he will see more clearly that Sievers' work was one primarily of systematization. Sievers himself says: "I had read Old English poetry for years exactly as I now scan it, and long before I had the slightest idea that what I did instinctively could be formulated into a system of set rules." (*Altgermanische Metrik, Vorwort,* p. 10.)

5. The first perpendicular marks the limit of the anacrusis.

SELECTIONS FOR READING.

VI. EXTRACTS FROM BEOWULF.

THE BANQUET IN HEOROT. [Lines 612-662.]

[The Heyne-Socin text has been closely followed. I have attempted no original emendations, but have deviated from the Heyne-Socin edition in a few cases where the Grein-Wülker text seemed to give the better reading.

The argument preceding the first selection is as follows: Hrothgar, king of the Danes, or Scyldings, elated by prosperity, builds a magnificent hall in which to feast his retainers; but a monster, Grendel by name, issues from his fen-haunts, and night after night carries off thane after thane from the banqueting hall. For twelve years these ravages continue. At last Beowulf, nephew of Hygelac, king of the Geats (a people of South Sweden), sails with fourteen chosen companions to Dane-land, and offers his services to the aged Hrothgar. "Leave me alone in the hall to-night," says Beowulf. Hrothgar accepts Beowulf's proffered aid, and before the dread hour of visitation comes, the time is spent in wassail. The banquet scene follows.]

    Þǣr wæs hæleþa hleahtor, hlyn swynsode,

    word wǣron wynsume. Ēode Wealhþēow forð,

    cwēn Hrōðgāres, cynna gemyndig;

  615 grētte gold-hroden guman on healle,

    ǫnd þā frēolīc wīf ful gesealde

    ǣrest Ēast-Dęna ēþel-wearde,

    bæd hine blīðne æt þǣre bēor-þęge,

    lēodum lēofne; hē on lust geþeah

  620 symbel ǫnd sęle-ful, sige-rōf kyning.

    Ymb-ēode þā ides Helminga

    duguðe ǫnd geogoðe dǣl ǣghwylcne,

    sinc-fato sealde, oð þæt sǣl ālamp

    þæt hīo1 Bēowulfe, bēag-hroden cwēn,

  625 mōde geþungen, medo2-ful ætbær;

grētte Gēata lēod,   Gode þancode
wīs-fæst wordum,   þæs þe hire se willa gelamp,
þæt hēo on ǣnigne   eorl gelȳfde
fyrena frōfre.   Hē þæt ful geþeah,
630 wæl-rēow wiga,   æt Wealhþēon,
ǫnd þā gyddode   gūðe gefȳsed;
Bēowulf maðelode,   bearn Ecgþēowes:
"Ic þæt hogode,   þā ic on holm gestāh,
sǣ-bāt gesæt   mid mīnra sęcga gedriht,
635 þæt ic ānunga   ēowra lēoda
willan geworhte,   oððe on wæl crunge
fēond-grāpum fæst.   Ic gefręmman sceal
eorlīc ęllen,   oððe ęnde-dæg
on þisse meodu2-healle   mīnne gebīdan."
640 Þām wīfe þā word   wel līcodon,
gilp-cwide Gēates;   ēode gold-hroden
frēolicu folc-cwēn   tō hire frēan sittan.
Þā wæs eft swā ǣr   inne on healle
þrȳð-word sprecen,3   þēod on sǣlum,
645 sige-folca swēg,   oþ þæt sęmninga

sunu Healfdęnes   sēcean wolde
ǣfen-ræste;   wiste þǣm āhlǣcan4
tō þǣm hēah-sęle   hilde geþinged,
siððan hīe sunnan lēoht   gesēon ne meahton
650 oððe nīpende   niht ofer ealle,
scadu-helma gesceapu   scrīðan cwōman,5
wan under wolcnum.   Werod eall ārās;
grētte þā *giddum*   guma ōðerne

- 140 -

Hrōðgār Bēowulf,   ǫnd him hǣl ābēad,

655 wīn-ærnes geweald,   ǫnd þæt word ācwæð:

"Nǣfre ic ǣnegum6 męn   ǣr ālȳfde,

siððan ic hǫnd ǫnd rǫnd   hębban mihte,

ðrȳþ-ærn Dęna   būton þē nū þā.

Hafa nū ǫnd geheald   hūsa sēlest,

660 gemyne mǣrþo,7   mægen-ęllen cȳð,

waca wið wrāðum.   Ne bið þē wilna gād,

gif þū þæt ęllen-weorc   aldre8 gedīgest."

> 623. **sinc-fato sealde**. Banning (*Die epischen Formeln im Beowulf*) shows that the usual translation, *gave costly gifts*, must be given up; or, at least, that the *costly gifts* are nothing more than *beakers of mead*. The expression is an epic formula for *passing the cup*.
>
> 638-39. **ęnde-ðæg ... mīnne**. This unnatural separation of noun and possessive is frequent in O.E. poetry, but almost unknown in prose.
>
> 641-42. **ēode ... sittan**. The poet might have employed **tō sittanne** (§ 108, (1)); but in poetry the infinitive is often used for the gerund. Alfred himself uses the infinitive or the gerund to express purpose after **gān, gǫngan, cuman**, and **sęndan**.
>
> 647-51. **wiste ... cwōman**. A difficult passage, even with Thorpe's inserted **ne**; but there is no need of putting a period after **geþinged**, or of translating **oððe** by *and*: *He (Hrothgar) knew that battle was in store* (**geþinged**) *for the monster in the high hall, after* [= *as soon as*] *they could no longer see the sun's light, or* [= *that is*] *after night came darkening over all, and shadowy figures stalking.* The subject of **cwōman** [= **cwōmon**] is **niht** and **gesceapu**.
>
> The student will note that the infinitive (**scrīðan**) is here employed as a present participle after a verb of motion (**cwōman**). This construction with **cuman** is frequent in prose and poetry. The infinitive expresses the kind of motion: **ic cōm drīfan** = *I came driving*.

1 = hēo.

2 = medu-.

3 = gesprecen.

4 = āglǣcan.

5 = cwōmon.

6 = ǣnigum.

7 = mǣrþe (acc. sing.).

8 = ealdre (instr. sing.).

The Fight Between Beowulf and Grendel. [Lines 740-837.]

[The warriors all retire to rest except Beowulf. Grendel stealthily enters the hall. From his eyes gleams "a luster unlovely, likest to fire." The combat begins at once.]

740 Ne þæt se āglǣca yldan þōhte,
ac hē gefēng hraðe forman sīðe
slǣpendne rinc, slāt unwearnum,
bāt bān-locan, blōd ēdrum dranc,
syn-snǣdum swealh; sōna hæfde
745 unlyfigendes eal gefeormod
fēt ǫnd folma. Forð nēar ætstōp,
nam þā mid handa hige-þihtigne
rinc on ræste; rǣhte ongēan
fēond mid folme; hē onfēng hraþe
750 inwit-þancum ǫnd wið earm gesæt.
Sōna þæt onfunde fyrena hyrde,
þæt hē ne mētte middan-geardes,
eorðan scēatta, on ęlran męn
mund-gripe māran; hē on mōde wearð

755 forht, on ferhðe;   nō þȳ ǣr fram meahte.
Hyge wæs him hin-fūs,   wolde on heolster flēon,
sēcan dēofla gedræg;   ne wæs his drohtoð þǣr,
swylce hē on ealder1-dagum   ǣr gemētte.
Gemunde þā se gōda   mǣg Higelāces
760 ǣfen-sprǣce,   ūp-lang āstōd
ǫnd him fæste wiðfēng;   fingras burston;
eoten wæs ūt-weard;   eorl furþur stōp.
Mynte se mǣra,   hwǣr hē meahte swā,
wīdre gewindan   ǫnd on weg þanon
765 flēon on fęn-hopu;   wiste his fingra geweald
on grames grāpum.   Þæt wæs gēocor sīð,
þæt se hearm-scaþa   tō Heorute2 ātēah.
Dryht-sęle dynede;   Dęnum eallum wearð
ceaster-būendum,   cēnra gehwylcum,
770 eorlum ealu-scerwen.   Yrre wǣron bēgen

rēþe rēn-weardas.   Ręced hlynsode;
þā wæs wundor micel,   þæt se wīn-sęle
wiðhæfde heaþo-dēorum,   þæt hē on hrūsan ne fēol,
fǣger fold-bold;   ac hē þæs fæste wæs
775 innan ǫnd ūtan   īren-bęndum
searo-þǫncum besmiðod.   Þǣr fram sylle ābēag
medu-bęnc mǫnig,   mīne gefrǣge,
golde geregnad,   þǣr þā graman wunnon;
þæs ne wēndon ǣr   witan Scyldinga,
780 þæt hit ā mid gemete   manna ǣnig,
betlīc ǫnd bān-fāg,   tōbrecan meahte,

listum tōlūcan,   nymþe līges fæðm
swulge on swaþule.   Swēg ūp āstāg
nīwe geneahhe;   Norð-Denum stōd
785 atelīc egesa,   ānra gehwylcum,
þāra þe of wealle   wōp gehȳrdon,
gryre-lēoð galan   Godes ondsacan,
sige-lēasne sang,   sār wānigean
helle hæfton.3   Hēold hine fæste,
790 sē þe manna wæs   mægene strengest
on þǣm dæge   þysses līfes.
Nolde eorla hlēo   ǣnige þinga
þone cwealm-cuman   cwicne forlǣtan,
nē his līf-dagas   lēoda ǣnigum

795 nytte tealde.   Þǣr genehost brǣgd
eorl Bēowulfes   ealde lāfe,
wolde frēa-drihtnes   feorh ealgian,
mǣres þēodnes,   ðǣr hīe meahton swā.
Hīe ðæt ne wiston,   þā hīe gewin drugon,
800 heard-hicgende   hilde-mecgas,
ond on healfa gehwone   hēawan þōhton,
sāwle sēcan: þone syn-scaðan
ǣnig ofer eorðan   īrenna cyst,
gūþ-billa nān,   grētan nolde;
805 ac hē sige-wǣpnum   forsworen hæfde,
ecga gehwylcre.   Scolde his aldor4-gedāl
on ðǣm dæge   þysses līfes
earmlīc wurðan5   ond se ellor-gāst
on fēonda geweald   feor sīðian.

810 Þā þæt onfunde, sē þe fela ǣror
mōdes myrðe manna cynne
fyrene gefremede (hē *wæs* fāg wið God),
þæt him se līc-homa lǣstan nolde,
ac hine se mōdega6 mǣg Hygelāces
815 hæfde be honda; wæs gehwæþer ōðrum
lifigende lāð. Līc-sār gebād
atol ǣglǣca7; him on eaxle wearð

syn-dolh sweotol; seonowe onsprungon;
burston bān-locan. Bēowulfe wearð
820 gūð-hrēð gyfeðe. Scolde Grendel þonan
feorh-sēoc flēon under fen-hleoðu,8
sēcean wyn-lēas wīc; wiste þē geornor,
þæt his aldres9 wæs ende gegongen,
dōgera dæg-rīm. Denum eallum wearð
825 æfter þām wæl-rǣse willa gelumpen.
Hæfde þā gefǣlsod, sē þe ǣr feorran cōm,
snotor ond swȳð-ferhð, sele Hrōðgāres,
genered wið nīðe. Niht-weorce gefeh,
ellen-mǣrþum; hæfde Ēast-Denum
830 Gēat-mecga lēod gilp gelǣsted;
swylce oncȳððe ealle gebētte,
inwid-sorge, þe hīe ǣr drugon
ond for þrēa-nȳdum þolian scoldon,
torn unlȳtel. Þæt wæs tācen sweotol,
835 syððan hilde-dēor hond ālegde,
earm ond eaxle (þǣr wæs eal geador

Grendles grāpe)   under gēapne hrōf.

740. **þæt**, the direct object of **yldan**, refers to the contest about to ensue. Beowulf, in the preceding lines, was wondering how it would result.

746. **ætstōp**. The subject of this verb and of **nam** is Grendel; the subject of the three succeeding verbs (**rǣhte, onfēng, gesæt**) is Beowulf.

751-52. The O.E. poets are fond of securing emphasis or of stimulating interest by indirect methods of statement, by suggesting more than they affirm. This device often appears in their use of negatives (**ne**, l. 13; p. 140, l. 3; **nō**, p. 140, l. 1), and in the unexpected prominence that they give to some minor detail usually suppressed because understood; as where the narrator, wishing to describe the terror produced by Grendel's midnight visits to Heorot, says (ll. 138-139), "Then was it easy to find one who elsewhere, more commodiously, sought rest for himself." It is hard to believe that the poet saw nothing humorous in this point of view.

755. **nō ... meahte**, *none the sooner could he away*. The omission of a verb of motion after the auxiliaries **magan, mōtan, sculan**, and **willan** is very frequent. *Cf.* Beowulf's last utterance, p. 147, l. 17.

768. The lines that immediately follow constitute a fine bit of description by indication of effects. The two contestants are withdrawn from our sight; but we hear the sound of the fray crashing through the massive old hall, which trembles as in a blast; we see the terror depicted on the faces of the Danes as they listen to the strange sounds that issue from their former banqueting hall; by these sounds we, too, measure the progress and alternations of the combat. At last we hear only the "terror-lay" of Grendel, "lay of the beaten," and know that Beowulf has made good his promise at the banquet (**gilp gelǣsted**).

769. **cēnra gehwylcum**. The indefinite pronouns (§ 77) may be used as adjectives, agreeing in case with their nouns; but they frequently, as here, take a partitive genitive: **ānra gehwylcum**, *to each one* (= *to*

each of ones); **ǣnige** (instrumental) **þinga**, *for any thing* (= *for any of things*); **on healfa gehwone**, *into halves* (= *into each of halves*); **ealra dōgra gehwām**, *every day* (= *on each of all days*); **ūhtna gehwylce**, *every morning* (= *on each of mornings*).

780. Notice that **hit**, the object of **tōbrecan**, stands for **wīn-sęle**, which is masculine. See p. 39, Note 2. **Manna** is genitive after **gemete**, not after **ǣnig**.

787-89. **gryre-lēoð ... hæfton** [= **hæftan**]. Note that verbs of hearing and seeing, as in Mn.E., may be followed by the infinitive. They heard *God's adversary sing* (**galan**) ... *hell's captive bewail* (**wānigean**). Had the present participle been used, the effect would have been, as in Mn.E., to emphasize the agent (the subject of the infinitive) rather than the action (the infinitive itself).

795-96. **þǣr ... lāfe**. Beowulf's followers now seem to have seized their swords and come to his aid, not knowing that Grendel, having forsworn war-weapons himself, is proof against the best of swords. *Then many an earl of Beowulf's* (= *an earl of B. very often*) *brandished his sword.* That no definite earl is meant is shown by the succeeding **hīe meahton** instead of **hē meahte**. See p. 110, Note.

799. *They did not know this* (**ðæt**), *while they were fighting*; but the first **Hīe** refers to the warriors who proffered help; the second **hīe**, to the combatants, Beowulf and Grendel. In apposition with **ðæt**, stands the whole clause, **þone synscaðan** (object of **grētan**) **... nolde**. The second, or conjunctional, **ðæt** is here omitted before **þone**. See p. 112, note on ll. 18-19.

837. **grāpe** = genitive singular, feminine, after **eal**.

1 = ealdor-.

2 = Heorote.

3 = hæftan.

4 = ealdor-.

5 = weorðan.

6 = mōdiga.

7 = āglǣca.

8 = -hliðu.

9 = ealdres.

BEOWULF FATALLY WOUNDED. [Lines 2712-2752.]

[Hrothgar, in his gratitude for the great victory, lavishes gifts upon Beowulf; but Grendel's mother must be reckoned with. Beowulf finds her at the sea-bottom, and after a desperate struggle slays her. Hrothgar again pours treasures into Beowulf's lap. Beowulf, having now accomplished his mission, returns to Sweden. After a reign of fifty years, he goes forth to meet a fire-spewing dragon that is ravaging his kingdom. In the struggle Beowulf is fatally wounded. Wiglaf, a loyal thane, is with him.]

Þā sīo1 wund ongǫn,
þe him se eorð-draca   ǣr geworhte,
swēlan ǫnd swellan.   Hē þǣt sōna onfand,
2715 þǣt him on brēostum   bealo-nīð wēoll
āttor on innan.   Þā se æðeling gīong,2
þæt hē bī wealle,   wīs-hycgende,
gesæt on sesse;   seah on ęnta geweorc,
hū þā stān-bogan   stapulum fæste
2720 ēce eorð-ręced   innan healde.
Hyne þā mid handa   heoro-drēorigne,
þēoden mǣrne,   þegn ungemete till,
wine-dryhten his   wætere gelafede,
hilde-sædne,   ǫnd his helm onspēon.
2725 Bīowulf3 maðelode;   hē ofer bęnne spræc,

wunde wæl-blēate;   wisse hē gearwe,
þæt hē dæg-hwīla   gedrogen hæfde

eorðan wynne;   þā wæs eall sceacen
dōgor-gerīmes,   dēað ungemete nēah:
2730 "Nū ic suna mīnum   syllan wolde
gūð-gewǣdu,   þǣr mē gifeðe swā
ǣnig yrfe-weard   æfter wurde
līce gelenge.   Ic ðās lēode hēold
fīftig wintra;   næs se folc-cyning
2735 ymbe-sittendra   ǣnig þāra,
þe mec gūð-winum   grētan dorste,
egesan ðēon.   Ic on earde bād
mǣl-gesceafta,   hēold mīn tela,
nē sōhte searo-nīðas,   nē mē swōr fela
2740 āða on unriht.   Ic ðæs ealles mæg,
feorh-bennum sēoc,   gefēan habban;
for-þām mē wītan ne ðearf   Waldend4 fīra
morðor-bealo5 māga,   þonne mīn sceaceð
līf of līce.   Nū ðū lungre geong6
2745 hord scēawian   under hārne stān,
Wīglāf lēofa,   nū se wyrm ligeð,
swefeð sāre wund,   since berēafod.

Bīo7 nū on ofoste,   þæt ic ǣr-welan,
gold-ǣht ongite,   gearo scēawige
2750 swegle searo-gimmas,   þæt ic ðȳ sēft mæge
æfter māððum-welan   mīn ālǣtan
līf ond lēod-scipe,   þone ic longe hēold."

   2716. **se æðeling** is Beowulf.

2718. **ęnta geweorc** is a stereotyped phrase for anything that occasions wonder by its size or strangeness.

2720. **healde**. Heyne, following Ettmüller, reads **hēoldon**, thus arbitrarily changing mood, tense, and number of the original. Either mood, indicative or subjunctive, would be legitimate. As to the tense, the narrator is identifying himself in time with the hero, whose wonder was "how the stone-arches ... *sustain* the ever-during earth-hall": the construction is a form of *oratio recta*, a sort of *miratio recta*. The singular **healde**, instead of **healden**, has many parallels in the dependent clauses of *Beowulf*, most of these being relative clauses introduced by **þāra þe** (= *of those that* ... + a singular predicate). In the present instance, the predicate has doubtless been influenced by the proximity of **eorð-ręced**, a *quasi*-subject; and we have no more right to alter to **healden** or **hēoldon** than we have to change Shakespeare's *gives* to *give* in

"Words to the heat of deeds too cold breath *gives*."

(*Macbeth*, II, I, 61.)

2722. The **þegn ungemete till** is Wiglaf, the bravest of Beowulf's retainers.

2725. **hē ofer bęnne spræc**. The editors and translators of *Beowulf* invariably render **ofer** in this passage by *about*; but Beowulf says not a word about his wound. The context seems to me to show plainly that **ofer** (cf. Latin *supra*) denotes here opposition = *in spite of*. We read in *Genesis*, l. 594, that Eve took the forbidden fruit **ofer Drihtenes word**. Beowulf fears (l. 2331) that he may have ruled unjustly = **ofer ealde riht**; and he goes forth (l. 2409) **ofer willan** to confront the dragon.

2731-33. **þǣr mē ... gelęnge**, *if so be that* (**þǣr ... swā**) *any heir had afterwards been given me* (**mē gifeðe ... æfter wurde**) *belonging to my body*.

2744-45. **geong** [= **gǫng**] **... scēawian**. See note on **ēode ... sittan**, p. 137, ll. 19-20. In Mn.E. *Go see, Go fetch*, etc., is the second verb imperative (coördinate with the first), or subjunctive (*that you may see*), or infinitive without *to*?

2751-52. **mīn ... līf.** See note on **ęnde-dæg ... mīnne**, p. 137, ll. 16-17.

1 = sēo.

2 = gēong.

3 = Bēowulf.

4 = Wealdend.

5 = morðor-bealu.

6 = gǫng (gang).

7 = Bēo.

BEOWULF'S LAST WORDS. [Lines 2793-2821.]

[Wiglaf brings the jewels, the tokens of Beowulf's triumph. Beowulf, rejoicing to see them, reviews his career, and gives advice and final directions to Wiglaf.]

Bīowulf1 maðelode,

gǫmel on giohðe   (gold scēawode):

2795 "Ic þāra frætwa   Frēan ealles ðanc,

Wuldur-cyninge,   wordum sęcge

ęcum Dryhtne,   þe ic hēr on starie,

þæs þe ic mōste   mīnum lēodum

ǣr swylt-dæge   swylc gestrȳnan.

2800 Nū ic on māðma hord   mīne bebohte

frōde feorh-lęge,   fręmmað gē nū

lēoda þearfe;   ne mæg ic hēr lęng wesan.

Hātað heaðo-mǣre   hlǣw gewyrcean,

beorhtne æfter bǣle   æt brimes nosan;

2805 sē scel2 tō gemyndum   mīnum lēodum

- 151 -

hēah hlīfian   on Hrones næsse,

þæt hit sǣ-līðend   syððan hātan3

Bīowulfes1 biorh1   þā þe brentingas

ofer flōda genipu   feorran drīfað."

2810 Dyde him of healse   hring gyldene

þīoden1 þrīst-hȳdig;   þegne gesealde,

geongum gār-wigan,   gold-fāhne helm,

bēah ond byrnan,   hēt hyne brūcan well.

"Þū eart ende-lāf   ūsses cynnes,

2815 Wǣgmundinga;   ealle wyrd forswēop

mīne māgas   tō metod-sceafte,

eorlas on elne;   ic him æfter sceal."

Þæt wæs þām gomelan   gingeste word

brēost-gehygdum,   ǣr hē bǣl cure,

2820 hāte heaðo-wylmas;   him of hreðre gewāt

sāwol sēcean   sōð-fæstra dōm.

> 2795-99. The expression **secgan þanc** takes the same construction as **þancian**; i.e., the dative of the person (**Frēan**) and the genitive (a genitive of cause) of the thing (**þāra frætwa**). Cf. note on **biddan**, p. 45. The antecedent of **þe** is **frætwa**. For the position of **on**, see § 94, (5). The clause introduced by **þæs þe** (*because*) is parallel in construction with **frætwa**, both being causal modifiers of **secge þanc**. The Christian coloring in these lines betrays the influence of priestly transcribers.

> 2800. *Now that I, in exchange for* (**on**) *a hoard of treasures, have bartered* (**bebohte**) *the laying down* (**-lege** > **licgan**) *of my old life*. The ethical codes of the early Germanic races make frequent mention of blood-payments, or life-barters. There seems to be here a suggestion of the "wergild."

2801. **fremmað gē**. The plural imperative (as also in **Hātað**) shows that Beowulf is here speaking not so much to Wiglaf in particular as, through Wiglaf, to his retainers in general,—to his *comitatus*.

2806. The desire for conspicuous burial places finds frequent expression in early literatures. The tomb of Achilles was situated "high on a jutting headland over wide Hellespont that it might be seen from off the sea." Elpenor asks Ulysses to bury him in the same way. Æneas places the ashes of Misenus beneath a high mound on a headland of the sea.

2807. **hit = hlǣw**, which is masculine. See p. 39, Note 2.

2810-11. **him ... þīoden**. The reference in both cases is to Beowulf, who is disarming himself (do-of > *doff*) for the last time; **þegne** = *to Wiglaf.*

Note, where the personal element is strong, the use of the dative instead of the more colorless possessive; **him of healse**, not **of his healse**.

2817. **ic ... sceal**. See note on **nō ... meahte**, p. 140, l. 1.

2820. **him of hreðre**. Cf. note on **him ... þīoden**, p. 147, ll. 10-11.

2820-21. For construction of **gewāt ... sēcean**, see note on **ēode ... sittan**, p. 137, ll. 19-20.

1 = īo, io = ēo, eo.

2 = sceal.

3 = hāten.

VII. THE WANDERER.

[Exeter MS. "The epic character of the ancient lyric appears especially in this: that the song is less the utterance of a momentary feeling than the portrayal of a lasting state, perhaps the reflection of an entire life, generally that of one isolated, or bereft by death or exile of protectors and friends." (Ten Brink, *Early Eng. Lit.*, I.) I adopt Brooke's threefold division (*Early Eng. Lit.*, p. 356): "It opens with a Christian prologue, and closes with a Christian epilogue, but the whole body of the poem was written, it seems to me, by a person who thought more of the goddess Wyrd than of God, whose life and way of thinking were uninfluenced by any distinctive Christian doctrine."

The author is unknown.]

PROLOGUE.

    Oft him ānhaga   āre gebīdeð,
    Metudes[1] miltse,   þēah þe hē mōdcearig
    geond lagulāde   lǫnge sceolde
    hrēran mid hǫndum   hrīmcealde sǣ,
5 wadan wræclǣstas: wyrd bið ful ārǣd!
    Swā cwæð eardstapa   earfeþa[2] gemyndig,
    wrāþra wælsleahta,   winemǣga hryres:

PLAINT OF THE WANDERER.

    "Oft ic sceolde āna   ūhtna gehwylce
    mīne ceare cwīþan;   nis nū cwicra nān,

10 þe ic him mōdsefan   mīnne durre
    sweotule[3] āsęcgan.   Ic tō sōþe wāt
    þæt biþ in eorle   indryhten þēaw,
    þæt hē his ferðlocan   fæste binde,
    healde his hordcofan,   hycge swā hē wille;
15 ne mæg wērig mōd   wyrde wiðstǫndan
    nē sē hrēo hyge   helpe gefręmman:
    for ðon dōmgeorne   drēorigne oft
    in hyra brēostcofan   bindað fæste.
    Swā ic mōdsefan   mīnne sceolde
20 oft earmcearig   ēðle bidǣled,
    frēomǣgum feor   feterum sǣlan,
    siþþan gēara iū   goldwine mīnne

hrūsan heolster biwrāh,   and ic hēan þonan
wōd wintercearig   ofer waþema gebind,
25 sōhte sele drēorig   sinces bryttan,
hwǣr ic feor oþþe nēah   findan meahte
þone þe in meoduhealle4   miltse wisse
oþþe mec frēondlēasne   frēfran wolde,
wenian mid wynnum.   Wāt sē þe cunnað
30 hū slīþen bið   sorg tō gefēran
þām þe him lȳt hafað   lēofra geholena:
warað hine wræclāst,   nāles wunden gold,
ferðloca frēorig,   nālæs foldan blǣd;
gemon hē selesecgas   and sincþege,
35 hū hine on geoguðe   his goldwine
wenede tō wiste: wyn eal gedrēas!

For þon wāt sē þe sceal   his winedryhtnes
lēofes lārcwidum   longe forþolian,
ðonne sorg and slǣp   somod ætgædre
40 earmne ānhagan   oft gebindað:
þinceð him on mōde   þæt hē his mondryhten
clyppe and cysse,   and on cnēo lecge
honda and hēafod,   swā hē hwīlum ǣr
in gēardagum   giefstōles brēac;
45 ðonne onwæcneð eft   winelēas guma,
gesihð him biforan   fealwe wǣgas,
baþian brimfuglas,   brǣdan feþra,
hrēosan hrīm and snāw   hagle gemenged.
Þonne bēoð þȳ hefigran   heortan benne,
50 sāre æfter swǣsne;   sorg bið genīwad;

þonne māga gemynd   mōd geondhweorfeð,
grēteð glīwstafum,   georne geondscēawað.
Secga geseldan   swimmað eft on weg;
flēotendra ferð5   nō þǣr fela bringeð
55 cūðra cwidegiedda;   cearo6 bið genīwad

þām þe sendan sceal   swīþe geneahhe
ofer waþema gebind   wērigne sefan.
For þon ic geþencan ne mæg   geond þās woruld
for hwan mōdsefa   mīn ne gesweorce,
60 þonne ic eorla līf   eal geondþence,
hū hī fǣrlīce   flet ofgēafon,
mōdge maguþegnas.   Swā þēs middangeard
ealra dōgra gehwām   drēoseð and fealleþ;
for þon ne mæg weorþan wīs   wer, ǣr hē āge
65 wintra dǣl in woruldrīce.   Wita sceal geþyldig,
ne sceal nō tō hātheort   nē tō hrædwyrde,
nē tō wāc wiga   nē tō wanhȳdig,
nē tō forht nē tō fægen   nē tō feohgīfre,
nē nǣfre gielpes tō georn,   ǣr hē geare cunne.
70 Beorn sceal gebīdan,   þonne hē bēot spriceð,
oþ þæt collenferð   cunne gearwe
hwider hreþra gehygd   hweorfan wille.
Ongietan sceal glēaw hæle   hū gǣstlīc bið,
þonne eall þisse worulde wela   wēste stondeð,
75 swā nū missenlīce   geond þisne middangeard
winde biwāune7   weallas stondaþ,

hrīme bihrorene,8   hryðge þā ederas.

Wōriað þā wīnsalo,9   waldend licgað

drēame bidrorene10;   duguð eal gecrong

80 wlonc bī wealle: sume wīg fornōm,

ferede in forðwege;   sumne fugel11 oþbær

ofer hēanne holm;   sumne sē hāra wulf

dēaðe gedǣlde;   sumne drēorighlēor

in eorðscræfe   eorl gehȳdde:

85 ȳþde swā þisne eardgeard   ælda Scyppend,

oþ þæt burgwara   breahtma lēase

eald enta geweorc   īdlu stōdon.

Sē þonne þisne wealsteal   wīse geþōhte,

and þis deorce līf   dēope geondþenceð,

90 frōd in ferðe12   feor oft gemon

wælsleahta worn,   and þās word ācwið:

'Hwǣr cwōm mearg?   hwǣr cwōm mago13? hwǣr cwōm māþþumgyfa?

hwǣr cwōm symbla gesetu?   hwǣr sindon seledrēamas?

Ēalā beorht bune!   ēalā byrnwiga!

95 ēalā þēodnes þrym!   hū sēo þrāg gewāt,

genāp under nihthelm,   swā hēo nō wǣre!

Stondeð nū on lāste   lēofre duguþe

weal wundrum hēah,   wyrmlīcum fāh:

eorlas fornōmon   asca þrȳþe,

100 wǣpen wælgīfru,   wyrd sēo mǣre;

and þās stānhleoþu14   stormas cnyssað;

hrīð hrēosende   hrūsan bindeð,

wintres wōma,   þonne won cymeð,

nīpeð nihtscūa,   norþan onsendeð

105 hrēo hæglfare   hæleþum on andan.

Eall is earfoðlīc   eorþan rīce,

onwęndeð wyrda gesceaft   weoruld under heofonum:

hēr bið feoh lǣne,   hēr bið frēond lǣne,

hēr bið mọn lǣne,   hēr bið mǣg lǣne;

110 eal þis eorþan gesteal   īdel weorþeð!'"

EPILOGUE.

Swā cwæð snottor on mōde,   gesæt him sundor æt rune.

Til biþ sē þe his trēowe gehealdeð;   ne sceal nǣfre his torn tō rycene

beorn of his brēostum ācȳþan,   nemþe hē ǣr þā bōte cunne;

eorl mid ęlne gefręmman.   Wel bið þām þe him āre sēceð,

115 frōfre tō Fæder on heofonum,   þǣr ūs eal sēo fæstnung stọndeð.

 7. The MS. reading is **hryre** (nominative), which is meaningless.

 8. For **ūhtna gehwylce**, see note on **cēnra gehwylcum**, p. 140.

 10. **þe ... him**. See § 75 (4). Cf. *Merchant of Venice*, II, v, 50-51.

 27. For **mine** (MS. **in**), which does not satisfy metrical requirements, I adopt Kluge's plausible substitution of **miltse; miltse witan** = *to show (know, feel), pity*. The **myne wisse** of *Beowulf* (l. 169) is metrically admissible.

 37. The object of **wāt** is **þinceð him on mōde**; but the construction is unusual, inasmuch as both **þæt's** (**þæt** pronominal before **wāt** and **þæt** conjunctional before **þinceð**) are omitted. See p. 112, ll. 18-19.

 41. **þinceð him on mōde** (see note on **him ... þīoden**, p. 147). "No more sympathetic picture has been drawn by an Anglo-Saxon poet than where the wanderer in exile falls asleep at his oar and dreams again of his dead lord and the old hall and revelry and joy and gifts,—then wakes to look once more upon

the waste of ocean, snow and hail falling all around him, and sea-birds dipping in the spray." (Gummere, *Germanic Origins*, p. 221.)

53-55. **Sęcga ... cwidegiedda** = *But these comrades of warriors* [= those seen in vision] *again swim away* [= *fade away*]; *the ghost of these fleeting ones brings not there many familiar words*; i.e. he sees in dream and vision the old familiar faces, but no voice is heard: they bring neither greetings to him nor tidings of themselves.

65. **Wita sceal geþyldig**. Either **bēon (wesan)** is here to be understood after **sceal**, or **sceal** alone means *ought to be*. Neither construction is to be found in Alfredian prose, though the omission of a verb of motion after **sculan** is common in all periods of Old English. See note on **nō ... meahte**, p. 140.

75. **swā nū**. "The Old English lyrical feeling," says Ten Brink, citing the lines that immediately follow **swā nū**, "is fond of the image of physical destruction"; but I do not think these lines have a merely figurative import. The reference is to a period of real devastation, antedating the Danish incursions. "We might fairly find such a time in that parenthesis of bad government and of national tumult which filled the years between the death of Aldfrith in 705 and the renewed peace of Northumbria under Ceolwulf in the years that followed 729." (Brooke, *Early Eng. Lit.*, p. 355.)

93. **cwōm ... gesetu**. Ettmüller reads **cwōmon**; but see p. 107, note on **wæs ... þā īgland**. The occurrence of **hwǣr cwōm** three times in the preceding line tends also to hold **cwōm** in the singular when its plural subject follows. Note the influence of a somewhat similar structural parallelism in *seas hides* of these lines (*Winter's Tale*, IV, IV, 500-502):

> "Not for ... all the *sun sees* or
>
> The close *earth wombs* or the profound *seas hides*
>
> In unknown fathoms, will I break my oath."

111. **gesæt ... rūne**, *sat apart to himself in silent meditation.*

114. **eorl ... gefremman**. Supply **sceal** after **eorl**.

1 = Metodes.

2 = earfoþa.

3 = sweotole.

4 = medu-.

5 = ferhð.

6 = cearu.

7 = See bewāwan.

8 = See behrēosan.

9 = wīnsalu.

10 = See bedrēosan.

11 = fugol.

12 = ferhðe.

13 = magu.

14 = -hliðu.

I. GLOSSARY.

OLD ENGLISH—MODERN ENGLISH.

[The order of words is strictly alphabetical, except that ð follows t. The combination æ follows ad.

Gender is indicated by the abbreviations, m. (= masculine), f. (= feminine), n. (= neuter). The usual abbreviations are employed for the cases, nom., gen., dat., acc., and instr. Other abbreviations are sing. (= singular), pl. (= plural), ind. (= indicative mood), sub. (= subjunctive mood), pres. (= present tense), pret. (= preterit tense), prep. (= preposition), adj. (= adjective), adv. (= adverb), part. (= participle), conj. (= conjunction), pron. (= pronoun), intrans. (= intransitive), trans. (= transitive).

Figures not preceded by § refer to page and line of the texts.

A B C D E F G H I K L
M N O P R S T Ð U W Y

A.

ā, *ever, always, aye.*

abbudisse, f., *abbess* [Lat. abbatissa].

ābēodan (§ 109), *bid, offer;*

him hǣl ābēad 138, 9 = *bade him hail, wished him health.*

ābrecan (§ 120, Note 2), *break down, destroy.*

ābūgan (§ 109, Note 1), *give way, start* [bow away].

ac, conj., *but.*

ācweðan (§ 115), *say, speak.*

ācȳðan (§ 126), *reveal, proclaim* [**cūð**].

ād, m., *funeral pile.*

adesa, m., *adze, hatchet.*

ǣ (**ǣw**), f., *law.*

ǣdre (**ēdre**), f., *stream, canal, vein;*

blōd ēdrum dranc 139, 4 = *drank blood in streams* (instr.).

ǣfæstnis, f., *piety.*

ǣfen-ræst, f., *evening rest.*

ǣfen-sprǣc, f., *evening speech.*

ǣfęst (ǣwfęst), *law-abiding, pious.*

ǣfęstnis, see ǣfæstnis.

ǣfre, *ever, always.*

ǣfter, prep. (§ 94, (1)), *after;*

ǣfter ðǣm, *after that, thereafter;*

æfter ðǣm ðe, conj., *after.*

æfter, adv., *after, afterwards.*

ǣghwā (§ 77, Note), *each, every.*

ǣghwilc (§ 77, Note), *each, any.*

ǣglǣca, see āglǣca.

ǣgðer (ǣghwæðer, āðer) (§ 77, Note), *each, either;*

ǣgðer ... ōðer ... ōðer, *either ... or ... or;*

ǣgðer ge ... ge (§ 95, (2)), *both ... and;*

ǣgðer ge ... ge ... ge, *both ... and ... and.*

ǣht, f., *property, possession* [āgan].

ǣlc (§ 77), *each.*

ælde (ielde) (§ 47), m. pl., *men;* gen. pl., ælda.

ælmihtig, *almighty.*

ǣmetta, m., *leisure* [*empti*-ness].

ǣnig (§ 77), *any;*

ǣnige ðinga 141, 22 = *for anything.*
(See 140, 15, Note.)

ǣr, adv., *before, formerly, sooner;*

nō þȳ ǣr 140, 1 = *none the sooner;*

ǣror, comparative, *before, formerly;*

ǣrest, superlative, *first*.

ǣr, conj. (§ 105, 2), *ere, before* = **ǣr ðǣm ðe**.

ǣr, prep, with dat., *before* (time);

ǣr ðǣm ðe, conj. (§ 105, 2), *before*.

ǣrcebisceop, m., *archbishop* [Lat. archiepiscopus].

ǣrendgewrit, n., *message, letter*.

ǣrendwreca (-raca), m., *messenger*.

ǣrest, adj. (§ 96, (4)), *first*.

ǣrnan (§ 127), *ride, gallop* [**iernan**].

ǣrra, adj. (§ 96, (4)), *former*.

ǣrwela, m., *ancient wealth*.

æsc, m., *ash, spear*; gen. pl., **asca**.

Æscesdūn, f., *Ashdown* (in Berkshire).

æstel, m., *book-mark* [Lat. hastula].

æt (§ 94, (1)), *at, in*;

with **leornian**, *to learn*, **geðicgan**, *to receive*, and other verbs of similar import,

æt = *from*: 115, 18; 137, 8, etc.

ætberan (§ 114), *bear to, hand*.

ætgæd(e)re, adv., *together*.

ætsteppan (§ 116), *step up, advance*; pret. sing., **ætstōp**.

æðele, *noble, excellent*.

æðeling, m., *a noble, prince*.

Æðelwulfing, m., *son of Ethelwulf*.

Æðered, m., *Ethelred*.

āfeallan (§ 117), *fall*.

āfierran (§ 127), *remove* [**feor**].

āgan (§ 136), *to own, possess*.

āgen, adj.-part., *own*; dat. sing., **āgnum** [**āgan**].

āgiefan (§ 115), *give back*.

- 163 -

āglǣca (ǣglǣca), m., *monster, champion.*

āhton, see **āgan.**

ālǣtan (§ 117), *let go, leave.*

aldor, see **ealdor.**

ālęcgan (§ 125, Note), *lay down* [**licgan**]; past part., **ālēd.**

Ālīesend, m., *Redeemer* [**ālīesan** = *release, ransom*].

ālimpan (§ 110), *befall, occur.*

ālȳfan (§ 126), *entrust, permit.*

ambor, m., *measure*; gen. pl., **ambra** (§ 27, (4)).

ambyre, *favorable.*

ān (§ 89), *one*;

āna, *alone, only*;

ānra gehwylcum 141, 15 = *to each one.*
(See 140, 15, Note.)

anda, m., *zeal, injury, indignation*;

hæleðum on andan 153, 6 = *harmful to men.*

andēfn, f., *proportion, amount.*

andgiet (-git), n., *sense, meaning.*

andgitfullīce, *intelligibly*;

-gitfullīcost, *superlative.*

andswaru, f., *answer.*

andwyrdan (§ 127), *to answer*; pret., **andwyrde.**

Angel, n., *Anglen* (in Denmark); dat. sing., **Angle** (§ 27 (4)).

Angelcynn, n., *English kin, English people, England.*

ānhaga (-hoga), m., *a solitary, wanderer* [**ān** + **hogian**, *to meditate*].

ānlīpig, *single, individual.*

ānunga (§ 93, (2)), *once for all* [**ān**].

apostol, m., *apostle* [Gr. ἀπὸστολος].

ār, f., *honor, property, favor;*

āre gebīdeð 148, 3 = *waits for divine favor* (gen.).

āræd, adj., *inexorable.*

ārǣdan (§ 126), *read.*

āręcc(e)an (§ 128), *translate, expound.*

ārfæstnis, f., *virtue.*

ārīsan (§ 102), *arise.*

asca, see **aesc**.

āsęcgan (§ 132), *say, relate.*

āsęttan (§ 127), *set, place.*

āsingan (§ 110), *sing.*

āspęndan (§ 127), *spend, expend.*

āstīgan (§ 102), *ascend, arise.*

āstǫndan (§ 116), *stand up.*

ātēah, see **ātēon**.

atelīc, *horrible, dire.*

ātēon (§ 118), *draw, draw away, take* (as a journey).

atol, *horrible, dire.*

āttor, n., *poison.*

ātuge, see **ātēon**.

āð, m., *oath.*

āðer, see **ǣgðer**.

āwęccan (§ 128), *awake, arouse;* pret. sing., **āweahte, āwęhte**.

aweg, *away.*

āwęndan (§ 127), *turn, translate.*

āwrītan (§ 102), *write, compose.*

āwyrcan (§ 128), *work, do, perform.*

B.

Bāchsęcg, m., *Bagsac.*

bæcbord, n., *larboard, left side of a ship.*

bǣl, n., *funeral fire, funeral pile.*

bān, n., *bone.*

bān-fāg, *adorned with bones* or *antlers.*

bān-loca, m., *flesh* [bone-locker].

Basengas, m. pl., *Basing* (in Hantshire).

be (**bĭ**) (§ 94, (1)), *by, about, concerning, near, along, according to*;

be norðan þǣm wēstenne (§ 94, (4)), *north of the waste* (*desert*);

be fullan, *fully, perfectly.*

bēag, see **būgan**.

bēag-hroden, *ring-adorned.*

bēah (**bēag**), m., *ring, bracelet, collar* [**būgan**].

bealo-nīð, m., *dire hatred, poison, venom.*

bearn, n., *child, son* [bairn].

bebēodan (§ 109), *command, bid, entrust* (with dat.).

bebīo-, see **bebēo-**.

bebohte, see **bebycgan**.

bebycgan (§ 128), *sell.*

bēc, see **bōc**.

becuman (§ 114), *come, arrive, befall.*

bedǣlan (§ 126), *separate, deprive.*

bedrēosan (§ 109), *deprive*; past part. pl., **bedrorene** (**bidrorene**) [dross, dreary].

befǣstan (§ 127), *fasten, implant.*

befēolan (§ 110), *apply one's self*;

ðāra ðe ðā spēda hæbben ðæt hīe ðǣm befēolan mægen 119, 20 = *of those who have the means by which they may apply themselves to it.*

beforan, prep. with dat., *before.*

bēgen (declined like **twēgen**, § 89), *both.*

- 166 -

begeondan (**begiondan**), prep. with dat., *beyond*.

begietan (§ 115), *get, obtain, find*.

beginnan (§ 110), *begin*.

beheonan (**behionan**), prep. with dat., *on this side of*.

behrēosan (§ 109), *fall upon, cover*; past part. pl., **behrorene** (**bihrorene**).

belimpan (§ 110), *pertain, belong*.

beniman (§ 114), *take, derive*.

benn, f., *wound* [**bana** = *murderer*].

bēon (**bīon**) (§ 134), *be, consist*.

beorh (**beorg, biorh**), m., *mound* [barrow].

beorht, *bright, glorious*.

Beormas, m. pl., *Permians*.

beorn, m., *man, hero, chief*.

bēor-þegu, f., *beer-drinking* [**þicgan** = *receive*].

bēot, n., *boast*.

beran (§ 114), *bear*.

berēafian (§ 130), *bereave*;

since berēafod 145, 22 = *bereft of treasure*.

beren, adj., *of a bear, bear*.

berstan (§ 110), *burst, crack*.

besmiðian (§ 130), *make hard* (as at the forge of a smith).

bet, see **wel** (§ 97, (2)).

bētan (§ 126), *make good, requite*; past part. pl., **gebētte**.

betera (**betra**), see **gōd** (§ 96, (3)).

betlīc, *excellent*.

betsta, see **gōd** (§ 96, (3)).

betuh (**betux**) (§ 94, (1)), *between*.

betwēonan (§ 94, (1)), *between*.

betȳnan (§ 126), *close, end* [**tūn** = *enclosure*].

bewāwan (§ 117), *blow upon*; past part. pl., **bewāune** (**biwāune, bewāwene**).

bewrēon (§ 118, 1), *enwrap*; pret. 3d sing., **bewrāh** (**biwrāh**).

bī, see **be**.

bi-, see **be-**.

bīdan (§ 102), *bide, await, expect, endure* (with gen.).

biddan (§ 115, Note 2), *bid, pray, request* (§ 65, Note 3);

bæd hine blīðne 136, 7 = *bade him be blithe*.

bindan (§ 110), *bind*.

bīo, see **bēo** (imperative sing.).

bisceop (**biscep**), m., *bishop* [Lat. episcopus].

bisceop-stōl, m., *episcopal seat, bishopric*.

bisigu, f., *business, occupation*; dat. pl., **bisgum**.

bītan (§ 102), *bite, cut*.

biwrāh, see **bewrēon**.

blǣd, m., *glory, prosperity* [**blāwan** = *blow, inflate*].

Blēcinga-ēg, f., *Blekingen*.

bliss, f., *bliss* [**blīðe**].

blīðe, *blithe, happy*.

blōd, n., *blood*.

bōc (§ 68, (1), Note 1), f., *book*.

bōcere, m., *scribe* [**bōc**].

bǫna (**bana**), m., *murderer* [bane].

bōt, f., *boot, remedy, help, compensation*.

brād (§ 96, (1)), *broad*.

brǣdan (§ 126), *extend, spread* [**brād**].

brǣdra, see **brād**.

brægd, see **bregdan**.

brēac, see **brūcan**.

breahtm, m., *noise, revelry*;

burgwara breahtma lēase 152, 10 = *bereft of the revelries of citizens.*

bregdan (§ 110), *brandish, draw* [braid]; pret. ind. 3d sing., **brægd**.

brenting, m., *high ship.*

brēost, n., *breast* (the pl. has the same meaning as the sing.).

brēost-cofa, m., *breast-chamber, heart, mind.*

brēost-gehygd, n., *breast-thought, thought of the heart, emotion.*

brim, n., *sea, ocean.*

brimfugol, m., *sea-fowl.*

bringan (§ 128), *bring.*

brōhte, brōhton, see **bringan**.

brōðor (brōður) (§ 68, (2)), m., *brother.*

brūcan (§ 109, Note 1), *use, enjoy* (§ 62, Note 1; but Alfred frequently employs the acc. with **brūcan**).

brycg, f., *bridge.*

brȳcð, see **brūcan**.

brytta, m., *distributor, dispenser* [**brēotan** = *break in pieces*].

būan (§ 126, Note 2), *dwell, cultivate* [bower].

būde, see **būan**.

bufan, prep. with dat. and acc., *above.*

būgan (§ 109, Note 1), *bow, bend, turn.*

bune, f., *cup.*

burg (burh) (§ 68, (1), Note), f., *city, borough*; dat. sing., **byrig**.

Burgenda, m. gen. pl., *of the Burgundians*;

Burgenda land, *Bornholm.*

burgware (§ 47), m. pl., *burghers, citizens.*

burh, see **burg**.

būtan (būton), prep. (§ 94, (1)), *without, except, except for, but.*

būtan (būton), conj., *except that, unless.*

būtū, *both* (= *both—two*.

The word is compounded of the combined neuters of **bēgen** and **twēgen**, but is m. and f. as well as n.).

bȳn (§ 126, Note 2), *cultivated*.

byrde, adj., *of high rank, aristocratic*.

byrig, see **burg**.

byrne, f., *byrnie, corselet, coat of mail*.

byrnwiga, m., *byrnie-warrior, mailed soldier*.

byrð, see **beran**.

C.

canōn, m., *sacred canon, Bible* [Lat. canon, Gr. κανών].

cearu (cearo), f., *care*.

ceaster-būend, m., *castle-dweller*.

cēne, *keen, bold, brave*.

cēosan (§ 109), *choose, accept, encounter*.

cild, n., *child*.

cirice, f., *church*; nom. pl., **ciricean**.

cirr (cierr), m., *turn, time, occasion* [char, chore, ajar = on char, on the turn].

cirran (§ 127), *turn*.

clǣne, *clean, pure*.

clǣne, adv., *entirely* ["clean out of the way," Shaks.].

clūdig, *rocky* [having boulders or masses like *clouds*].

clyppan (§ 127), *embrace, accept* [clip = clasp for letters, papers, etc.].

cnapa, m., *boy* [knave].

cnēo (cnēow), n., *knee*; acc. pl., **cnēo**.

cniht, m., *knight, warrior*.

cnyssan (§ 125), *beat*.

collenferð (-ferhð), *proud-minded, fierce*.

costnung, f., *temptation.*

Crēcas (**Crēacas**), m. pl., *Greeks.*

cringan (§ 110), *cringe, fall.*

Crīst, m., *Christ.*

Crīsten, *Christian*; nom. pl. m., **Crīstene**, **Crīstne**.

cuma, m., *new-comer, stranger.*

cuman (§ 114), *come.* (See p. 138, Note on ll. 2-6.)

cunnan (§ 137), *know, can, understand.*

cunnian (§ 130), *make trial of, experience* [**cunnan**].

cure, see **cēosan**.

cūð, *well-known, familiar* [past part. of **cunnan**: cf. uncouth].

cūðe, cūðen, cūðon, see **cunnan**.

cwǣden, cwǣdon, see **cweðan**.

cwalu, f., *death, murder* [**cwelan**].

cwealm-cuma, m., *murderous comer.*

cwelan (§ 114), *die* [to quail].

cwēn, f., *queen.*

Cwēnas, m. pl., *a Finnish tribe.*

cweðan (§ 115), *say, speak* [quoth, bequeath].

cwic, *living, alive* [quicksilver; the quick and the dead].

cwidegiedd, n., *word, utterance* [**cweðan** and **gieddian**, both meaning *to speak*].

cwīðan (§ 126), *bewail* (trans.).

cwōm, see **cuman**.

cyle (**ciele**), m., *cold* [chill];

cyle gewyrcan 110, 7 = *produce cold, freeze.*

cyme, m., *coming* [**cuman**].

cyn(n), n., *kin, race.*

cyn(n), adj. (used only in pl.), *fitting things, etiquette, proprieties, courtesies*;

cynna gemyndig 136, 3 = *mindful of courtesies.*

cynerīce, n., *kingdom.*

cyning, m., *king.*

cyssan (§ 125), *kiss.*

cyst, f., *the choice, the pick, the best* [**cēosan**].

cȳðan (§ 126), *make known, display,* [**cūð**];
2d sing. imperative, **cȳð**.

D.

dǣd, f., *deed.*

dæg, m., *day.*

dæg-hwīl, f., *day-while, day*;

hē **dæg-hwīla gedrogen hæfde eorðan wynne** 145, 2 = *he had spent his days of earth's joy.*

dæg-rīm, n., **number of days** [day-rime];

dōgera daeg-rīm 143, 7 = *the number of his days.*

dæl, n., *dale.*

dǣl, m., *part, deal, division.*

dēad, *dead.*

dēað, m., *death.*

dēman (§ 126), *deem, judge.*

Dęnamearc, see **Dęnemearc**.

Dęne (§ 47), m. pl., *Danes.*

Dęnemearc (**Dęnemearce**), f., *Denmark*; dat. sing., **Dęnemearce** (strong), **Dęnemearcan** (weak).

Dęnisc, *Danish*;

ðā **Dęniscan**, *the Danes.*

dēofol, m., n., *devil*; gen. sing., **dēofles** (§ 27, (4)).

dēope, *deeply, profoundly* [**dēop**].

dēor, n., *wild animal* [deer].

deorc, *dark, gloomy*.

dōgor, n., *day*; gen. pl., **dōgora, dōgera, dōgra**.

dōgor-gerīm, n., *number of days, lifetime*.

dōm, m., *doom, judgment, glory*.

dōmgeorn, adj., *eager for glory* [*doom-yearning*].

dōn (§ 135), *do, cause, place, promote, remove*.

dorste, dorston, see **durran**.

drēam, m., *joy, mirth* [dream].

drēogan (§ 109), *endure, enjoy, spend* [Scotch dree].

drēorig, *dreary, sad*.

drēorighlēor, adj., *with sad face* [**hlēor** = *cheek, face, leer*].

drēosan (§ 109), *fall, perish* [dross].

drīfan (§ 102), *drive*.

drihten, see **dryhten**.

drincan (§ 110), *drink*.

drohtoð (**-að**), m., *mode of living, occupation* [**drēogan**].

drugon, see **drēogan**.

dryhten (**drihten**), m., *lord, Lord*; dat. sing., **dryhtne**.

dryht-sęle, m., *lordly hall*.

duguð, f., *warrior-band, host, retainers* [**doughtiness**].

In **duguð** and **geogoð**, the higher (older) and lower (younger) ranks are represented, the distinction corresponding roughly to the mediæval distinction between knights and squires.

durran (§ 137), *dare*.

duru, f., *door*.

dyde, see **dōn**.

dynnan (§ 125), *resound* [din].

dȳre (**dīere, dēore, dīore**), *dear, costly*.

E.

ēa, f., *river*; gen. sing., **ēas**; dat. and acc. sing., **ēa**.

ēac, *also, likewise* [a nickname = an eek-name. See § 65, Note 2];

ēac swilce (swelce) 112, 3 = *also.*

ēaca, m., *addition* [ēac];

tō ēacan = *in addition to* (§ 94, (4)).

ēage, n., *eye.*

eahta, *eight.*

ēalā, *oh! alas!*

ealað, see ealu.

eald (§ 96, (2)), *old.*

ealdor (aldor), n., *life;*

gif ðū ðæt ęllenweorc aldre gedīgest 138, 17 = *if thou survivest that feat with thy life* (instr.).

ealdor-dæg (aldor-, ealder-), m., *day of life.*

ealdor-gedāl (aldor-), n., *death* [life-deal].

ealdormǫn, m., *alderman, chief, magistrate.*

ealgian, (§ 130), *protect, defend.*

eall (eal), *all;*

ealne weg, *all the way* (§ 98, (1));

ealneg (< ealne weg), *always;*

ealles (§ 98, (3)), adv., *altogether, entirely.*

Eall (eal) is frequently used with partitive gen. = *all of:* 143, 19; 145, 3.

ealu (ealo) (§ 68), n., *ale;* gen. sing., ealað.

ealu-scerwen, f., *mortal panic* [ale-spilling].

eard, m., *country, home* [eorðe].

eardgeard, m. *earth* [earth-yard].

eardian (§ 130), *dwell* [eard].

eardstapa, m., *wanderer* [earth-stepper].

ēare, n., *ear.*

earfoð (earfeð), n. *hardship, toil*; gen. pl., **earfeða**.

earfoðlīc, adj., *full of hardship, arduous*.

earm, m., *arm*.

earm, adj., *poor, wretched*.

earmcearig, *wretched, miserable*.

earmlīc, *wretched, miserable*.

earnung, f., *merit* [earning].

ēast, *east*.

ēastan (§ 93, (5)), *from the east*.

Ēast-Dęne (§ 47), *East-Danes*.

ēasteweard, *eastward*.

ēastrihte (ēastryhte) (§ 93, (6)), *eastward*.

Ēastron, pl., *Easter*.

ēaðe, *easily*.

ēaðmōdlīce, *humbly*.

eaxl, f., *shoulder* [axle].

Ebrēisc, adj., *Hebrew*.

ēce, *eternal, everlasting*.

ęcg, f., *sword* [edge].

edor, m., *enclosure, dwelling*; nom. pl., **ederas**.

ēdrum, see **ǣdre**.

efne, adv., *just, only* [evenly].

eft, adv., *again, afterwards* [aft].

ęgesa, m., *fear, terror* [awe].

ęllen, n., *strength, courage*;

mid ęlne = *boldly*;

on ęlne 147, 17 = *mightily, suddenly*, or *in their (earls') strength (prime)*.

ęllen-mǣrðu, f. *fame for strength, feat of strength*.

ęllen-weorc, n., *feat of strength*.

ęllenwōdnis, f., *zeal, fervor.*

ęllor-gāst, m., *inhuman monster* [alien ghost].

ęln, f., *ell* [el-bow].

ęlne, *see* **ęllen**.

ęlra, adj. comparative, *another* [***ęle** cognate with Lat. alius];

on ęlran męn 139, 14 = *in another man.*

emnlong (-lang), *equally long;*

on emnlange = *along* (§ 94, (4)).

ęnde, m., *end.*

ęndebyrdnes, f., *order.*

ęnde-dæg, m., *end-day, day of death.*

ęnde-lāf, f., *last remnant* [end-leaving].

ęngel, m., *angel* [Lat. angelus].

Ęnglafeld (§ 51), m., *Englefield* (in Berkshire).

Ęngle (§ 47), m. pl., *Angles.*

Ęnglisc, adj., *English;*

on Ęnglisc 117, 18 and 19 = *in English, into English.*

Ęngliscgereord, n., *English language.*

ęnt, m., *giant.*

ēode, see **gān**.

eodorcan (§ 130), *ruminate.*

eorl, m., *earl, warrior, chieftain.*

eorlīc, *earl-like, noble.*

eorð-draca, m., **dragon** [earth-drake].

eorðe, f., *earth.*

eorð-ręced, n., *earth-hall.*

eorðscræf, n., *earth-cave, grave.*

eoten, m., *giant, monster.*

- 176 -

ēow, see ðū.

Ēowland, n., *Öland* (an island in the Baltic Sea).

ęrian (§ 125), *plow* [to ear].

Estland, n., *land of the Estas* (on the eastern coast of the Baltic Sea).

Estmęre, m., *Frische Haff*.

Estum, dat. pl., *the Estas*.

etan (§ 115), *eat* [ort].

ęttan (§ 127), *graze* [etan].

ēðel, m., *territory, native land* [allodial].

ēðel-weard, m., *guardian of his country*.

F.

fæc, n., *interval, space*.

fæder (§ 68, (2)), m., *father*.

fægen, *fain, glad, exultant*.

fæger (fǣger), *fair, beautiful*.

fǣlsian (§ 130), *cleanse*.

fǣrlīce, *suddenly* [fǣr = *fear*].

fæst, *fast, held fast*.

fæste, adv., *fast, firmly*.

fæstnung, f., *security, safety*.

fæt, n., *vessel* [wine-fat, vat].

fǣtels, m., *vessel;* acc. pl., fǣtels.

fæðm, m., *embrace, bosom* [fathom = the space *embraced* by the extended arms].

fāg (fāh), *hostile;*

hē wæs fāg wið God 142, 18 = *he was hostile to God*.

fāh (fāg), *variegated, ornamented*.

Falster, *Falster* (island in the Baltic Sea).

fandian (§ 130), *try, investigate* [findan].

faran (§ 116), *go* [fare].

- 177 -

feallan (§ 117), *fall, flow.*

fealu, *fallow, pale, dark*; nom. pl. m., **fealwe**.

fēawe (**fēa, fēawa**), pl., *few.*

fela (indeclinable), *much, many* (with gen.).

feld (§ 51), m., *field.*

fell (**fel**), n., *fell, skin, hide.*

fēng, see **fōn**.

fęn-hlið, n., *fen-slope.*

fęn-hop, n., *fen-retreat.*

feoh, n., *cattle, property* [fee]; gen. and dat. sing., **fēos, fēo**.

feohgīfre, *greedy of property, avaricious.*

feohtan (§ 110), *fight.*

fēol, see **feallan**.

fēond (§ 68, (3)), m., *enemy, fiend.*

fēond-grāp, f., *fiend-grip.*

feor (§ 96, (4)), adj., *far, far from* (with dat.).

feor, adv., *far, far back* (time).

feorh, m., n., *life.*

feorh-bęnn, f., *life-wound, mortal wound.*

feorh-lęgu, f., *laying down of life.* (See p. 146, Note on l. 13.)

feorh-sēoc, *life-sick, mortally wounded.*

feorm (**fiorm**), f., *use, benefit (food, provisions)* [farm].

feormian (§ 130), *eat, devour.*

feorran, *from afar.*

fēowertig, *forty*; gen., **fēowertiges** (§ 91, Note 1).

ferhð (**ferð**), m., *heart, mind, spirit.*

fęrian (§ 125), *carry, transport* [to ferry];

fęrede in forðwege 152, 5 = *carried away.*

fers, n., *verse* [Lat. versus].

fersc, *fresh*.

ferðloca (**ferhð-**), m., *heart, mind, spirit* [heart-locker].

fēt, see **fōt**.

fetor, f., *fetter* [**fōt**]; instr. pl., **feterum**.

feðer, f., *feather*; acc. pl., **feðra**.

fierd, f., *English army* [**faran**].

fīf, *five*.

fīftīene, *fifteen*.

fīftig, *fifty*; gen. sing., **fīftiges** (§ 91, Note 1); dat. pl., **fīftegum** (§ 91, Note 3).

findan (§ 110), *find*.

finger, m., *finger*.

Finnas, m. pl., *Fins*.

fiorm, see **feorm**.

fīras, m. pl., *men* [**feorh**]; gen. pl., **fīra**; dat. pl., **fīrum**.

firrest (**fierrest**), see **feor** (§ 96, (4)).

first, m., *time, period*.

fiscað (**fiscnað**), m., *fishing*.

fiscere, m., *fisherman*.

fiscnað, see **fiscað**.

flēon (§ 118, II.), *flee*.

flēotan (§ 109), *float*.

flęt, n., *floor of the hall*.

flōd, m., *flood, wave*.

folc, n., *folk, people*.

folc-cwēn, f., *folk-queen*.

folc-cyning, m., *folk-king*.

folcgefeoht, n., *folk-fight, battle, general engagement*.

fold-bold, n., *earth-building, hall*.

folde, f., *earth, land, country* [**feld**].

folm, f., *hand* [**fēlan** = *feel*].

fōn (§ 118), *seize, capture, take* [fang];

tō rīce fōn = *come to (ascend) the throne.*

for (§ 94, (1)), *for, on account of;*

for ðǣm (ðe), for ðon (ðe), *because;*

for ðon, for ðȳ, for ðǣm (for-ðām), *therefore.*

fōr, see **faran**.

forbærnan (§ 127), *burn thoroughly* [**for** is intensive, like Lat. per].

forgiefan (-gifan) (§ 115), *give, grant.*

forhergian (§ 130), *harry, lay waste.*

forhogdnis, f., *contempt.*

forht, *fearful, afraid.*

forhwæga, *about, at least.*

forlǣtan (§ 117), *abandon, leave.*

forlēt, forlēton, see **forlǣtan**.

forma, *first;*

forman sīðe, *the first time* (instr.).

forniman (§ 114), *take off, destroy.*

forspendan (§ 127), *spend, squander.*

forstondan (-standan) (§ 116), *understand.*

forswāpan (§ 117), *sweep away;* pret. 3d sing. indic., **forswēop**.

forswerian (§ 116), *forswear* (with dat.); past part., **forsworen**.

forð, *forth, forward.*

forðolian (§ 130), *miss, go without* (with dat.) [not to *thole* or experience].

forðweg, m., *way forth;*

in forðwege, *away.*

fōt (§ 68, (1)), m. *foot.*

Frǣna, m., *Frene.*

frætwe, f. pl., *fretted armor, jewels* [fret].

fram, see **frǫm**.

frēa, m., *lord, Lord.*

frēa-drihten, m., *lord, master.*

frēfran (§ 130), *console, cheer* [**frōfor**].

fremde, *strange, foreign;*

ðā **fremdan**, *the strangers.*

fremman (§ 125), *accomplish, perform, support* [to frame].

fremsumnes (-nis), f., *kindness, benefit.*

frēo (frīo), *free;* gen. pl., **frēora (frīora)**.

frēodōm, m., *freedom.*

frēolīc, *noble* [free-like].

frēomǣg, m., *free kinsman.*

frēond (§ 68, (3)), m., *friend.*

frēondlēas, *friendless.*

frēondlīce, *in a friendly manner.*

frēorig, *cold, chill* [**frēoran**].

frīora, see **frēo**.

frið, m., n., *peace, security* [bel-*fry*].

frōd, *old, sage, prudent.*

frōfor, f., *comfort, consolation, alleviation;*

fyrena frōfre 137, 7 = *as an alleviation of outrages* (dat.).

frǫm (fram) (§ 94, (1)), *from, by.*

frǫm, adv., *away, forth.*

fruma, m., *origin, beginning* [**frǫm**].

frumsceaft, f., *creation.*

fugela, see **fugol**.

fugelere, m., *fowler.*

fugol (fugel), m., *fowl, bird*; gen. pl., **fugela**.

ful, n., *cup, beaker*.

fūl, *foul*.

fūlian (§ 130), *grow foul, decompose*.

full (ful), adj., *full* (with gen.);

be **fullan**, *fully, perfectly*.

full (ful) adv., *fully, very*.

fultum, m., *help*.

furðor (furður), adv., *further*.

furðum, adv., *even*.

fylð, see **feallan**.

fyren (firen), f., *crime, violence, outrage*.

fyrhtu, f., *fright, terror*; dat. sing., **fyrhtu**.

fyrst, adj., superlative, *first, chief*.

fȳsan (§ 126), *make ready, prepare* [**fūs** = *ready*];

gūðe gefȳsed 137, 9 = *ready for battle*.

G.

gād, n., *lack*.

gǣst, see **gāst**.

gafol, n., *tax, tribute*.

galan (§ 116), *sing* [nightingale].

gālnes, f., *lust, impurity*.

gān (§ 134), *go*.

gār, m., *spear* [gore, gar-fish].

gār-wiga, m., *spear-warrior*.

gāst (gǣst), m., *spirit, ghost*.

gāstlīc (gǣstlīc), *ghastly, terrible*.

ge, *and*; see **ǣgðer**.

gē, *ye*; see **ðū**.

geador, *together*.

geǣmetigian (§ 130), *disengage from* (with acc. of person and gen. of thing) [empty].

geærnan (§ 127), *gain by running* [**iernan**].

gēap, *spacious*.

gēar, n., *year*; gen. pl., **gēara**, is used adverbially = *of yore, formerly*.

gēardæg, m., *day of yore*.

geare (**gearo**, **gearwe**), *readily, well, clearly* [yarely].

Gēat, m., *a Geat, the Geat* (i.e. Beowulf).

Gēatas, m. pl., *the Geats* (a people of South Sweden).

Gēat-mecgas, m. pl., *Geat men* (= the fourteen who accompanied Beowulf to Heorot).

gebēorscipe, m., *banquet, entertainment*.

gebētan (§ 126), *make amends for* [**bōt**].

gebīdan (§ 102), *wait, bide one's time* (intrans.); *endure, experience* (trans., with acc.).

gebind, n., *commingling*.

gebindan (§ 110), *bind*.

gebrēowan (§ 109), *brew*.

gebrowen, see **gebrēowan**.

gebūd, gebūn, see **būan** (§ 126, Note 2).

gebyrd, n., *rank, social distinction*.

gecēosan (§ 109), *choose, decide*.

gecnāwan (§ 117), *know, understand*.

gecoren, see **gecēosan**.

gecringan (§ 110), *fall, die* [cringe].

gedǣlan (§ 126), *deal out, give*;

dēaðe gedǣlde 152, 7 = *apportioned to death* (dat.), or, *tore* (?) *in death* (instr.).

gedafenian (§ 130), *become, befit, suit* (impersonal, usually with dat., but with acc. 112, 10).

gedīgan (§ 126), *endure, survive.*

gedōn (§ 135), *do, cause, effect.*

gedræg, n., *company.*

gedrēosan (§ 109), *fall, fail.*

gedriht (gedryht), n., *band, troop.*

gedrogen, see **drēogan**.

gedrync, n., *drinking.*

geęndian (§ 130), *end, finish.*

gefaran (§ 116), *go, die.*

gefēa, m., **joy**.

gefeaht, see **gefeohtan**.

gefeh, see **gefēon**.

gefēng, see **gefōn**.

gefeoht, n., *fight, battle.*

gefeohtan (§ 110), *fight.*

gefēon (§ 118, v.), *rejoice at* (with dat.); pret. 3d sing., **gefeah, gefeh**.

gefēra, m., *companion, comrade* [co-farer].

geflīeman (§ 126), *put to flight* [**flēon**].

gefohten, see **gefeohtan**.

gefōn (§ 118, vii.), *seize.*

gefōr, see **gefaran**.

gefrǣge, n., *hearsay, report;*

mīne gefrǣge (instr.) 141, 7 = *as I have heard say, according to my information.*

gefręmman (§ 125), *perform, accomplish, effect.*

gefultumian (§ 130), *help* [**fultum**].

gefylce, n., *troop, division* [**folc**]; dat. pl., **gefylcum, gefylcium**.

gefyllan (§ 127), *fill* (with gen.); past part. pl., f., **gefylda**.

geglęngan (§ 127), *adorn.*

gehātland, n., *promised land* [**gehātan** = *to promise*].

gehealdan (§ 117), *hold, maintain.*

gehīeran (gehȳran) (§ 126), *hear.*

gehīersumnes, f., *obedience.*

gehola, m., *protector* [**helan**].

gehwā (§ 77, Note), *each*;

on healfa gehwone 142, 7 (see Note 140, 15. Observe that the pron. may, as here, be masc. and the gen. fem.).

gehwæðer (§ 77, Note), *each, either, both.*

gehwylc (gehwilc) (§ 77, Note), *each* (with gen. pl. See Note 140, 15).

gehwyrfan (§ 127), *convert, change.*

gehȳdan (§ 126), *hide, conceal, consign.*

gehygd, f., n., *thought, purpose.*

gehȳran, see **gehīeran**.

gehȳrnes, f., *hearing*;

eal ðā hē in gehȳrnesse geleornian meahte 115, 14 = *all things that he could learn by hearing.*

gelǣdan (§ 126), *lead.*

gelǣred, part.-adj., *learned*; superlative, **gelǣredest**.

gelafian (§ 130), *lave.*

gelęnge, *along of, belonging to* (with dat.).

geleornian (-liornian) (§ 130), *learn.*

gelīce, *likewise; in like manner to* (with dat.).

gelīefan (gelȳfan) (§ 126), *believe*;

ðæt hēo on ǣnigne eorl gelȳfde 137, 6 = *that she believed in any earl.*

gelimpan (§ 110), *happen, be fulfilled.*

gelimplīc, *proper, fitting.*

gelȳfan, see **gelīefan**.

gelȳfed, *weak, infirm* [left (hand)].

gēmde, see **gīeman**.

gemet, n., *meter, measure, ability.*

gemētan (§ 126), *meet.*

gemǫn, see **gemunan**.

gemunan (§ 136), *remember;* indic. pres. 1st and 3d sing., **gemǫn**; pret. sing., **gemunde**.

gemynd, n., *memory, memorial;*

tō gemyndum 147, 5 = *as a memorial.*

gemyndgian (-mynian) (§ 130), *remember;*

mid hine gemyndgade 115, 15 = *he treasured in his memory;*

gemyne mǣrðo 138, 15 = *be mindful of glory* (imperative 2d sing.).

gemyndig, *mindful of* (with gen.).

genāp, see **genīpan**.

geneahhe, *enough, often;*

genehost, superlative, *very often.*

genip, n., *mist, darkness.*

genīpan (§ 102), *grow dark.*

genīwian (§ 130), *renew.*

genōh, *enough.*

genumen, see **niman**.

geoc, n., *yoke.*

gēocor, *dire, sad.*

geogoð, f., *youth, young people, young warriors.* (See **duguð**.)

geond (giond) (§ 94, (2)), *throughout* [yond].

geondhweorfan (§ 110), *pass over, traverse, recall;*

ðonne māga gemynd mōd geondhweorfeð 150, 15 = *then his mind recalls the memory of kinsmen.*

geondscēawian (§ 130), survey, review;

georne geondscēawað 150, 16 = *eagerly surveys them.*

geondðęnc(e)an (§ 128), *think over, consider.*

geong (§ 96, (2)), *young;*

giengest, (**gingest**), superlative, *youngest, latest, last.*

geong = **gǫng**, see **gǫngan** (imperative 2d sing.).

gēong (**gīong**), see **gǫngan** (pret. 3d sing.).

georn (**giorn**), *eager, desirous, zealous, sure* [yearn].

georne, *eagerly, certainly;*

wiste ðē geornor 143, 5 = *knew the more certainly.*

geornfulnes, f., *eagerness, zeal.*

geornlīce, *eagerly, attentively.*

geornor, see **georne**.

geręcednes, f., *narration* [**ręccan**].

gerisenlīc, *suitable, becoming.*

gerȳman (§ 126), *extend,* (trans.) [**rūm**].

gesæliglīc, *happy, blessed* [silly].

gesamnode, see **gesǫmnian**.

gesceaft, f., *creature, creation, destiny* [**scieppan**].

gesceap, n., *shape, creation, destiny* [**scieppan**].

gescieldan (§ 127), *shield, defend.*

gesealde, see **gesęllan**.

geseglian (§ 130), *sail.*

geselda, m., *comrade.*

gesęllan (§ 128), *give.*

gesēon (**gesīon**) (§ 118), *see,* **observe**; pres. indic. 3d sing., **gesihð**.

geset, n., *habitation, seat.*

gesęttan (§ 127), *set, place, establish.*

gesewen, see **sēon**, **gesēon** (past part.).

gesewenlīc, *seen, visible* [seen-like].

gesiglan (§ 127), *sail*.

gesihð, see **gesēon**.

gesittan (§ 115, Note 2), *sit* (trans., as *to sit a horse, to sit a boat*, etc.); *sit, sit down* (intrans.).

geslægen, see **slēan** (§ 118).

gesǫmnian (§ 130), *assemble, collect*.

gesǫmnung, f., *collection, assembly*.

gestāh, see **gestīgan**.

gestaðelian (§ 130), *establish, restore* [**standan**].

gesteal, n., *establishment, foundation* [stall].

gestīgan (§ 102), *ascend, go* [stile, stirrup, sty (= a *rising* on the eye)].

gestrangian (§ 130), *strengthen*.

gestrēon, n., *property*.

gestrȳnan (§ 126), *obtain, acquire* [**gestrēon**].

gesweorcan (§ 110), *grow dark, become sad*;

For ðon ic geðęncan ne mæg geond ðās woruld for hwan mōdsefa mīn ne gesweorce 151, 3-4 = *Therefore in this world I may not understand wherefore my mind does not grow "black as night."* (Brooke.)

geswīcan (§ 102), *cease, cease from* (with gen.).

getæl, n., *something told, narrative*.

getruma, m., *troop, division*.

geðanc, m., n., *thought*.

geðeah, see **geðicgan**.

geðęnc(e)an (§ 128), *think, remember, understand, consider*.

geðēodan (§ 126), *join*.

geðēode (-ðīode), n., *language, tribe*.

geðēodnis, f., *association*;

but in 112, 2 this word is used to render the Lat. *appetitus* = *desire*.

geðicg(e)an (§ 115, Note 2), *take, receive*; pret. indic. 3d sing., **geðeah**.

geðungen, part.-adj., *distinguished, excellent* [**ðēon**, *to thrive*].

geðyldig, *patient* [**ðolian**].

geweald (**gewald**), n., *control, possession, power* [wield].

geweorc, n., *work, labor*.

geweorðian (§ 130), *honor* [to attribute *worth* to].

gewīcian (§ 130), *dwell*.

gewin(n), n., *strife, struggle*.

gewindan (§ 110), *flee* [wend].

gewissian (§ 130), *guide, direct*.

gewītan (§ 102), *go, depart*.

geworht, see **gewyrcan**.

gewrit, n., *writing, Scripture*.

gewunian (§ 130), *be accustomed, be wont*.

gewyrc(e)an (§ 128), *work, create, make, produce*.

gid(d), n., *word, speech*.

giefan (§ 115), *give*.

giefstōl, m., *gift-stool, throne*.

giefu (**gifu**), f., *gift*.

gielp (**gilp**), m., n., *boast* [yelp].

gīeman (**gēman**) (§ 126), *endeavor, strive*.

gīet (**gīt**, **gȳt**), *yet, still*.

gif (**gyf**), *if* [not related to *give*].

gifeðe (**gyfeðe**), *given, granted*.

gilp, see **gielp**.

gilp-cwide, m., *boasting speech* [*yelp*-speech].

gingest, see **geong** (adj.).

giohðo (**gehðu**), f., *care, sorrow, grief*.

giū (**iū**), *formerly, of old*.

glæd (glǽd), *glad.*

glēaw, *wise, prudent.*

glīwstæf, m., *glee, joy*; instr. pl. (used adverbially), **glīwstafum** 150, 16 = *joyfully.*

God, m., *God.*

gōd (§ 96, (3)), *good*;

mid his gōdum 115, 12 = *with his possessions (goods).*

godcund, *divine* [God].

godcundlīce, *divinely.*

gold, n., *gold.*

gold-ǣht, f., *gold treasure.*

gold-fāh, *gold-adorned.*

gold-hroden, part.-adj., *gold-adorned.*

goldwine, m., *prince, giver of gold, lord* [gold-friend].

gomel (gomol), *old, old man.*

gǫngan (gangan) (§ 117), *go* [gang]; imperative 2d sing., **geong**; pret. sing., **gēong, gīong, gēng**; past part., **gegǫngen, gegangen**.

The most commonly used pret. is **ēode**, which belongs to **gān** (§ 134).

Gotland, n., *Jutland* (in *Ohthere's Second Voyage*), *Gothland* (in *Wulfstan's Voyage*).

gram, *grim, angry, fierce, the angry one.*

grāp, f., *grasp, clutch, claw.*

grētan (§ 126), *greet, attack, touch.*

grōwan (§ 117, (2)), *grow.*

gryre-lēoð, n., *terrible song* [grisly lay].

guma, m., *man, hero* [groom; see § 65, Note 1].

gūð, f., *war, battle.*

gūð-bill, n., *sword* [war-bill].

gūð-gewǣde, n., *armor* [war-weeds].

gūð-hrēð, f., *war-fame.*

gūð-wine, m., *sword* [war-friend].

gyddian (§ 130), *speak formally*, **chant** [giddy; the original meaning of *giddy* was *mirthful*, as when one sings].

gyf, see **gif**.

gyfeðe, see **gifeðe**.

gyldan (**gieldan**) (§ 110), *pay*; indic. 3d sing., **gylt**.

gylden, *golden* [**gold**].

H.

habban (§ 133), *have*.

hād, m., *order, rank, office, degree* [-hood, -head].

hæfta, m., *captive*.

hægel (**hagol**), m., *hail*; instr. sing., **hagle**.

hæglfaru, f., *hail-storm* [hail-faring].

hæle, see **hæleð**.

hǣl, f., *hail, health, good luck*.

hæleð (**hæle**), m., *hero, warrior*.

hǣt, see **hātan**.

hǣðen, *heathen*.

Hǣðum (**æt Hǣðum**), *Haddeby* (= *Schleswig*).

hāl, *hale, whole*.

hālettan (§ 127), *greet, salute* [to hail].

Halfdęne, *Halfdane* (proper name).

hālga, m., *saint*.

Hālgoland, *Halgoland* (in ancient Norway).

hālig, *holy*.

hālignes, f., *holiness*.

hām, m., *home*; dat. sing., **hāme**, **hām** (p. 104, Note); used adverbially in **hām ēode** 112, 18 = *went home*.

hand, see **hǫnd**.

hār, *hoary, gray.*

hāt, *hot.*

hātan (§ 117, Note 2), *call, name, command*; pret. sing., **heht, hēt**.

hātheort, *hot-hearted.*

hātte, see **hātan**.

hē, hēo, hit (§ 53), *he, she, it.*

hēafod, n., *head.*

hēah (§ 96, (2)), *high*; acc. sing, m., **hēanne**.

hēah-sęle, m., *high hall.*

hēahðungen, *highly prosperous, aristocratic* [**hēah** + past part. of **ðēon** (§ 118)].

healdan (§ 117), *hold, govern, possess*;
144, 9 = *hold up, sustain.*

healf, adj., *half.*

healf, f., *half, side, shore.*

heall, f., *hall.*

heals, m., *neck.*

hēan, *abject, miserable.*

hēanne, see **hēah**.

heard, *hard.*

heard-hicgende, *brave-minded* [hard-thinking].

hearm-scaða, m., *harmful foe* [harm-scather].

hearpe, f., *harp.*

heaðo-dēor, *battle-brave.*

heaðo-mǣre, *famous in battle.*

heaðo-wylm, m., *flame-surge, surging of fire* [battle-welling].

hēawan (§ 117), *hew, cut.*

hębban, hōf, hōfon, gehafen (§ 117), *heave, lift, raise.*

hęfig, *heavy, oppressive.*

heht, see **hātan**.

helan (§ 114), *conceal*.

hęll, f., *hell*.

helm, m., *helmet*.

Helmingas, m. pl., *Helmings* (Wealtheow, Hrothgar's queen, is a Helming).

help, f., *help*.

helpan (§ 110), *help* (with dat.).

heofon, m., *heaven*.

heofonlīc, *heavenly*.

heofonrīce, n., *kingdom of heaven*.

hēold, see **healdan**.

heolstor (-ster), n., *darkness, concealment, cover* [holster].

heora (hiera), see **hē**.

heord, f., **care, guardianship** [hoard].

heoro-drēorig, *bloody* [sword-dreary].

Heorot, *Heorot, Hart* (the famous hall which Hrothgar built).

heorte, f., *heart*.

hēr, *here, hither;*

in the *Chronicle* the meaning frequently is *at this date, in this year.* 99, 1.

hęre, m., *Danish army*.

hęrenis, f., *praise*.

hęrgian (§ 130), *raid, harry, ravage* [**hęre**].

hęrgung, f., *harrying, plundering*.

hęrian (hęrigean) (§ 125), *praise*.

hērsumedon, see **hīersumian**.

hēt, see **hātan**.

hider (hieder), *hither*.

hiera, see **hē**.

hīeran (hȳran) (§ 126), *hear, belong*.

- 193 -

hierde, m., *shepherd, instigator* [keeper of a *herd*].

hierdebōc, f., *pastoral treatise* [shepherd-book, a translation of Lat. *Cura Pastoralis*].

hīerra, see **hēah**.

hīersumian (**hȳr-, hēr-**) (§ 130), *obey* (with dat.).

hige (**hyge**), m., *mind, heart.*

hige-ðihtig, *bold-hearted.*

hild, f., *battle.*

hilde-dēor, *battle-brave.*

hilde-mecg, m., *warrior.*

hilde-sæd, *battle-sated.*

hin-fūs, *eager to be gone* [hence-ready].

hira, see **hē**.

hlǣw (**hlāw**), m., *mound, burial mound* [Lud*low* and other place-names, *low* meaning *hill*].

hlāford, m., *lord, master* [loaf-ward?].

hleahtor, m., *laughter.*

hlēo, m., *refuge, protector* [lee].

hlīfian (§ 130), *rise, tower.*

hlyn, m., *din, noise.*

hlynsian (§ 130), *resound.*

hof, n., *court, abode.*

hogode, see **hycgan**.

holm, m., *sea, ocean.*

hǫnd (**hand**), f., *hand;*

on gehwæðre hǫnd, *on both sides.*

hord, m., n., *hoard, treasure.*

hordcofa, m., *breast, heart* [hoard-chamber]

hors, n., *horse.*

horshwæl, m., *walrus.*

hrædwyrde, *hasty of speech* [**hræd** = *quick*].

hrægel, n., *garment*; dat. sing., **hrægle**.

hrān, m., *reindeer*.

hraðe, *quickly, soon* [*rath*-er].

hrēo (**hrēoh**), *rough, cruel, sad*.

hrēosan (§ 109), *fall*.

hrēran (§ 126), *stir*.

hreðer, m., n., *breast, purpose*; dat. sing., **hreðre**.

hrīm, m., *rime, hoarfrost*.

hrīmceald, *rime-cold*.

hring, m., *ring, ring-mail*.

hrīð, f. (?), *snow-storm*.

hrōf, m., *roof*.

Hrones næss, literally *Whale's Ness, whale's promontory*; see **næss**.

hrūse, f., *earth* [**hrēosan**: deposit].

hryre, m., *fall, death* [**hrēosan**].

hrȳðer, n., *cattle* [rinder-pest].

hryðig, *ruined* (?), *storm-beaten*; nom. pl. m., **hryðge**.

hū, *how*.

Humbre, f., *river Humber*.

hund, *hundred*.

hunig, n., *honey*.

hunta, m., *hunter*.

huntoð (**-tað**), m., *hunting*.

hūru, adv., *about*.

hūs, n., *house*.

hwā, hwæt (§ 74), *who? what?* **swā hwæt swā** (§ 77, Note), *whatsoever*;

indefinite, *any one, anything*;

for hwan (instr.), *wherefore*.

hwæl, m., *whale*.

hwælhunta, m., *whale-hunter*.

hwælhuntað, m., *whale-fishing*.

hwǣr, *where?* **hwǣr ... swā**, *wheresoever*;

wel hwǣr, *nearly everywhere*.

hwæthwugu, *something*.

hwæðer, *whether, which of two?*

hwæðre, *however, nevertheless*.

hwēne, see **hwōn**.

hweorfan (§ 110), *turn, go*.

hwider, *whither*.

hwīl, f., *while, time*;

ealle ðā hwīle ðe, *all the while that*;

hwīlum (instr. pl.), *sometimes*.

hwilc (hwylc, hwelc) (§ 74, Note 1), *which? what?*

hwōn, n., *a trifle*;

hwēne (instr. sing.), *somewhat, a little*.

hwǫnan, *when*.

hȳ, see **hīe**.

hycgan (§ 132), *think, resolve*; pret. 3d sing., **hogode**.

hȳd, f., *hide, skin*.

hyge, see **hige**.

hyra (hiera), see **hē**.

hȳran, see **hīeran**.

hyrde, see **hierde**.

hys (his), see **hē**.

hyt (hit), see **hē**.

I.

ic (§ 72), *I.*

īdel, *idle, useless, desolate.*

ides, f., *woman, lady.*

ieldra, adj., see **eald**.

ieldra, m., *an elder, parent, ancestor.*

iernan (yrnan) (§ 112), *run.*

īglǫnd (īgland), n., *island.*

ilca (ylca), *the same* [of that ilk].

Ilfing, *the Elbing.*

in, *in, into* (with dat. and acc.);

in on, *in on, to, toward.*

inbryrdnis (-nes), f., *inspiration, ardor.*

indryhten, *very noble.*

ingǫng, m., *entrance.*

innan, adv., *within, inside*;

on innan, *within.*

innanbordes, adv.-gen., *within borders, at home.*

inne, adv., *within, inside.*

intinga, m., *cause, sake.*

inweardlīce, *inwardly, fervently.*

inwid-sorg (inwit-sorh), f., *sorrow caused by an enemy.*

inwit-ðanc, m., *hostile intent.*

Īraland, n., *Ireland* (but in *Ohthere's Second Voyage, Iceland* is probably meant).

īren, n., *iron, sword*; gen. pl., **īrenna, īrena**.

īren-bend, m., f., *iron-band.*

īu, see **gīu**.

K.

kynerīce, see **cynerīce**.

kyning, see **cyning**.

kyrtel, m., *kirtle, coat.*

L.

Lǣden, *Latin.*

Lǣdengeðēode (-ðīode), n., *Latin language.*

Lǣdenware (§ 47), m. pl., *Latin people, Romans.*

lǣfan (§ 126), *leave.*

lǣge, see **licgan**.

Lǣland, n., *Laaland* (in Denmark).

lǣn, n., *loan*;

tō lǣne 121, 2 = *as a loan.*

lǣne, adj., *as a loan, transitory, perishable.*

lǣran (§ 126), *teach, advise, exhort* [**lār**].

lǣssa, lǣsta, see **lȳtel**.

lǣstan (§ 127), *last, hold out* (intrans.); *perform, achieve* (trans.).

lǣtan (§ 117), *let, leave.*

lāf, f., *something left, remnant, heirloom* (often a *sword*);

tō lāfe, *as a remnant, remaining.*

lagulād, f., *sea* [lake-way, **lād** = *leading, direction, way*].

land, see **lǫnd**.

lang, see **lǫng**.

Langaland, n., *Langeland* (in Denmark).

lār, f., *lore, teaching.*

lārcwide, m., *precept, instruction,* [**cwide** < **cweðan**].

lārēow, m., *teacher* [**lār** + **ðēow**].

lāst, m., *track, footprint* [shoemaker's last];

on lāst(e), *in the track of, behind* (with dat.).

lāð, *loathsome, hateful.*

lēas, *loose, free from, bereft of* (with gen.).

lēasung, f., *leasing, deception, falsehood.*

lęcgan (§ 125, Note), *lay.*

lēfdon, see **līefan**.

leger, n., *lying in, illness* [**licgan**].

lęng, see **lǫnge**.

lęngra, see **lǫng**.

lēod, m., *prince, chief.*

lēod, f., *people, nation* (the plural has the same meaning).

lēod-scipe, m., *nation* [people-ship].

lēof, *dear* [lief].

leoht, adj., *light.*

lēoht, n., *light, brightness.*

leornere, m., *learner, disciple.*

leornian (§ 130), *learn.*

leornung (liornung), f., *learning.*

lēoð, n., *song* [lay?].

lēoðcræft, m., *poetic skill* [lay-craft].

lēoðsǫng, n., *song, poem.*

lēt, see **lǣtan**.

libban (§ 133), *live;* pres. part., **lifigende**, *living, alive.*

līc, n., *body, corpse* [lich-gate, Lichfield].

licgan (§ 115, Note 2), *lie, extend, flow, lie dead;* 3d sing. indic. pres., **ligeð, līð**.

līchama (-hǫma), m., *body* [body-covering].

līcian (§ 130), *please* (with dat.) [like].

līc-sār, n., *body-sore, wound in the body.*

līefan (lēfan) (§ 126), *permit, allow* (with dat.) [grant *leave* to].

līf, n., *life.*

līf-dagas, m. pl., *life-days.*

lifigende, see **libban**.

līg, m., *flame, fire.*

ligeð, see **licgan**.

lim, n., *limb.*

list, f., *cunning*; dat. pl., **listum**, is used adverbially = *cunningly.*

līð, see **licgan**.

lof, m., *praise, glory.*

lǫnd (land), n., *land, country.*

lǫng (lang) (§ 96, (2)), *long.*

lǫnge (lange) (§ 97, (2)), *long*;

lǫnge on dæg, *late in the day.*

lufan, see **lufu**.

lufian (lufigean) (§ 131), *love.*

luflīce, *lovingly.*

lufu, f., *love*; dat. sing. (weak), **lufan**.

lungre, *quickly.*

lust, m., *joy* [lust];

on lust, *joyfully.*

lȳt, indeclinable, *little, few* (with partitive gen.).

lȳtel (lītel) (§ 96, (2)), *little, small.*

M.

mā, see **micle** (§ 97, (2)).

mæg, see **magan**.

mǣg, m., *kinsman*; nom. pl., **māgas** (§ 27, (2)).

mægen n., *strength, power* [might and *main*].

mægen-ęllen, n., *main strength, mighty courage*.

mǣgð, f., *tribe*.

mægðhād, m., *maidenhood, virginity*.

mǣl-gesceaft, f., *appointed time* [**mǣl** = *meal, time*].

mǣran (§ 126), *make famous, honor*.

mǣre, *famous, glorious, notorious*.

mǣrðo (**mǣrðo, mǣrð**), f., *glory, fame*.

mæssepr̄eost, m., *mass-priest*.

mǣst, see **micel**.

magan (§ 137), *be able, may*.

māgas, see **mǣg**.

magu (**mago**), m., *son, man*.

maguðegn, m., *vassal, retainer*.

man(n), see **mǫn(n)**.

mancus, m., *mancus, half-crown*; gen. pl., **mancessa**.

māndǣd, f., *evil deed*.

manig, see **mǫnig**.

manigfeald, see **mǫnigfeald**.

māra, see **micel**.

maðelian (§ 130), *harangue, speak*.

māðum (**māððum**), m., *gift, treasure, jewel*; gen. pl., **māðma**.

māððumgyfa, m., *treasure-giver, lord*.

māððum-wela, m., *wealth of treasure*.

mē, see **ic**.

meaht, f., *might, power*.

meahte, see **magan**.

mearc, f., *boundary, limit* [mark, march].

mearg (mearh), m., *horse*; nom. pl., **mēaras**.

mearð, m., *marten*.

mec, see **ic**.

medmicel, *moderately large, short, brief.*

medu (medo), m., *mead.*

medu-benc, f., *mead-bench.*

medu-ful, n., *mead-cup.*

medu-heall, f., *mead-hall.*

men, see **mọn(n)**.

mengan (§ 127), *mingle, mix.*

menigu (menigeo), f., *multitude* [many].

menniscnes, f., *humanity, incarnation* [man].

meolc, f., *milk.*

Mēore, *Möre* (in Sweden).

mere, m., *lake, mere, sea* [mermaid].

Meretūn, m., *Merton* (in Surrey).

mētan (§ 126), *meet, find.*

Metod (Meotod, Metud), m., *Creator, God.*

metod-sceaft, f., *appointed doom, eternity.*

micel (§ 96, (3)), *great, mighty, strong, large* [mickle];

māra, *more, stronger, larger.*

micle (micele), *greatly, much.*

miclum, (§ 93, (4)), *greatly.*

mid, *with, amid, among* (with dat. and acc.).

middangeard, m., *earth, world* [middle-yard].

middeweard, *midward, toward the middle.*

Mierce, m. pl., *Mercians.*

mihte, see *magan.*

mīl, f., *mile* [Lat. mille].

mildheortnes, f., *mild-heartedness, mercy.*

milts, f., *mildness, mercy.*

mīn (§ 76), *my, mine.*

mislīc, *various.*

missenlīc, *various.*

mōd, n., *mood, mind, courage.*

mōdcearig, *sorrowful of mind.*

mōdega, mōdga, see **mōdig**.

mōdgeðanc, m., *purpose of mind.*

mōdig, *moody, brave, proud.*

mōdor, f., *mother.*

mōdsefa, m., *mind, heart.*

mǫn(n) (**man, mann**) (§ 68; § 70, Note), m., *man, one, person, they.*

mōna, m., *moon.*

mōnað (§ 68, (1), Note), m., *month* [**mōna**]; dat. sing., **mōnðe**.

mǫn(n)cynn, n., *mankind.*

mǫndryhten, m., *liege lord.*

mǫnian (**manian**) (§ 130), *admonish.*

mǫnig (**manig, mǫneg, mænig**), *many.*

mǫnigfeald (**manig-**), *manifold, various.*

mōnðe, see **mōnað**.

mōr, m., *moor.*

morgen, m., *morning*; dat. sing., **morgen(n)e**.

morðor-bealu (**-bealo**), n., *murder* [murder-bale]; see **ðurfan**.

mōste, see **mōtan**.

mōtan (§ 137), *may, be permitted, must.*

mund-gripe, m., *hand-grip.*

munuc, m., *monk* [Lat. monachus].

- 203 -

munuchād, m., *monkhood, monastic rank.*

mūð, m., *mouth.*

myntan (§ 127), *be minded, intend*; pret. indic. 3d sing., **mynte.**

mynster, n., *monastery* [Lat. monasterium]; dat. sing., **mynstre.**

mȳre, f., *mare* [**mearh**].

myrð, f., *joy, mirth*;

mōdes myrðe 142, 17 = *with joy of heart.*

N.

nā (nō), *not* [**ne ā** = *n-ever*];

nā ne, *not, not at all.*

nabban (p. 32, Note), *not to have.*

nǣdre, f., *serpent, adder.*

næfde, see **nabban.**

nǣfre, *never.*

nǣnig (§ 77), *no one, no, none.*

nǣre, nǣren, nǣron, see § 40, Note 2.

næs = **ne wæs**, see § 40, Note 2.

næss, m., *ness, headland.*

nāht, see **nōht.**

nālæs (nāles), *not at all* [**nā ealles**].

nam, see **niman.**

nama, see **nǫma.**

nāmon, see **niman.**

nān, *not one, no, none* [**ne ān**].

nānwuht, n., *nothing* [no whit].

ne, *not.*

nē, *nor*;

nē ... nē, *neither ... nor.*

nēah (§ 96, (4)), *near.*

nēah, adv., *nigh, near, nearly, almost;* comparative, **nēar**, *nearer.*

neaht, see **niht**.

nēalēcan (-lǣcan) (§ 126), *draw near to, approach* (with dat.).

nēar, see **nēah**, adv.

nēat, n., *neat, cattle.*

nęmnan (§ 127), *name.*

nemðe, (nymðe), *except, unless.*

nęrian (§ 125), *save, preserve.*

nēten, see **nīeten**.

nīedbeðearf, *needful, necessary.*

nīehst, see **nēah** (§ 96, (4)).

nīeten (nēten), n., *neat, beast, cattle.*

nigontīene, *nineteen.*

niht (neaht) (§ 68, (1), Note), *night.*

nihthelm, m., *night-helm, shade of night.*

nihtscūa, m., *shadow of night.*

niht-weorc, n., *night-work.*

niman (§ 114), *take, gain* [nimble, numb].

nīpan (§ 102), *grow dark, darken.*

nis, see § 40, Note 2.

nīð, m., *malice, violence.*

nīwe, *new, novel, startling.*

nō, see **nā**.

nōht (nāht, nā-wiht), n., *not a whit, naught, nothing; not, not at all.*

nōhwæðer (nāhwæðer), *neither;*

nōhwæðer nē ... ne ... nē ... ne 118, 8 = *neither ... nor.*

nolde, noldon = ne wolde, ne woldon, see **willan**.

nǫma (nama), m., *name.*

norð (§ 97, (1)), *north, in the north, northwards.*

norðan (§ 93, (5)), *from the north;*

be norðan, see § 94, (4).

Norð-Dęne, m. pl., *North-Danes.*

norðeweard, *northward.*

Norðhymbre, m. pl., *Northumbrians.*

Norðmanna, see **Norðmǫn.**

Norðmęn, see **Norðmǫn.**

norðmest, see **norð.**

Norðmǫn (-man) (§ 68, (1)), *Norwegian.*

norðor, see **norð.**

norðryhte, *northward.*

norðweard, *northward.*

Norðweg, *Norway.*

nose, f., *cape, naze* [ness, nose].

notu, f., *office, employment.*

nū, *now; now that, seeing that;*

nū ðā 138, 13 = *now then.*

nȳhst (nīehst), see **nēah.**

nymðe, see **nemðe.**

nysse, see **nytan.**

nyste, see **nytan.**

nyt(t), *useful, profitable.*

nytan (nitan < ne witan, § 136), *not to know;*
3d sing. pret., **nysse, nyste.**

O.

of (§ 94, (1)), *of, from, concerning.*

ofer (§ 94, (2)), *over, across, after, in spite of* (see 144, 14);

ofer eorðan 142, 9 = *on earth.*

ofer, adv., *over, across.*

oferfēran (§ 126), *go over, traverse.*

oferfrēosan (§ 109), *freeze over.*

oferfroren, see **oferfrēosan**.

ofgiefan (§ 115), *give up, relinquish.*

ofost, f., *haste.*

ofslægen, see **ofslēan**.

ofslēan (§ 118), *slay off, slay.*

ofslōge, see **ofslēan**.

oft, *oft, often*; superlative, **oftost**.

on (§ 94, (3)), *in, into, on, against, to, among, during;*

on fīf oððe syx 109, 6 = *into five or six parts;*

on weg 140, 10 = *away;*

on innan 144, 5 = *within;*

on unriht 145, 15 = *falsely.*

onbærnan (§ 126), *kindle, inspire.*

oncȳðð, f., *distress, suffering.*

ǫnd (and), *and.*

ǫndsaca, m., *adversary.*

ǫndswarian (§ 130), *answer.*

ǫndweard, adj., *present.*

onfēng, see **onfōn**.

onfeohtan (§ 110), *fight.*

onfindan (§ 110), *find out, discover;* pret. indic. 3d sing., **onfunde**.

onfōn (§ 118), *receive, seize violently.*

onfunde, see **onfindan**.

ongēan, prep., *against, towards* (with dat. and acc.).

ongēan, adv., *just across, opposite.*

Ǫngelcynn (Angel-), n., *Angle kin, English people, England.*

Ǫngelðēod (Angel-), f., *the English people or nation.*

ongemang (-mǫng), *among* (with dat.).

ongietan (-gitan) (§ 115), *perceive, see, understand.*

onginnan (§ 110), *begin, attempt.*

onlūtan (§ 109), *bow, incline* (intrans.) [lout = a stooper].

onrīdan (§ 102), *ride against, make a raid on.*

onsęndan (§ 127), *send.*

onslǣpan (onslēpan) (§ 126), *fall asleep, sleep.*

onspǫnnan (§ 117), *loosen* [unspan]; pret. 3d sing. indic., **onspēon**.

onspringan (§ 110), *spring apart, unspring.*

onstāl, m., *institution, supply.*

onstęllan (§ 128), *establish*; pret. 3d sing. indic., **onstealde**.

onwæcnan (§ 127), *awake* (intrans.).

onweald (-wald), m., *power, authority* [wield].

onwęndan (§ 127), *change, overturn* [to wind].

ōr, n., *beginning.*

oð (§ 94, (2)), *until, as far as* (of time and place);

oð ðæt, oð ðe, *until.*

oðberan (§ 114), *bear away.*

ōðer, *other, second;*

ōðer ... ōðer, *the one ... the other.*

oðfæstan (§ 127), *set to* (a task).

oðfeallan (§ 117) *fall off, decline.*

oððe, *or;*

oððe ... oððe, *either ... or.*

P.

plega, m., *play, festivity.*

port, m., *port* [Lat. portus].

R.

rād, f., *raid.*

rǣcan (§ 126), *reach*; pret. 3d sing., **rǣhte**.

ræst, see **ręst**.

Rēadingas, m. pl., *Reading* (in Berkshire).

ręccan (§ 128), *narrate, tell*; pret. pl. indic., **ręhton, reahton**.

ręccelēas, *reckless, careless.*

ręced, n., *house, hall.*

regnian (rēnian) (§ 130), *adorn, prepare*; past part., **geregnad**.

regollīc (-lec), *according to rule, regular.*

rēn-weard, m., *mighty warden, guard, champion.*

ręst (ræst), f., *rest, resting-place, bed.*

rēðe, *fierce, furious.*

rīce, *rich, powerful, aristocratic.*

rīce, n., *realm, kingdom* [bishopric].

rīcsian (§ 130), *rule.*

rīdan (§ 102), *ride.*

rīman (§ 126), *count* [rime].

rinc, m., *man, warrior.*

rōd, f., *rood, cross*;

rōde tācen, *sign of the cross.*

Rōmware, m. pl., *Romans.*

rǫnd (rand), m., *shield.*

rūn, f., *rune, secret meditation* [to round = to whisper].

rycene (ricene), *quickly, rashly.*

ryhtnorðanwind, m., *straight north-wind.*

S.

sǣ, f., *sea.*

sǣ-bāt, m., *sea-boat.*

sǣd, n., *seed.*

sǣde, see **sęcgan**.

sǣl, m., f., *time, happiness* [sil-ly];

on sǣlum 137, 22 = *joyous, merry.*

sǣlan (§ 126), *bind.*

sǣ-līðend (§ 68, (3)), m., *seafarer* (nom. and acc. pl. same as nom. and acc. sing.).

sam ... sam, *whether ... or.*

same, *similarly*;

swā same, *just the same, in like manner.*

samod, see **sǫmod**.

sanct, m., f., *saint* [Lat. sanctus]; gen. sing., **sanctæ**, f., **sancti**, m.

sang, see **sǫng**.

sār, f., n., *sore, pain, wound.*

sār, adj., *sore, grievous.*

sāre, *sorely.*

sāwan (§ 117,) *sow.*

sāwol, f., *soul*; oblique cases, sing., **sāwle** (§ 39, Note).

scacan (sceacan) (§ 116), *shake, go, depart*; past part., **scacen, sceacen**.

scadu-helm, m., *cover of night, shadow-covering* [shadow-helm];

scadu-helma gesceapu, see Note on 138, 2-6.

sceal, see **sculan**.

scēap, n., *sheep.*

scēat, m., *corner, region, quarter* [sheet];

eorðan scēatta 139, 14 = *in the regions of earth* (gen. used as locative).

scēawi(g)an (§ 130), *view, see* [shew].

scēawung, f., *seeing*.

sceolde, see **sculan**.

scēop (**scōp**), see **scieppan**.

scēowyrhta, m., *shoe-maker*.

scęððan (§ 116), *injure, scathe* (with dat.).

scieppan (§ 116), *create*.

Scieppend, m., *Creator*.

scīnan (§ 102), *shine*.

scip (**scyp**), n., *ship*.

scipen, n., *stall*.

sciprāp, m., *ship-rope, cable*.

scīr, f., *shire, district*.

Sciringeshēal, m., *Sciringesheal* (in Norway).

scolde, see **sculan**.

scǫmu, f., *shame, dishonor*.

Scōnēg, f., *Skaane* (southern district of the Scandinavian peninsula).

scopgereord, n., *poetic language*.

scrīðan (§ 102), *stride, stalk*.

sculan (§ 136; § 137, Note 2), *shall, have to, ought*.

Scyldingas, m. pl., *Scyldings, Danes*.

scyp, see **scip**.

Scyppend, see **Scieppend**.

sē, sēo, ðæt (§ 28; § 28, Note 3), *the; that; he, she, it; who, which, that;*

ðæs, *from then, afterwards, therefore;*

ðæs ðe (p. 110, l. 2), *with what;*

ðȳ ... ðæt (p. 110, ll. 7-8), *for this reason ... because;*

tō ðǣm ... swā, *to such an extent ... as;*

ðy (ðē), *the* (adverbial, with comparatives);

ðȳ ... ðȳ, *the ... the.*

seah, see **sēon**.

sealde, see **sęllan**.

searo-gimm, m., *artistic gem, jewel.*

searo-nīð, m., *cunning hatred, plot.*

searo-ðǫnc, m., *cunning thought, device.*

Seaxe, m. pl., *Saxons, Saxony.*

sēc(e)an (§ 128), *to seek, visit, meet.*

sęcg, m., *man, warrior.*

sęcgan (§ 132), *say, tell.*

sefa, m., *mind, spirit.*

sēfte, *more easily* (comparative of **sōfte**).

segel, m., n., *sail;* dat. sing. = **segle**.

seglian (§ 130), *sail.*

sęle, m., *hall.*

sęledrēam, m., *hall joy, festivity.*

sęle-ful, n., *hall cup.*

sęlesęcg, m., *hall warrior, retainer.*

sēlest, *best* (no positive).

self (**sylf**), *self, himself* (declined as strong or weak adjective).

sęllan (**syllan**) (§ 128), *give* [sell, han(d)sel].

sęmninga, *forthwith, straightway.*

sęndan (§ 127), *send.*

sēo, see **sē**.

sēoc, *sick.*

seofon (**syfan**), *seven.*

seolh, m., *seal;* gen. sing. = **sēoles** (§ 27, (3)).

sēon (§ 118), *see, look.*

- 212 -

seonu, f., *sinew*; nom. pl., **seonowe**.

sess, m., *seat*.

sibb, f., *friendship, peace* [gos*sip*].

sidu (**siodu**), m., *custom, morality, good conduct*.

sīe, see **bēon**.

siex, *six*;

syxa (**siexa**) **sum**, see **sum**.

siextig, *sixty*.

sige, m., *victory*.

sige-folc, n., *victorious people*.

sige-lēas, *victory-less, of defeat*.

sige-rōf, **victory-famed**, *victorious*.

sige-wǣpen, n., *victory-weapon*.

siglan (§ 127), *sail*.

Sillende, *Zealand*.

sinc, n., *treasure, prize*.

sinc-fǣt, n., see 137, 1 [treasure-vat].

sinc-ðęgu, f., *receiving of treasure* [**ðicgan**].

sind, sint, sindon, see **bēon**.

singan (§ 110), *sing*.

sittan (§ 115, Note 2), *sit, take position*.

sīð, m., *journey, time*;

forman sīðe 139, 2 = *the first time* (instr. sing.).

sīðian (§ 130), *journey*.

siððan, *after that, afterwards, after*.

slǣp, m., *sleep*.

slǣpan (§ 117), *sleep*.

slēan (§ 118), *slay* [slow-worm].

slītan (§ 102), *slit, tear to pieces*.

slīðen, *savage, perilous.*

smæl, *narrow.*

smalost, see **smæl**.

snāw, m., *snow.*

snot(t)or, *wise, prudent.*

sōhte, see **sēcan**.

sǫmod (samod), *together.*

sōna, *soon.*

sǫng, m., n., *song, poem.*

sǫngcræft, m., *art of song and poetry.*

sorg (sorh), f., *sorrow.*

sōð, *true.*

sōð, n., *truth;*

tō sōðe, *for a truth, truly, verily.*

sōð-fæst, *truthful, just.*

sōðlīce, *truly.*

spēd, f., *possessions, success, riches* [speed].

spēdig, *rich, prosperous.*

spell, n., *story, tale* [gospel].

spēow, see **spōwan**.

spere, n., *spear.*

spor, n., *track, footprint.*

spōwan (§ 117), *succeed* (impersonal with dat.).

sprǣc, f., *speech, language.*

sprecan (§ 115), *speak.*

spyrian (spyrigean) (§ 130), *follow* (intrans.) [**spor**].

stæf, *staff, rod*; pl. = *literature, learning.*

stælhrān, m., *decoy-reindeer.*

stælwierðe, *serviceable* (see p. 56, Note 2).

- 214 -

stǣr, n., *story, narrative* [Lat. historia].

stæð, n., *shore*.

stān, m., *stone, rock*.

stān-boga, m., *stone-arch* [stone-bow].

standan, see **stǫndan**.

stānhlið (-hleoð), n., *stone-cliff*.

stapol, m., *column* [staple].

starian (§ 125), *stare, gaze*.

stęde, m., *place*.

stelan (§ 114), *steal*.

stęnt, see **stǫndan**.

stēorbord, n., *starboard, right side of a ship*.

stęppan (§ 116), *step, advance*; pret. indic. 3d sing., **stōp**.

stilnes, f., *stillness, quiet*.

stǫndan (§ 116), *stand*.

stōp, see **stęppan**.

storm, m., *storm*.

stōw, f., *place* [stow, and in names of places].

strang, see **strǫng**.

stręngest, see **strǫng**.

strǫng (§ 96, (2)), *strong*.

styccemǣlum, *here and there*.

sum (§ 91, Note 2), *some, certain, a certain one*;

hē syxa sum 104, 25 = *he with five others*.

sumera, see **sumor**.

sumor, m., *summer*; dat. sing. = **sumera**.

sumorlida, m., *summer-army*.

sundor, *apart*.

sunne, f., *sun.*

sunu, m., *son.*

sūð, *south, southwards.*

sūðan (§ 93, (5)), *from the south;*

be sūðan, *south of* (§ 94, (4)).

sūðeweard, *southward.*

sūðryhte, *southward.*

swā (swǣ), *so, as, how, as if;*

swā swā, *just as, as far as;*

swā ... swā, *the ... the, as ... as;*

swā hwæt swā, *whatsoever* (§ 77, Note).

swǣs, *beloved, own.*

swæð, n., *track, footprint* [swath].

swaðul, m.? n.?, *smoke.*

swealh, see **swelgan**.

swefan (§ 115), *sleep, sleep the sleep of death.*

swefn, n., *sleep, dream.*

swēg, m., *sound, noise.*

swegle, *bright, clear.*

swēlan (§ 126), *burn* [sweal].

swelgan (§ 110), *swallow;* pret. indic. 3d sing., **swealh**; subj., **swulge**.

swellan (§ 110), *swell.*

Swēoland, n., *Sweden.*

Swēom, m., dat. pl., *the Swedes.*

sweotol, *clear.*

sweotole, *clearly.*

swęrian (§ 116), *swear.*

swēte, *sweet.*

swētnes (**-nis**), f., *sweetness*.

swift (**swyft**), *swift*.

swilc (**swylc**) (§ 77), *such*.

swilce, *in such manner, as, likewise; as if, as though* (with subj.).

swimman (§ 110), *swim*.

swīn (**swȳn**), n., *swine, hog*.

swīnsung, f., *melody, harmony*.

swīðe (**swȳðe**), *very, exceedingly, greatly*.

swīðost, *chiefly, almost*.

swōr, see **swęrian**.

swulge, see **swelgan**.

swuster (§ 68, (2)), f., *sister*.

swylce (**swelce**), see **swilce**.

swȳn, see **swīn**.

swynsian (§ 130), *resound*.

swȳðe, see **swīðe**.

swȳð-ferhð, *strong-souled*.

sylf, see **self**.

syll, f., *sill, floor*.

syllan, see **sęllan**.

symbel, n., *feast, banquet*.

symle, *always*.

synd, see **bēon**.

syn-dolh, n., *ceaseless wound, incurable wound*.

syndriglīce, *specially*.

synn, f., *sin*.

syn-scaða, m., *ceaseless scather, perpetual foe*.

syn-snǣd, f., *huge bit* [ceaseless bit].

syððan, see **siððan**.

syx, see **siex**.

syxtig, see **siextig**.

T.

tācen, n., *sign, token*; dat. sing., **tācne** (§ 33, Note).

tǣcan (§ 128), *teach*.

tam, *tame*.

tela, *properly, well* [til].

tęllan (§ 128), *count, deem* [tell]; pret. 3d sing., **tealde**.

Tęmes, f., *the Thames*.

tēon, *arrange, create*; pret. sing., **tēode**.

Terfinna, m., gen. pl., *the Terfins*.

tēð, see **tōð**.

tīd, f., *tide, time, hour*.

tīen (**tȳn**), *ten*.

til(l), *good*.

tīma, m., *time*.

tintreglīc, *full of torment*.

tō (§ 94, (1)), *to, for, according to, as*;

tō hrōfe 114, 2 = *for (as) a roof* [cf. Biblical *to wife*, modern *to boot*].

tō, adv., *too*.

tōbrecan (p. 81, Note 2), *break to pieces, knock about*.

tōdǣlan (§ 126), *divide*.

tōemnes (**tō emnes**) (§ 94, (4)), *along, alongside*.

tōforan (§ 94, (1)), *before*.

tōgeðēodan (§ 126), *join*.

tōhopa, m., *hope*.

tōlicgan (§ 115, Note 2), *separate, lie between*;
3d sing, indic. = **tōlīð**.

tōlīð, see tōlicgan.

tolūcan (§ 109, Note 1), *destroy* [the prefix tō reverses the meaning of lūcan, *to lock*].

torn, m., *anger, insult.*

tōð (§ 68, (1)), m., *tooth.*

tōweard (§ 94, (1)), *toward.*

tōweard, adj., *approaching, future.*

trēow, f., *pledge, troth.*

trēownes, f., *trust.*

Trūsō, *Drausen* (a city on the Drausensea).

tūn, m., *town, village.*

tunge, f., *tongue.*

tūngerēfa, m., *bailiff* [town-reeve; so sheriff = shire-reeve].

tungol, n., *star.*

twā, see twēgen.

twēgen, (§ 89), *two, twain.*

twēntig, *twenty.*

tȳn, see tīen.

Ð.

ðā, *then, when;*

ðā ... ðā, *when ... then;*

ðā ðā, *then when = when.*

ðā, see sē.

ðǣr, *there, where;*

ðǣr ðǣr, *there where = where;*

ðǣr ... swā 142, 4 = *wheresoever,* 145, 6 = *if so be that.*

ðæs, *afterwards, therefore, thus, because;* see sē.

ðæt (ðætte = ðæt ðe), *that, so that.*

- 219 -

ðafian (§ 130), *consent to.*

ðanc, see **ðǫnc**.

ðancian (ðǫncian) (§ 130), *thank.*

ðanon, see **ðǫnan**.

ðās, see **ðēs**.

ðē, see **sē** (instr. sing.) and **ðū**.

ðe (§ 75), *who, whom, which, that.*

ðēah, *though, although;*

ðēah ðe, *though, although.*

ðearf, see **ðurfan**.

ðearf, f., *need, benefit.*

ðēaw, m., *habit, custom* [thews].

ðegn (ðegen), m., *servant, thane, warrior.*

ðęnc(e)an (§ 128), *think, intend.*

ðening (-ung), f., *service;*

the pl. may mean *book of service* (117, 17).

ðēod, f., *people, nation.*

ðēoden, m., *prince, lord.*

ðēodscipe, m., *discipline.*

ðēon (ðȳwan) (§ 126), *oppress* [ðēow].

ðēow, m., *servant.*

ðēowa, m., *servant.*

ðēowotdōm (ðīowot-), m., *service.*

ðēs (§ 73), *this.*

ðider, *thither.*

ðiderweard, *thitherward.*

ðīn (§ 76), *thine.*

ðing, n., *thing;*

ǣnige ðinga, see 140, 15, Note.

ðingan (§ 127), *arrange, appoint.*

ðis, see ðēs.

ðissum, see ðēs.

ðōhte, ðōhton, see ðęncean.

ðolian (§ 130), *endure* [thole].

ðǫnan, *thence.*

ðǫnc, m., *thanks.*

ðone, see **sē**.

ðonne, *than, then, when;*

ðonne ... ðonne, *when ... then.*

ðrāg, f., *time.*

ðrēa-nȳd, f., *compulsion, oppression, misery* [throe-need].

ðrēora, see ðrīe.

ðridda, *third.*

ðrie (ðrȳ) (§ 89), *three.*

ðrīm, see ðrīe.

ðrīst-hȳdig, *bold-minded.*

ðrītig, *thirty.*

ðrōwung, f., *suffering.*

ðrȳ, see ðrīe.

ðrym(m), m., *renown, glory, strength.*

ðrȳð, f., *power, multitude* (pl. used in sense of sing.);

asca ðrȳðe 152, 23 = *the might of spears.*

ðrȳð-ærn, n., *mighty house, noble hall.*

ðrȳð-word, n., *mighty word, excellent discourse.*

ðū (§ 72), *thou.*

ðūhte, see ðyncan.

ðurfan (§ 136), *need;* pres. indic. 3d sing., ðearf; pret. 3d sing., ðorfte;

- 221 -

for-ðām mē wītan ne ðearf Waldend fīra morðor-bealo māga 145, 17 = *therefore the Ruler of men need not charge me with the murder of kinsmen.*

ðurh (§ 94, (2)), *through.*

ðus, *thus.*

ðūsend, *thousand.*

ðȳ, see **sē.**

ðyder, see **ðider.**

ðyncan (§ 128), *seem, appear* (impersonal);

mē ðyncð, *methinks, it seems to me;*

him ðūhte, *it seemed to him.*

U.

ūhta, m., *dawn;* gen. pl., **ūhtna.**

unbeboht, *unsold* [**bebycgan** = *to sell*].

uncūð, *unknown, uncertain* [uncouth].

under, *under* (with dat. and acc.).

understǫndan (§ 116), *understand.*

underðēodan (-ðīedan) (§ 126), *subject to;* past part. **underðēoded** = *subjected to, obedient to* (with dat.).

unforbærned, *unburned.*

unfrið, m., *hostility.*

ungefōge, *excessively.*

ungemete, *immeasurably, very.*

ungesewenlīc, *invisible* [past part. of **sēon** + **līc**].

unlyfigend, *dead, dead man* [unliving].

unlȳtel, *no little, great.*

unriht, n., *wrong;*

on unriht, see **on.**

unrihtwīsnes, f., *unrighteousness.*

unspēdig, *poor.*

unwearnum, *unawares.*

ūp (ūpp), *up.*

ūpāstīgnes, f., *ascension* [**stīgan**].

ūp-lang, *upright.*

ūre (§ 76), *our.*

usses = gen. sing. neut. of **ūser**, see **ic**.

ūt, *out, outside.*

ūtan, *from without, outside.*

ūtanbordes, *abroad.*

ūtgǫng, m., *exodus.*

uton, *let us* (with infin.) [literally *let us go* with infin. of purpose (see 137, 19-20, Note); **uton** = **wuton**, corrupted form of 1st pl. subj. of **wītan**, *to go*].

ūt-weard, *outward bound, moving outwards.*

W.

wāc, *weak, insignificant.*

wacian (§ 130), *watch, be on guard;* imperative sing., **waca**.

wadan (§ 116), *go, tread* [wade].

wæg, m., *wave.*

Wægmundigas, m. *Wægmundings* (family to which Beowulf and Wiglaf belonged).

wæl, n., *slaughter, the slain.*

wæl-blēat, *deadly* [slaughter-pitiful].

wælgīfre, *greedy for slaughter.*

wæl-rǣs, m., *mortal combat* [slaughter-race].

wæl-rēow, *fierce in strife.*

wælsliht (-sleaht), m., *slaughter.*

wælstōw, f., *battle-field* [slaughter-place];

wælstōwe gewald, *possession of the battle-field.*

wǣpen, n., *weapon.*

- 223 -

wǣre, see **bēon**.

wæs, see **bēon**.

wæter, n., *water*.

waldend, see *wealdend*.

wan (wǫn), *wan, dark*.

wanhȳdig, *heedless, rash*.

wānigean (wānian) (§ 130), *bewail, lament* (trans.) [whine].

warian (§ 130), *attend, accompany*.

wāt, see **witan**.

waðum, m., *wave*; gen. pl., **waðema**.

weal(l), m., *wall, rampart*.

wealdend (§ 68, (3)), *wielder, ruler, lord*.

wealh, m., *foreigner, Welshman*.

wealhstōd, m., *interpreter, translator*.

weallan (§ 117), *well up, boil, be agitated*; pret. 3d. sing. indic., **wēoll**.

wealsteal(l), m., *wall-place, foundation*.

weard, m., *ward, keeper*.

wearð, see **weorðan**.

weaxan (§ 117), *wax, grow*.

weg, m., *way*;

hys weges, see § 93, (3);

on weg, see **on**.

wel(l), *well, readily*.

wela, m., *weal, prosperity, riches*.

welm, see **wielm**.

wēnan (§ 126), *ween, think, expect*.

węndan (§ 127), *change, translate* [wend, **windan**].

węnian (§ 130), *entertain*;

- 224 -

węnian mid wynnum 149, 20 = *entertain joyfully*;

węnede tō wiste 149, 27 = *feasted* (trans.).

Weonodland (Weonoðland), n., *Wendland*.

weorc, n., *work, deed*.

weorold (weoruld), see **woruld**.

weorpan (§ 110), *throw*.

weorðan (§ 110), *be, become*.

wer, m., *man* [werwulf].

wērig, *weary, dejected*.

werod, n., *army, band*.

wesan, see **bēon**.

Wesseaxe, m. pl., *West Saxons*; gen. pl. = **Wesseaxna**.

west, *west, westward*.

westanwind, m., *west wind*.

wēste, *waste*.

wēsten, n., *waste, desert*.

Westsǣ, f., *West Sea* (west of Norway).

Westseaxe, m. pl., *West Saxons, Wessex*.

wīc, n., *dwelling* [bailiwick].

wīcian (§ 130), *stop, lodge, sojourn* [**wīc**].

wīdre, adv., *farther, more widely* (comparative of **wīde**).

wīdsǣ, f., *open sea*.

wielm (welm), m., *welling, surging flood* [**weallan**].

wīf, n., *wife, woman*.

wīg, m., n., *war, battle*.

wiga, m., *warrior*.

wild, *wild*.

wildor, n., *wild beast, reindeer*; dat. pl. = **wildrum** (§ 33, Note).

willa, m., *will, pleasure*; gen. pl., **wilna** (**138**, 16).

willan (§ 134; § 137, Note 3), *will, intend, desire.*

wilnung, f., *wish, desire;*

for ðǣre wilnunga 119, 4 = *purposely.*

Wiltūn, m., *Wilton* (in Wiltshire).

wīn, n., *wine.*

wīn-ærn, n., *wine-hall.*

Wīnburne, f., *Wimborne* (in Dorsetshire).

wind, m., *wind.*

wine, m., *friend.*

Winedas, m. pl., *the Wends, the Wend country.*

wine-dryhten, m., *friendly lord.*

winelēas, *friendless.*

winemǣg, m., *friendly kinsman.*

wīngeard, m., *vineyard.*

winnan (§ 110), *strive, fight* [win].

wīnsæl, n., *wine-hall.*

wīn-sęle, m., *wine-hall.*

winter, m., *winter;* dat. sing. = **wintra.**

wintercearig, *winter-sad, winter-worn.*

wīs, *wise.*

wīsdōm, m., *wisdom.*

wīse, *wisely.*

wīse, f., *manner, matter, affair* [in this wise].

wīs-fæst, *wise* [wise-fast; cf. shame-faced = shamefast].

wīs-hycgende, *wise-thinking.*

Wīsle, f., *the Vistula.*

Wīslemūða, m., *the mouth of the Vistula.*

wisse, see **witan.**

wist, f., *food, feast.*

wita, m., *wise man, councillor.*

witan (§ 136), *know, show, experience.*

wītan (§ 102), *reproach, blame* (with acc. of thing, dat. of person).

wīte, n., *punishment.*

Wītland, n., *Witland* (in Prussia).

wið (§ 94, (3)), *against, toward, with;*

wið ēastan and wið ūpp on emnlange ðǣm bȳnum lande, *toward the east, and upwards along the cultivated land;*

wið earm gesæt 139, 11 = *supported himself on his arm;*

genered wið nīðe (dat.) 143, 11 = *had preserved it from (against) violence.*

wiðerwinna, m., *adversary.*

wiðfōn (§ 118), *grapple with* (with dat.).

wiðhabban (§ 133), *withstand, resist* (with dat.).

wiðstondan (§ 116), *withstand, resist* (with dat.).

wlonc, *proud.*

wōd, see **wadan.**

wolcen, n., *cloud* [welkin]; dat. pl., **wolcnum.**

wolde, see **willan.**

wōma, m., *noise, alarm, terror.*

won, see **wan.**

wōp, n., *weeping.*

word, n., *word.*

wōrian (§ 130), *totter, crumble.*

worn, m., *large number, multitude.*

woruld, f., *world;*

tō worulde būtan ǣghwilcum ende 102, 18 = *world without end.*

woruldcund, *worldly, secular.*

woruldhād, m., *secular life* [world-hood].

woruldrīce, n., *world-kingdom, world.*

woruldðing, n., *worldly affair.*

wræclāst, m., *track or path of an exile.*

wrāð, *wroth, angry; foe, enemy.*

wrītan (§ 102), *write.*

wucu, f., *week.*

wudu, m., *wood, forest.*

wuldor, n., *glory.*

Wuldorfæder (§ 68, (2)), m., *Father of glory*; gen. sing., **Wuldorfæder.**

Wuldur-cyning, m., *King of glory.*

wulf, m., *wolf.*

wund, f., *wound.*

wund, *wounded.*

wunden, *twisted, woven, convolute* (past part. of **windan**).

wundor, n., *wonder, marvel.*

wundrian (§ 130), *wonder at* (with gen.).

wurdon, see **weorðan.**

wurðan, see **weorðan.**

wylf, f., *she wolf.*

wyllað, see **willan.**

wyn-lēas, *joyless.*

wynn, f., *joy, delight.*

wynsum, *winsome, delightful.*

wyrc(e)an (§ 128), *work, make, compose.*

wyrd, f., *weird, fate, destiny.*

wyrhta, m., *worker, creator* [-wright].

wyrm, m., *worm, dragon, serpent.*

wyrmlīca, m., *serpentine ornamentation.*

wyrð (**weorð**), *worthy*; see 114, 7-9, Note.

Y.

ylca, see **ilca**.

yldan (§ 127), *delay, postpone* [**eald**].

yldu, f., *age* [eld].

ymbe (**ymb**) (§ 94, (2)), *about, around, concerning* [*um*while];

ðæs ymb iii niht 99, 2 = *about three nights afterwards.*

ymb-ēode, see **ymb-gān**.

ymbe-sittend, *one who sits (dwells) round about another, neighbor.*

ymb-gān (§ 134), *go about, go around, circle* (with acc.).

yrfe-weard, m., *heir.*

yrnan, see **iernan**.

yrre, *ireful, angry.*

yteren, *of an otter* [*otor*].

ȳðan (§ 126), *lay waste* (as by a deluge) [**ȳð** = *wave*].

II. GLOSSARY.

MODERN ENGLISH—OLD ENGLISH.

A B C D E F G H I K L
M N O P Q R S T V W Y

A.

a, *ān* (§ 77).

abide, *bīdan* (§ 102), *ābīdan*.

about, *be* (§ 94, (1)), *ymbe* (§ 94, (2));

to write about, *wrītan be*;

to speak about (= of), *sprecan ymbe*;

about two days afterwards, *ðæs ymbe twēgen dagas*.

adder, *nǣdre* (§ 64).

afterwards, *ðæs* (§ 93, (3)).

against, *wið* (§ 94, (3)), *on* (§ 94, (3)).

Alfred, *Ælfred* (§ 26).

all, *eall* (§ 80).

also, *ēac*.

although, *ðēah* (§ 105, 2).

always, *ā*; *ealne weg* (§ 98, (1)).

am, *eom* (§ 40).

an, see **a**.

and, *ǫnd* (*and*).

angel, *ęngel* (§ 26).

animal, *dēor* (§ 32).

are, *sind, sint, sindon* (§ 40).

army, *werod* (§ 32);

Danish army, *hęre* (§ 26);

English army, *fierd* (§ 38).

art, *eart* (§ 40).

Ashdown, *Æscesdūn* (§ 38).

ask, *biddan* (§ 65, Note 3; § 115, Note 2).

away, *aweg*.

B.

battle-field, *wælstōw* (§ 38).

be, *bēon* (§ 40);

not to be, see § 40, Note 2.

bear, *beran* (§ 114).

because, *for ðǣm (ðe), for ðon (ðe)*.

become, *weorðan* (§ 110).

before (temporal conjunction), *ǣr, ǣr ðǣm ðe* (§ 105, 2).

begin, *onginnan* (§ 107, (1); § 110).

belong to, *belimpan tō* + dative (§ 110).

best, see **good**.

better, see **good**.

bind, *bindan* (§ 110).

bird, *fugol* (§ 26).

bite, *bītan* (§ 102).

body, *līc* (§ 32).

bone, *bān* (§ 32).

book, *bōc* (§ 68).

both ... and, *ǣgðer ge ... ge*.

boundary, *mearc* (§ 38).

boy, *cnapa* (§ 64).

break, *brēotan* (§ 109), *brecan, ābrecan* (§ 114).

brother, *brōðor* (§ 68, (2)).

but, *ac*.

by, *from (fram)* (§ 94, (1); § 141, Note 1).

C.

Cædmon, *Cædmon* (§ 68, (1)).

call, *hātan* (§ 117, (1)).

cease, cease from, *geswīcan* (§ 102).

child, *bearn* (§ 32).

choose, *cēosan* (§ 109).

Christ, *Crīst* (§ 26).

church, *cirice* (§ 64).

come, *cuman* (§ 114).

comfort, *frōfor* (§ 38).

companion, *gefēra* (§ 64).

consolation, *frōfor* (§ 38).

create, *gescieppan* (§ 116).

D.

Danes, *Dene* (§ 47).

day, *dæg* (§ 26).

dead, *dēad* (§ 80).

dear (= **beloved**), *lēof* (§ 80).

deed, *dǣd* (§ 38).

die, *cwelan* (§ 114).

division (of troops), *gefylce* (§ 32), *getruma* (§ 64).

do, *dōn* (§ 134).

door, *dor* (§ 32), *duru* (§ 52).

drink, *drincan* (§ 110).

during, *on* (§ 94, (3)). See also § 98.

dwell in, *būan on* (§ 126, Note 2).

E.

earl, *eorl* (§ 26).

endure, *drēogan* (§ 109).

England, *Englalǫnd* (§ 32).

enjoy, *brūcan* (§ 62, Note 1; § 109, Note 1).

every, *ǣlc* (§ 77).

eye, *ēage* (§ 64).

F.

father, *fæder* (§ 68, (2)).

field, *feld* (§ 51).

fight, *feohtan, gefeohtan* (§ 110).

find, *findan* (§ 110).

finger, *finger* (§ 26).

fire, *fȳr* (§ 32).

fisherman, *fiscere* (§ 26).

foreigner, *wealh* (§ 26).

freedom, *frēodōm* (§ 26).

friend, *wine* (§ 45), *frēond* (§ 68, (3)).

friendship, *frēondscipe* (§ 45).

full, *full* (with genitive) (§ 80).

G.

gain the victory, *sige habban, sige niman.*

gift, *giefu* (§ 38).

give, *giefan* (with dative of indirect object) (§ 115).

glad, *glæd* (§ 81).

glove, *glōf* (§ 38).

go, *gān* (§ 134), *faran* (§ 116).

God, *God* (§ 26).

good, *gōd* (§ 80).

H.

Halgoland, *Hālgoland* (§ 32).

hall, *heall* (§ 38).

hand, *hǫnd* (§ 52).

hard, *heard* (§ 80).

have, *habban* (§ 34);

not to have, *nabban* (p. 32, Note).

he, *hē* (§ 53).

head, *hēafod* (§ 32).

hear, *hīeran* (§ 126).

heaven, *heofon* (§ 26).

help, *helpan* (with dative) (§ 110).

herdsman, *hierde* (§ 26).

here, *hēr*.

hither, *hider*.

hold, *healdan* (§ 117, (2)).

holy, *hālig* (§ 82).

horse, *mearh* (§ 26), *hors* (§ 32).

house, *hūs* (§ 32).

I.

I, *ic* (§ 72).

in, *on* (§ 94, (3)).

indeed, *sōðlīce*.

injure, *scęððan* (with dative) (§ 116).

it, *hit* (§ 53).

K.

king, *cyning* (§ 26).

kingdom, *rīce* (§ 32), *cynerīce* (§ 32).

L.

land, *lǫnd* (§ 32).

language, *sprǣc* (§ 38), *geðēode* (§ 32).

large, *micel* (§ 82).

leisure, *ǣmetta* (§ 64).

let us, *uton* (with infinitive).

limb, *lim* (§ 32).

little, *lytel* (§ 82).

live in, *būan on* (§ 126, Note 2).

lord, *hlāford* (§ 26).

love, *lufian* (§ 131).

love (noun), *lufu* (§ 38).

M.

make, *wyrcan* (§ 128).

man, *secg* (§ 26), *mǫn* (§ 68, (1)).

many, *mǫnig* (§ 82).

mare, *mȳre* (§ 64).

mead, *medu* (§ 51).

Mercians, *Mierce* (§ 47).

milk, *meolc* (§ 38).

month, *mōnað* (§ 68, (1), Note 1).

mouth, *mūð* (§ 26).

much, *micel* (§ 96, (3)), *micle* (§ 97, (2)).

murderer, *bǫna* (§ 64).

my, *mīn* (§ 76).

N.

natives, *lǫndlēode* (§ 47).

nephew, *nefa* (§ 64).

new, *nīwe* (§ 82).

Northumbrians, *Norðymbre* (§ 47).

not, *ne*.

O.

of, see **about**.

on, *on* (§ 94, (3)), *ofer* (§ 94, (2)).

one, *ān* (§ 89);

the one ... the other, *ōðer ... ōðer.*

other, *ōðer* (§ 77).

our, *ūre* (§ 76).

ox, *oxa* (§ 64).

P.

place, *stōw* (§ 38).

plundering, *hergung* (§ 38).

poor, *earm* (§ 80), *unspēdig* (§ 82).

prosperous, *spēdig* (§ 82).

Q.

queen, *cwēn* (§ 49).

R.

reindeer, *hrān* (§ 26).

remain, *bīdan* (§ 102), *ābīdan*.

retain possession of the battle-field, *āgan wælstōwe gewald*.

rich, *rīce* (§ 82), *spēdig* (§ 82).

ride, *rīdan* (§ 102).

S.

say, *cweðan* (§ 115), *secgan* (§ 133).

scribe, *bōcere* (§ 26).

seal, *seolh* (§ 26).

see, *sēon* (§ 118), *gesēon*.

serpent, *nǣdre* (§ 64).

servant, *ðēowa* (§ 64), *ðegn* (§ 26).

shall, *sculan* (§ 136; § 137, Note 2).

she, *hēo* (§ 53).

shepherd, *hierde* (§ 26).

ship, *scip* (§ 32).

shire, *scīr* (§ 38).

shoemaker, *scēowyrhta* (§ 64).

side, on both sides, *on gehwæðre hǫnd*.

six, *siex* (§ 90).

slaughter, *wæl* (§ 32), *wælsliht* (§ 45).

small, *lȳtel* (§ 82).

son, *sunu* (§ 51).

soul, *sāwol* (§ 38).

speak, *sprecan* (§ 115).

spear, *gār* (§ 26), *spere* (§ 32).

stand, *stǫndan* (§ 116).

stone, *stān* (§ 26).

stranger, *wealh* (§ 26), *cuma* (§ 64).

suffer, *drēogan* (§ 109).

sun, *sunne* (§ 64).

swift, *swift* (§ 80).

T.

take, *niman* (§ 110).

than, *ðonne* (§ 96, (6)).

thane, *ðegn* (§ 26).

that (conjunction), *ðæt*.

that (demonstrative), *sē, sēo, ðæt* (§ 28).

that (relative), *ðe* (§ 75).

the, *se, sēo, ðæt* (§ 28).

then, *ðā, ðonne*.

these, see **this**.

they, *hīe* (§ 53).

thing, *ðing* (§ 32).

thirty, *ðrītig*.

this, *ðēs, ðēos, ðis* (§ 73).

those, see **that** (demonstrative).

thou, *ðū* (§ 72).

though, *ðēah* (§ 105, 2).

three, *ðrīe* (§ 89).

throne, ascend the throne, *tō rīce fōn*.

throw, *weorpan* (§ 110).

to, *tō* (§ 94, (1)).

tongue, *tunge* (§ 64).

track, *spor* (§ 32).

true, *sōð* (§ 80).

truly, *sōðlīce*.

two, *twēgen* (§ 89).

V.

very, *swīðe*.

vessel, *fæt* (§ 32).

victory, *sige* (§ 45).

W.

wall, *weall* (§ 26).

warrior, *secg* (§ 26), *eorl* (§ 26).

way, *weg* (§ 26).

weapon, *wǣpen* (§ 32).

well, *wel* (§ 97, (2)).

Welshman, *Wealh* (§ 26).

went, see **go**.

westward, *west, westrihte*.

whale, *hwæl* (§ 26).
what? *hwæt* (§ 74).
when, *ðā, ðonne*.
where? *hwǣr*.
which, *ðe* (§ 75).
who? *hwā* (§ 74).
who (relative), *ðe* (§ 75).
whosoever, *swā hwā swā* (§ 77, Note).
will, *willan* (§ 134; § 137, Note 3).
Wilton, *Wiltūn* (§ 26).
win, see **gain**.
wine, *wīn* (§ 32).
wisdom, *wīsdōm* (§ 26).
wise, *wīs* (§ 80).
with, *mid* (§ 94, (1));
to fight with (= **against**), *gefeohtan wið* (§ 94, (3)).
withstand, *wiðstǫndan* (with dative) (§ 116).
wolf, *wulf* (§ 26), *wylf* (§ 38).
woman, *wīf* (§ 32).
word, *word* (§ 32).
worm, *wyrm* (§ 45).
Y.
ye, *gē* (§ 72).
year, *gēar* (§ 32).
yoke, *geoc* (§ 32).
you, *ðū* (singular), *gē* (plural) (§ 72).
your, *ðīn* (singular), *ēower* (plural) (§ 76).

linenote

```
vi   v   iv  iii  ii   i    1   2   3   4   5   6
 |   |   |   |   |   |    X
 |   |   |   |   |   |    XX   X   X
 |   |   |   |   |   |    XXX  XX  XX  X   X
----------------------    XXXX XXX XXX XX  XX  X
_e_ _d_                   _c_ _b_         _a_
```

Where the horsemen   The six parts of the property
  assemble.   placed within one mile.

———————